The Gift
of Hope

The Gift of Hope

UNEXPECTED GIFTS

Kristen McKanagh

JOVE
New York

A JOVE BOOK
Published by Berkley
An imprint of Penguin Random House LLC
penguinrandomhouse.com

ISBN: 9780593199862

First Edition: April 2021

Printed in the United States of America
1   3   5   7   9   10   8   6   4   2

Book design by Gaelyn Galbreath

To Kristine.
Thank you for taking a chance with
me on a new, and beloved, genre!

Chapter One

✳

THE KNOCK AT the door was expected, but a bit early.

"I'll get it," Hope Beiler tried to quietly shout down the stairs from her doorway. Her sister was always saying she was too loud, but she was trying. She needn't have bothered this time. The front door squealed a protest at the use. Over the indistinguishable murmur of voices, Hope mentally added the task of oiling the hinges to her unending to-do list.

She would just have to hurry to finish getting ready. Hopping around her room, she put on her shoes as quickly as she could. Voices drifted up to her, but she couldn't make out the words. Hopefully Mammi wasn't in one of her moods and was keeping her comments to the weather—or something equally neutral . . . or normal.

Her grandmother had moved in this year. While Hope loved Mammi with all her heart and was grateful for her cheerful if somewhat scattered presence every day, she was also never entirely sure what might come out of Mammi's mouth, particularly when guests arrived.

Snatching her hard-saved money off the dresser, Hope hurried down the stairs to find Mammi standing there with her hands on her hips, talking to Sarah and Rachel Price. Tucking back an errant strand of her wayward strawberry-colored curls, which never wanted to stay pinned under her white kapp, Hope made her way to Mammi's side in time to catch the words "Find my Hope a husband."

She had to hide her snort of laughter.

A husband wasn't exactly high on Hope's list of worries, not these days at least. That topic was better than last week, when Mammi had asked Elam Hershberger if he thought he saw a turkey every time he looked in the mirror. To be fair, the poor man had a hunk of skin that sort of hung under his neck, but still . . .

"We'll try," Sarah said, glancing at Hope over Mammi's shoulder, eyes twinkling with amusement. "But she is wonderful picky. She seems almost . . ." She paused and wrinkled her nose in thought.

"Hopeless," Mammi filled in. Then nodded solemnly as though her granddaughter weren't standing right there listening. "There must be *some* young man."

As if men grew on trees like apples, and you simply had to pluck one from its branch, rotten or not.

Hope lifted her gaze heavenward, sending up a quick prayer for patience. She was always praying for patience but found that to be more and more the case lately.

"Dat needs me at home too much," she said firmly. "A husband can wait."

Her mamm's sudden passing last year had been hard on them all, but hardest on her dat. Levi Beiler had shrunken in on himself without his fraa at his side, turning into a ghost of the strong, dependable provider and father he'd always been. With only the two girls—she and her sister,

Hannah—he had to work the family farm alone. Hannah was getting married, focused on preparing for the wedding. Mammi was a dear but getting older and less able. Which left Hope, who tried to help in her own way.

Speaking of which . . . "Where is Dat?" she asked Mammi.

"He's already in the north field," she was informed.

She exchanged a quick glance with her grossmammi that said everything. Every day her father went to "work the fields," but as far as she could tell, not much was getting done.

She hadn't voiced her concerns out loud, though. No need to burden others with worry when little could be done. The signs hadn't become obvious until recently because, after Mamm's passing, the community had gathered around them in so many ways. The blessing of a close-knit community. Their Amish neighbors and friends had helped get the farm through summer and fall harvest, after which winter had been relatively slow with no need for extra hands. But now that spring had come . . .

Unfortunately, Hope was fairly certain Mammi had noticed as well.

Mammi might be prone to saying odd things and having an outlook that bordered on overly optimistic, but beneath that, she was surprisingly sharp. Not much got by Rebecca Beiler. While neither Hope nor her grandmother had voiced any of their concerns outright, they'd both done their best to fill the gap left by both of Hope's parents.

The general air of neglect in the fields was equally true around the house. Not the cleanliness or tidiness, which the women were on top of. But the place was quickly falling into a state of disrepair—the roof needed patching, a gutter was hanging on by a thread, and there were various other fixes that they were waiting on Dat to get to.

Hope tried her best. In addition to her usual chores, she'd been trying her hand at repairs, but she could only do so much in a day. Also, several larger repairs needed a man's muscles, like digging up the massive dead rosebush in the front yard. She'd reminded Dat about it until he'd asked her not to repeat herself, but still the rosebush sat outside, untended.

Nothing she could do about that either.

In addition, the wedding preparations were a lot. Getting ready to host and feed over three hundred people took planning, coordinating with their close community of friends and neighbors, and money they didn't have, which meant getting creative.

Things would get better, though. Dat was in mourning and would find his way home again eventually, with Gotte's help, the wedding would pass, and everything would get back to normal.

As her mamm used to say, "Difficulty is only a miracle in its first stage."

"Can I get anything from town for you, Mammi?"

"Nae, denki." Her grandmother patted her shoulder. "Enjoy your outing with your friends."

"I will," Hope promised.

Other than Gmay every other Sunday, and the daily walks to her spot in the woods where she went to think, this was the first she'd been away from the house in some time. She'd stopped attending singeon with the other youngie Sunday evenings. Enjoying the social time felt selfish when so much needed doing at home.

She leaned in and placed a kiss on her grandmother's cheek, the skin soft and paper thin under her lips, a reminder her mammi wasn't as young as she liked to act. "Keep an eye on Dat?"

"I always keep an eye on that boy. It's what gute maters do, even when their sons arc grown." Mammi winked.

Hope chuckled at the image of her strong, silent father as a boy.

With a deep breath, trying to rid herself of the anxious feeling that the house might collapse without her there to hold it together, Hope followed Sarah and Rachel down the stairs. As she hit the third step, she wobbled slightly. Peering closer, she discovered the wooden tread was starting to split right along the overhang. Yet another thing to add to her list of concerns and fixes.

Maybe while she was in town, she could ask about how to fix a breaking stairstep and even get the supplies she'd need.

Except there was no money for it. So perhaps not.

"Your grossmammi is precious, Hope," Sarah said, pulling her from her thoughts.

Giving herself a mental shake, she smiled. "Yes, she is."

Sarah and Rachel lived just down the lane and had been her closest friends, along with Hannah, since childhood. They knew about many of the troubles in the Beiler house. Dawdi had passed away a few years ago, leaving her grandmother alone, and after Mamm . . . Regardless of the sad circumstances leading to it, having Mammi here now was a blessing in the midst of sorrow.

"Denki for the ride," she said to Sarah and Rachel's father as she climbed into the waiting buggy.

"My pleasure, Hope." He pulled the wide brim of his hat lower over his eyes to shield against the bright sun and snapped the reins to set the horses to an easy pace.

Intending to enjoy the day shopping for wedding gifts for Hannah, the girls planned to walk the three-mile trip home afterward.

Hope turned her face to the warmth of the sun and let the pleasant chirping of the birds sing her worries away. While the air remained brisk in mid-spring, which meant she'd brought a sweater with her, the sun would keep them warm well enough. This was always Hope's favorite time of the year, when small green shoots sprouted in the fields and the last of winter snow, clinging to the shadowy bases of trees, melted away. Soon enough, flowers would bring color to their community of Charity Creek.

Many blessings to thank Gotte for today. Hope laid her worries aside, determined to enjoy her outing.

"How did you keep Hannah from coming with us?" Sarah asked. "It wonders me she could not join us today?"

Wedding shopping meant keeping her schwester away. "She and Noah are looking at a house he wishes to buy for them."

"How wunderbaar!" Rachel clapped her hands. "Hannah is lucky to have caught Noah Fisher."

"I think he's lucky to have caught Hannah," Hope said, though in her sweet way. Hannah was perfect. Exactly what Hope tried to be, though she often fell short. Especially in the kitchen.

"True," Rachel agreed easily. "Too bad he is an only child."

All three of them nodded. Poor Noah's mamm had died in childbirth when he was born. Hope had wondered if Noah and Hannah had bonded over that small sadness they had in common. The loss of a parent.

"I wish I was picking a house with my handsome husband," Sarah sighed.

She earned a sharp glance from her dat for the trouble. "I hope I've raised dochders who wish for helpmates, men who can walk beside them in life and faith, rather than wishing for houses or material things."

Sarah lowered her eyes. "Yes, Dat."

Rachel wasn't as meek as her younger sister, and merely chuckled. "Handsome wouldn't be so bad."

"Ach." Zachariah Price shook his head, though Hope caught a small twitch of his beard that she thought might be hidden amusement.

"What do you think you'll get for Hannah?" Rachel asked Hope.

"Something she could use in the new house maybe. Or in her garden."

Thankfully, talk turned to the wedding and gift ideas and plans for the future. Hope let Sarah and Rachel's cheerful chatter pour over her as she debated her own purchase in town today. The Amish lived a plain and simple life with not a lot of fluff, but a new house would require many useful things. They planned to visit A Thankful Heart—the only Amish-owned and -run gift store for several towns around, popular with the Amish and Englischer locals and tourists alike. Granted, the Kanagys owned it, and Dat wouldn't care for her giving them any business. She could hear his gruff voice now saying, "No dochder of mine should have anything to do with the Kanagys, even if I *have* forgiven them."

He said he had, but anyone in their family could tell he still harbored bitterness. Not that her parents had ever explained why. As far as Hope could tell, the Kanagys, whom she knew because they were part of the same church, were honest people of faith. Well . . . all except Aaron Kanagy maybe. Granted, she didn't know the Kanagys well, mostly because of the tension between the two families making them acquaintances more than friends. Still, their shop had to have some small item appropriate for Hannah on her wedding day.

The way Hope saw it, she had no other choice. Given the pittance in her purse, saved over time for rainy days, finding anything would be difficult. She'd thought she might paint something, but Hope's paints had dried up these last months, thanks to lack of use, and she hadn't wanted to waste money on new ones.

She straightened in her seat, determined to find at least a little something.

Despite it being a Wednesday in the middle of spring, Charity Creek was as busy as she'd ever seen, bustling with cars and people on foot, as well as several buggies. The town itself was small enough to recognize most anyone—both Amish and, to a certain extent, Englischers—who lived in the area. Everyone in everybody else's business, especially within her Amish community. However, they were in the heart of Indiana Amish country of the Elkhart-LaGrange counties and drew tourists and outsiders for various reasons. Especially their lovely little downtown with its shops and places to eat. But this was more than usual. Perhaps the weather had drawn people out—a hint of coming warmth and skies as blue as she remembered her mother's eyes.

Zachariah pulled his buggy up right outside A Thankful Heart, and Hope jumped out, giving a quick wave to Luke Raber, who stood across the street and thankfully nodded in return but didn't come over. As she waited for Sarah and Rachel, Hope peered in the shop window, already mentally discarding items as inappropriate wedding gifts.

Then a small, simply carved chair, obviously intended for a child, caught her eye and sparked an idea. Perhaps the new couple could use a simple piece of furniture for the new home. Noah's family were selling their farmland, as most of his sisters had married and moved away and his dat had started working in the nearby factory, as many Amish men in this area had out of necessity. A farmer born and raised, Noah intended to move to the Beiler farm and help her dat, who'd only had two girls. Luckily, a small home on three acres that backed up to their southern border had been put on the market. If that didn't work out, Noah intended to build eventually.

"Did you hear me, Hope?" Sarah's voice pulled her from her thoughts.

She turned away from the window with what she hoped was an interested smile plastered to her lips. "I'm sorry. I was caught up with this little chair."

"Which one?" Sarah and Rachel pressed closer to peer through the glass and Hope pointed it out to them.

"Oh," Rachel said. "That is sweet. Aaron must've made it, for sure and certain. He does all the woodworking for the store."

Hope tried not to let her smile slip at the sound of Aaron's name, and a picture immediately formed in her mind. Dark hair, laughing dark eyes, a too-easily-given grin, and strong hands made for hard work. Why couldn't it have been one of Aaron's brothers, Joshua or Daniel, who'd carved the chair? She could've dealt with one of them much better.

"Why do you need a child's chair, though?" Rachel turned to her with a frown.

Hope quickly shook her head. "I don't, but I was thinking I could have whoever made that build a small table or a rocking chair perhaps. For Hannah."

"She would love that," Sarah enthused. "I'm sure Aaron could build you something right quick."

Hope shook her head.

She had no intention of asking Aaron Kanagy any such

thing. Just the thought of him still made her wince, the sting of her hurt pride not dimmed by time. No doubt he hadn't meant for her to overhear him telling his friends that he had no interest in her after singeon one night about a year ago. He hadn't known that Hope had been standing outside to escape Barnabas Miller's attentions. She'd been taking a needed break around the corner from where the group of boys he was with had gathered, mid-conversation, talking about girls they were interested in. One of the boys brought up her name.

"Hope Beiler is okay, I guess," Aaron had said, his voice unenthusiastic.

Hope's heart had shriveled in the same way she'd shrunk herself into the shadows, the burn of mortification heating her skin.

True, her curls were a tad unruly and brightly colored, and she was on the short side and skinny with it. Next to Hannah, with her golden hair and flawless ways, Hope had often felt inadequate. Regardless, Aaron shouldn't have said such a thing to all those other boys. No one would want to show interest in her after that.

The memory still had the power to turn her ears hot and no doubt bright red, and she was suddenly grateful for her kapp, which covered them.

"I'll ask at the Troyers' store where they make larger furniture," she said firmly, glad for the excuse. "They might have something already finished."

"I guess so." Sarah puckered her brows, but then a sly glint came out to play. "But wouldn't you want to spend time with Aaron? I would."

Hope was well aware how all the Kanagy boys—men in their early twenties now, actually—were considered quite the catches. They never wanted for girls to talk to at the various community events and frolics. Even Daniel, who tended to keep to himself.

Rachel widened her eyes dramatically. "Hmmm . . . But think if it led to more, and he fell hopelessly in love with you, and you married him."

When they turned to Hope with such expectant expressions, words of denial popped out of her mouth. "Aaron Kanagy is the last man I could ever think to marry."

The instant she'd said it, Hope clapped a hand over her mouth and wished she could pull the words back in and swallow them whole.

Unfortunately, Sarah and Rachel, instead of appearing shocked, exchanged glances filled with a knowing that set Hope's teeth on edge. "What's wrong with Aaron?" Rachel asked.

Hope lowered her hand. "Nothing. That was an unkind thing to say. Please don't repeat it. I would feel terrible."

The words spoken in haste made her no better than Aaron telling those boys she was just okay. Worse even. Hope glanced around, relieved to find no one else close enough to overhear.

"But you don't like him?" Sarah prodded, confusion evident in her tone.

"Nae. He's . . . fine . . ." Hope stumbled over herself to get words out. "He's not who I would . . . choose, is all."

She barely kept from closing her eyes in despair. What could she say to fix this?

"You're so picky, you don't choose anyone," Sarah pointed out. "I, for one, wouldn't mind his interest."

"Me neither." Rachel waggled her eyebrows.

Hope managed a laugh that sounded just the right type of light and airy. "Then *you* commission him. Let's save the gift shop for last and see if anything in Troyers' will do?"

At least her friends allowed her to lead them away. Hope couldn't possibly go in there right now. Not with them watching her extra closely, especially if Aaron was working today. Given her behavior, they no doubt assumed she either disliked him or harbored a secret crush.

Too bad, since she'd so wanted a closer look at the little chair. Affording anything in Troyers' was not an option. She'd have to be extra persnickety and reject everything in there, which no doubt would earn her more teasing.

Or maybe she'd manage to find a small item. Probably tiny. Because asking Aaron Kanagy for anything was not an option.

Chapter Two

❦

WHAT DID I ever do to Hope Beiler?

Aaron had just finished a project in the small workshop they'd added on behind the store last year for him to make the wooden toys and other items they sold. Fatigue dragging at his heels, he'd walked down the side of the old stone building toward the main entrance on the street. Right before turning the corner, he'd caught a bit of the girls' discussion of his chair and had smiled and stopped, not wanting to interrupt. Maybe also to appreciate the compliments they'd paid his work.

Now he wished he hadn't. Pride always cometh before a fall.

The last man Hope would ever think to marry. Why?

As far as he could remember, he'd never said a word wrong to her. In fact, he'd always liked Hope. Cheerful and sweet, she was kind to everyone around her. While other boys had teased her about her curls, he'd thought of her as the most colorful girl in the community, which suited her personality.

He would even have liked to be friends. However, the private tension between their fathers had kept him from trying. Other than that, Aaron honestly had no idea why Hope didn't like him.

A twinge poked at his heart like how, when he'd been a boy, he used to poke a stick at the bullfrogs in the stream near their house. No doubt his pride protesting Hope's attitude. He should strive to be humbler.

Not *everyone* had to like him.

Luckily, the girls had moved on down the street to the Troyers' furniture store. With an impatient hum, Aaron rolled his sleeves down and continued into his family's shop. He paused at the child's chair Hope had been admiring. That was, until she'd found out *he* had made it. Still smarting, Aaron scooped it up and carried it to the back room, where he found his mamm and his older bruder, Daniel.

His mother raised her eyebrows at the chair in his hand. "Did someone finally buy it?"

As soon as she spoke, Aaron realized his mistake.

Of course she'd want to know. After making the sturdy seat, he'd set it out on the floor beside the carved toys he made, just to see if anyone might be interested in bigger items. Not that he'd told anyone in his family that he was testing the market. Unfortunately, the chair had sat unclaimed for a full month now. The thing was becoming a bit of a joke among them. One Aaron laughed along with good-naturedly, even as he gritted his teeth in private.

"It's dusty," was all he could think to give in explanation for moving it.

Mamm gave a little snort, eyes twinkling, though not unkindly. "I should say so," she teased. "Where have you been?"

"In the workshop."

"Ach du lieva, you spend too much time in there." She waved her hand as if she were shooing a fly.

Aaron hunched a shoulder. "I like working with the wood, Mamm."

"But you will wear yourself to nothing."

Aaron had to resist the urge to rub at his eyes, which felt like they'd been run over with sandpaper. Mamm was right about the hours. He was certainly burning his candle at both ends, going through more batteries for the lantern than he had a right to.

"I heard you leave this morning long before sunrise and you appear now right in time to take over from your bruder. What were you working on?"

He'd wanted to finish a small table that would be perfect to set beside couches or to possibly use as a bedside table. This one he'd designed with several drawers and a small writing platform that could be pulled out when needed. He'd also worked on several toys for the shop, simply so he wouldn't have to lie now.

"A new train set," he said. "It's nearly finished."

Guilt gnawed at his insides. He hadn't lied, but omission could also be a lie. Perhaps his chair wasn't selling because Gotte could see his heart and was teaching him a lesson. Which lesson that might be—honoring his parents, avoiding the sin of pride, a lying tongue, or perhaps not straying from the path he'd been set upon—Aaron wasn't entirely sure.

Daniel, who stood in the back corner counting inventory, said nothing, though Aaron got the sense his bruder saw more than he let on.

Aaron had been debating for months now if he should tell his parents that he didn't want to work in the gift shop that had been in their family for several generations. A

Thankful Heart was gute business and meant a solid future. Though his parents had been careful not to build the business too big, as was the Amish way. No need for more than what their family could use. More than enough, though, to share with his brothers and eventually provide for their own wives and families. Mamm had been hinting more and more that she longed for grandbabies.

Was he ungrateful, wanting to walk away from this blessing and start a different life?

Aaron's passion didn't lie in stocking those shelves with trinkets and treasures or useful tools and sweet candies—not that anything was wrong with that. What he loved most, though, was taking plain wood and shaping it into something usable and beautiful. Gotte must've felt a small measure of this kind of satisfaction when He sculpted the heavens and the earth and all the living creatures.

The trouble was, he knew what his dat would say to his dream of starting a furniture business. He'd point out the Troyers' shop down the street. The town didn't need another Amish-made furniture provider, and they shouldn't compete with another family from their community. Plenty to go around already. And Dat would be right.

But Aaron still wanted the chance to try, maybe in Lillistz or Lampton, a few towns over.

If he could make a few larger pieces and try to sell them here, then he'd have a better idea if his designs and craftsmanship could draw enough business. Though that small chair sitting unsold for so long had him debating if he should give up his dream.

Besides, his family was starting to notice. He was putting in too many hours, exhaustion becoming his constant companion. He couldn't keep this up, for sure and certain.

"I look forward to seeing it." Mamm's voice pulled him out of his musings, and he had to think a moment.

Right . . . the train set. At least he was almost finished with that as well. "It'll be ready tomorrow."

She nodded vaguely, her mind already moving to other matters. "Dat and Joshua are over in Skokegan talking to a blacksmith there to see if any of his goods would be a fit for our shop."

"What do you need done first?" All three of the brothers could run the shop on their own, but anytime Mamm was around, they deferred to her. Even Dat deferred to Mamm, though the shop had been passed down through his family.

She tapped a pencil against her mouth, thinking. "For now, help Daniel rearrange and restock the back shelves of lotion and candles. The lavender sachets are selling well, and I want to put them next to the lavender and honey soap to see if that helps those sell better."

Hiding a sigh, Aaron grabbed the rolling cart he'd made to help stocking shelves go more quickly. Together he and Daniel piled it with items, then rolled it out to the shop floor. There they removed the items on the shelves, grouping them with like items on the cart. The scent of lavender, which the ladies seemed to love but gave Aaron a headache, filled the air around them.

The bells over the door rang, but Mamm got it, and continued to help customers as a steady stream came and went. Pleasant weather always brought more visitors.

Focused on his task, Aaron crossed his arms and considered the now empty shelves. "I think we should put the candles on the lower shelves. They're bigger and will be seen down there."

So saying, he grabbed a candle and crouched down.

"I think you should tell Mamm that you want to make furniture," Daniel said quietly.

Aaron stilled where he was squatting, candle in hand and halfway to a shelf, and stared at his bruder. "What?"

"Don't deny it. You're in that workshop early and leave late every day."

"I get all my chores done before and after."

Daniel ignored that. "You can't be making *that* many toys."

Aaron rose to his feet and glanced toward the front of the shop, where Mamm was busy showing a customer how the candy barrels worked. "I can't make furniture," he said in a low voice. "In order to spend the time I need, someone else would have to take my place working in the shop. I'm not making Mamm and Dat pay for extra hands when mine are perfectly fine."

Except guilt still plucked at him about hiding this piece of himself from his family.

"Are you happy?"

Aaron stared at Daniel. The oldest of the three, Daniel had always been the steady, quiet one. But he was just as devoted to their kind, hardworking parents as Aaron and Joshua were. "I'm happy to be part of my family business yet," Aaron insisted.

Even as the words left his lips, they tasted sour, not entirely the truth.

"Maybe I could help?"

Aaron and Daniel both stiffened at the sound of a soft, feminine voice behind them, then slowly turned to find, of all people, Hope Beiler standing there.

Given what he'd overheard outside, Aaron straightened as though his spine had been nailed to a rail post.

Meanwhile, Hope shifted under his stare with a pretty

blush staining her cheeks darker by the second. She'd always been a tiny thing, not much more than five feet at a guess. He thought of her like a delicate little bird. On Sundays, sometimes he could hear her singing, slightly off-key and hooty like an owl . . . and yet adorable because she obviously took such joy from it.

A strawberry blond curl escaped from under her kapp, giving her a bit of a flyaway air. She bounced on her toes as though she wanted to run out of the store, but after a second, she tipped up her chin in a gesture that indicated an inner stubbornness he wouldn't have guessed about her, even though he'd known her his whole life.

When neither he nor Daniel said a word, she cleared her throat. "I apologize for eavesdropping. I wouldn't have said anything, except I think we might be able to help each other."

The woman who declared in no uncertain terms that he was the last man she'd ever marry wanted to help him?

Daniel elbowed him in the ribs.

"Oh?" Aaron coughed. "What do you think you heard?"

Hope glanced around her and the color in her cheeks deepened, spreading down her neck, splotchy against her pale skin. "Could we speak outside, in . . . private?"

If she got any redder, she could pass for a ripe berry.

Aaron shook his head. "I can't leave—"

"I'll take care of this." Daniel cut him off, gesturing at the shelves they were reorganizing.

"Denki." Hope smiled at Daniel suddenly, and Aaron had to ease the tightness that suddenly constricted his lungs.

What would he do if she ever smiled at him that way? As if he was her hero. Sunshine in a bottle, that smile.

She turned to Aaron, and the sunshine dimmed as though

the shadow of clouds passed over her features. Eyebrows raised in expectation.

Fine. He'd hear what she had to say, then take her back to her friends, wherever they had disappeared to.

With a last glance at his bruder's innocent expression, Aaron waved her ahead and showed her the way outside and back around to his workshop. Only, instead of talking to him, Hope gasped and moved to inspect the table he'd finished this morning.

"Oh!" She turned wide eyes filled with surprising interest up to him, then focused back on the table. "This is wonderful gute."

She ran a light hand over the wood, and Aaron watched closely. He'd sanded that table until not a splinter could be found, but what if he'd missed a spot?

Slowly Hope got to her feet, her gaze still on the table. "You have a gift. Gotte-given. It would be a shame to waste it."

The last man I'd ever think to marry.

The words rang in his head like a clanging gong drowning out her words now. Did she really like his work, or was she buttering him up for whatever offer she intended to make?

Aaron crossed his arms and stared at her. "You said you thought we could help each other?"

Hope lifted her gaze to his. Even in the dim light of his workshop, her eyes sparkled as though she was about to start a bit of innocent mischief and wanted him to join the fun. "I need a wedding gift for my schwester, and I would like to commission you to build a bed frame for her and her new husband."

Interest caught at him like fire to tinder. A commission? His first real piece of furniture?

But the wedding was in a few months. Less even. He'd never have the time. How did she think this helped anything? "You overheard my conversation with Daniel?"

She nodded.

"Then you know I don't have time to work on a piece that large. The shop." He waved his hand in the general direction.

"I know. I also have a problem. I don't have . . ." She paused and bit her lip, wrinkling her nose as if debating with herself. "I don't have money to pay for the bed or anything else really."

His first instinct was to offer it to her at no cost. Helping a neighbor. But he hadn't been exaggerating about not having the time. Disappointment weighing him down, Aaron reached to open the door. "Ach vell, I can't help—"

"But I'd like to offer a trade." She rushed to interrupt him before he could usher her back outside.

A trade? Aaron paused and studied the face tipped up to him. He found himself getting lost in those wide, imploring eyes. Hope lived up to her name, her expression filled with the emotion. To turn her away now would be like kicking a puppy or crushing a butterfly under the wheel of his buggy.

"What do you mean a trade?" he asked in a voice gone gruff.

"I could . . . work in the shop for you. Then you would have time to work on the bed frame and maybe a few other pieces." She nibbled at her bottom lip, searching his expression. "Would . . . would that work?"

All day to himself to design and build furniture and maybe give rise to his dream? Except he'd be going against his parents' wish for him to eventually run the store with his brothers by pursuing this carpentry dream. That didn't feel honest to him. Granted, he'd just be testing the waters to see if a furniture store would be worth the work and time. No harm in that.

In front of him, Hope seemed to hold her breath.

He'd be helping her give her sister a present for an important occasion in her life. Was this what Gotte wanted him to do?

Hope continued to gnaw at her lip, her anxiousness almost a physical presence. "Worse than failure is the failure to try," she said. "Mamm used to say that."

I'll work on the bed, and if I have time, a few other pieces as well, but only after I finish any items for the shop, Aaron reasoned to himself.

"Jah," he said. "I think that would work."

The words were out of his mouth before he'd finished thinking this through. *Please let me be doing the right thing.*

The beaming grin that lit up Hope's face stole his breath the same way that happened when he got kicked by a horse as a kid. That sunshine smile warmed his heart, and, suddenly, somehow, he knew this was the right path to take.

"Denki," Hope said in a rush, relief lacing her voice. Then doubts chased themselves through her expression again.

"Is there a problem?" he asked. Already?

Hope blinked, reminding him of a little lost owl, then her expression cleared, and she shook her head. What was going on in that head of hers?

"Nae," she said. "I was thinking about what I'll need to do at home so I can be away."

Chapter Three

※

WHAT DID I do?

Hope asked herself for the thousandth time as she stood at the kitchen sink drying dishes after supper. That question had been chasing itself around in her head like a cat after a mouse ever since she had left Aaron at the shop.

In fact, that question ruined most of the rest of her day, causing anxiety to swirl around inside her like a storm about to break. A new experience for her. The girl she had been before her mother's death would've gone blithely ahead with her plans, assuming good intentions would a positive outcome make.

But she'd lost that girl somewhere along the way.

She'd finished her shopping with Sarah and Rachel, and they had walked home with their parcels. Hope had walked home empty-handed, not able to think of buying another thing.

What had possessed her to make that deal with Aaron Kanagy of all people?

She knew what, though. Desperation and circumstance. She had poked around Troyers' for all of five minutes, aghast at prices she couldn't hope to afford, then left Sarah and Rachel there as she hurried back to the gift shop. She would buy that chair and tell Hannah it was for her future children. If it didn't cost too much, maybe she could also afford paints to decorate it.

But as soon as she entered the shop, she'd discovered the chair was already gone. Disappointment dragging at her steps, she'd gone searching for one of the Kanagys to ask about it, only to stumble upon Aaron's conversation with Daniel.

Granted, Hope could be impetuous, but this plan was narrish. Crazy. Except the circumstances leading up to her overhearing that conversation made it feel as though Gotte had set her in Aaron's path in order that they might help one another.

Dishes already cleaned and dried and put away, Hope swept the kitchen. Hannah had gone out to the coop to feed the chickens and bed them down for the night, leaving the house quiet.

Hope cast a searching glance over her shoulder at where her dat was sitting in front of the fireplace. Mid-spring continued to be chilly, especially as evening crept across the sky and temperatures dropped. This had been his favorite spot since Mamm's death. He sat with his Bible open in his lap, but not reading; instead he was staring into the crackling flames in the fireplace.

Just as he did every night.

Hope worried at her lower lip. She needed to leave right quick. She'd agreed to meet Aaron in the woods after supper and chores to discuss their arrangement. He was going to ask his mamm's permission for her to work in the shop. She was supposed to do the same.

Only she didn't want to pile onto Dat's worries. He held on to a resentment toward the Kanagys that Hope had never understood. Their faith was one of forgiveness—though they were human, too, making that harder sometimes. Mamm used to soothe Dat's initial response to them, or ignore him, insisting they would shop at the Kanagys' store and treat the family with neighborly charity.

Hope had always been an obedient daughter, and the thought of arguing with her father sat like an anvil in the pit of her stomach.

Maybe she should tell Aaron she changed her mind. This was a deerich idea. A silly thing to pursue.

Except this was something she could do for Hannah. She'd always looked up to her sister, who'd treated her better than any younger sister had a right to expect. Hope could easily picture the pleasure in Hannah's eyes when she saw the new bed frame for her new house.

A loud chuckle sounded from upstairs, and Hope paused in her sweeping as an idea occurred to her. Mammi, of course. Maybe she didn't need to bother Dat with this. Mammi and Hannah would be the most affected by her absence during the day. She'd talk to Mammi and get her permission.

This would all work out.

With a deep breath, Hope pull her shoulders back. *Please let me be making the right decision*—she sent the quick prayer up to Gotte.

Except she didn't have time to ask her grandmother, who no doubt would have many questions. She would talk to Mammi after she returned home. Perhaps Aaron's mamm had said no to the idea anyway.

Hope wrapped a scarf she had knitted herself this winter around her neck and pulled on her sweater.

"I'm going to my bridge," she called to no one in particular. They were used to her disappearing to her favorite place each evening. Even in the cold of winter, unless Dat thought it dangerous, she still spent time there.

She did her best thinking in her spot.

"Come home before dark." Mammi's voice reached her from her room upstairs.

"Jah. I will," Hope called back.

Not waiting, Hope was out the back door and across the side yard to the line of woods their plain two-story house—with its whitewashed wood siding, red brick chimney, and large front porch that caught the morning sun—nestled up to. She followed the well-worn, familiar trail through dense forest of maple, elm, and pine. Not too far from home, a small stream lazily meandered between the trees. Crystal clear waters gurgled over rocks polished smooth by the passage of time, Hope's favorite sound in the world, except maybe her mater's voice.

She followed the water south a short distance to where she'd arranged to meet with Aaron. After a turn in the path, a small clearing opened up where her bridge waited, guarded by a pair of gnarled trees that had grown together, wrapped around each other as though embracing. Hope's steps slowed as she realized Aaron already waited there for her.

He stood on her bridge, leaning his elbows on the rail, watching in the other direction. Even hunched over, she could tell how tall he was. Over six foot if she had to guess. Lean, with strong shoulders highlighted only by his white shirt and black suspenders.

He hadn't even turned around yet to show her his handsome face with laughing dark eyes, a wide grin that invited you to laugh with him, and a jaw perhaps a tad too stubbornly made.

With a determined breath, she willed her heart to quit its thumping. *Aaron means nothing to you.*

At least . . . nothing beyond the bed frame for Hannah. That's what mattered.

That "okay, I guess" had hurt too much, done too much damage to her self-worth. She had worried all year after that that no other boys would want her because of his cruel words. She'd end up an old maid aendi, helping raise her nieces and nephews.

"Hello," she called out, happy her voice came out normal.

Aaron straightened and turned. As soon as he set eyes on her, he smiled and waved, and her darn heart went hooey all over again. Hopping around inside her chest. Fickle thing.

"Hello." Aaron waited patiently as she walked the last little way to join him on the bridge. Strangely intimate sharing the small space that had been hers alone for so long. As though she'd invited him into her world, and he was filling it up with his broad shoulders and big smile.

"I forgot this was here," he said, running a hand over the rail.

The Kanagys' home was on the other side of the woods and farther down. Several miles from her own home by road, but only a half mile or so by foot through the trees.

"Dat built it for me when I was a child," she said.

Aaron's smile widened, teeth flashing white in the shadows. "I always wondered who put it here. Why did he? This stream is hardly wider than a yardstick."

Hope stopped short of stepping onto the bridge with him. "Mamm always worried about me."

He raised his eyebrows in questioning expectation, obviously wanting to know more. Though she wasn't sure why he cared, really.

Hope gave a mental shrug. "When I was young, I used

to sneak out of the house and come play on the banks of the stream. I always loved how peaceful it seemed here. One time, Mamm found me on the other bank."

The stream itself was small and could be easily leapt by an adult.

Aaron glanced down at the water as though assessing it through the eyes of a child.

"I was only three years old, and she worried I might slip and hit my head on a rock or drown, but no matter how they tried to keep me inside, I always managed to get out." Hope allowed a small smile at the memory of the stories her parents would tell of her antics.

"I didn't know we had a magician in our community," Aaron teased.

She shouldn't like it when he teased. He didn't mean anything by it. After all, he teased all the girls. But her heart gave a happy little leap all the same.

Hope pushed the feeling aside with sensible determination. "Mammi told Dat about a natural bridge that had been formed by a pine tree that fell across the stream and said she would show me so I could cross safely. But Mamm insisted Dat make it into a bridge with rails, so they wouldn't have to worry about me falling off. Since they couldn't seem to make me stay in the house, she decided that was the best they could do."

Hope ran her hand over the smooth wood. Made of pine from the original tree, the bridge had aged with time and the elements, but still stood sturdily over the water. Dat hadn't simply made a plain bridge, straight and simple. He'd made it bow above the water, and the rails crisscrossed, but in a way that made Hope think of hugs. What's more, he'd carved Hope's name into one of the beams on the back side.

Their little secret, he'd told her, because Mamm and Hannah would be jealous.

"And you still come here often?" Aaron asked.

The memories faded from her lips. Why had she shared all that with Aaron? It must be because the man was a surprisingly gute listener. That didn't mean he needed to know more, though. "What did your parents say about my working in the shop?" she asked.

Aaron's smile faded as well, turning to a small frown as he studied her quietly. Hope tried not to shift uncomfortably under such a direct gaze. "Mamm says she would appreciate having another woman in the shop. You can start as early as tomorrow if you would like."

That easily, Hope was working for the Kanagys.

She glanced upward waiting for lightning to strike her dead, given the tension between the two families. But the skies remained clear and beautiful, fading from blue to pink to orange as the sun lowered in the sky, casting longer shadows in the woods where they stood. When Aaron also glanced upward, as though trying to figure out what she was searching for, she jerked her gaze back down.

She still had to talk to Mammi. "Will the day after tomorrow be okay?"

"Jah. That is fine."

"How long do you think the bed frame will take?"

Aaron ran a hand over his chin, the day's worth of stubble making a raspy noise above the soft bubbling of the stream. "That depends."

"On?"

He grinned. "How fancy you want it."

From out of nowhere, he produced a small pad of paper and a pencil. Flipping to a clean page, he looked up at her, his dark eyes expectant.

"I hadn't thought about it. It should have a headboard and footboard."

"What size?"

"I heard Noah tell Mammi he wants to buy a queen-size mattress for their bed." Heat rushed into Hope's cheeks, and she hoped Aaron couldn't see the blush that was surely staining her face as red as raspberries got in the summer. She'd only been thinking of Hannah when she had decided she wanted a bed frame and hadn't thought through what an intimate piece of furniture that was, and the fact that she would have to be discussing a bed with Aaron, of all people.

Aaron didn't appear to notice, making a note of it on his pad. "Do you want something simple and straight? Maybe like this?"

His hand flew lightly over the paper, bringing to life a lovely, clean design—squared off but with a floating frame around the headboard and footboard that looked almost like a picture frame, but let the light through between the slats.

"That's perfect." Hope forgot to keep her distance, stepping in close to see. "Especially for Noah." Her soon-to-be brother-in-law was straight and narrow but yielding. However, the bed was also for Hannah, who was more flowery yet. "What if we added a small touch?"

Without thinking, she snatched the pad and pencil from his hand and drew in a swirling pattern over each thick post at the four corners, then handed the pad back to him. "Would that be too difficult?"

Aaron stared at the paper, then looked back up at Hope with a light in his eyes that caught at her, holding her suddenly still and slightly breathless. He searched her face, but she didn't know what he thought to find.

"Do you like to draw?" he asked slowly.

Whatever she thought might be in his head, that had not been it. "I used to. I haven't had much time since—"

She stopped and swallowed. Talking about Mamm still hurt too much.

Aaron had been at the funeral. He and his family had offered their condolences, and his mamm had brought several meals over the weeks and months afterward. She could only pray he let the subject drop now.

"Ach vell . . . I think I could do this, though I might need help tracing the design for the carvings."

Hope blew out a silent breath of relief. "That is the best news."

"When is the wedding again?" he asked.

"In June." There was something optimistic about a June wedding, starting your life together as the world turned fragrant and green and warm and new life entered the world.

"Do you think you could work in the shop until then?" he asked.

Six weeks. That was longer than she had expected. But for Hannah, she would do anything. "I think that will be all right, though I might have to take days off here and there to get things done around the house."

Aaron grinned and held out his hand to shake. "Then we have a deal, Hope Beiler."

Hope slid her small hand into his with visible reluctance, her skin soft and warm against his, and suddenly Aaron worried that the calluses formed through long hours working with wood might offend her.

Strangely, he also didn't want to let go.

He wanted to keep her there with him, maybe get a chance to pull another unwilling smile from her. When she wasn't being determined to keep him at a distance, her natural enthusiasm surfaced. Her face had practically glowed in the few minutes she'd taken to sketch her swirling design over his own.

That had knocked him sideways. He knew Hope liked to sing, if slightly off-key, and told fun stories, but she was also an artist? How had such a creative personality been hidden from the community? Why was she not making things for the gift shop already?

Especially if her family needed money.

Yet another shock when it came to Hope. He, like everyone else, assumed the Beilers' farm was doing fine. What had changed? Or rather . . . when had things changed for them? Had it been after her mother's sudden death? Or before?

Several times today, he had been tempted to offer another round of condolences for her mother, whom she obviously missed. Only Hope's reluctance to talk about it was obvious, and so he let it go.

His mother had been more than pleased when he had mentioned the plan to her, looking upon it as an opportunity to help one of their Amish neighbors. In fact, she'd practically been tickled pink about having another woman in the shop.

"I'm surrounded by big, burly men who don't know light green from mint," she'd said with a *tsk* and shake of her head.

"I'm not sure about the burly part, but not knowing the shades of green is true enough," he'd said. Only last week he'd had to call his mother into the front of the shop to help a woman looking for a quilt that was mint green; the one he'd shown her apparently was not.

At the mention of Hope, Mamm might have had a matrimonial matchmaking light in her eyes as well, but Hope's attitude toward him no doubt would put that idea to rest right quick.

"Should I talk to Dat tonight?" he'd asked his mother.

Mamm had pursed her lips then shaken her head. "No. I will talk to him after supper."

Aaron wasn't too surprised. His dat and Hope's dat had always kept their distance from each other, putting a natural distance between the families beyond that of neighbors worshipping in the same gmay, though he had no idea why. But if his mother agreed, his father would not be standing in the way of that. When it came to the shop, his mother lovingly ruled the roost.

Hopefully Dat didn't object too much. Aaron wouldn't want to hurt Hope's feelings by having to cancel their deal. Even if she didn't like him.

Why didn't she like him anyway?

"Um . . ." Hope's eyes went wide, and she slowly pulled her hand from his grip, and Aaron suddenly realized that he'd been standing here holding her hand and staring at the poor girl in silence for longer than was comfortable or appropriate.

Before he could say anything, not that he knew exactly what he could say to excuse his behavior, she took a step back. "I should be getting home."

Part of Aaron wanted to call her back, think of a way to talk to her for longer. Here in the woods it almost felt as though they were in their own tranquil world. The other part of him was still stinging over her words. Had that just been earlier today?

"I'll see you day after tomorrow," he said.

Hope swallowed, fear tracing lines across her features. "What if I'm not enough help in the shop?"

Unable to help himself, Aaron tipped his head back and laughed. "When my mamm learned who wanted to come work with us, she said no other girl in the district could be better. That Hope Beiler had her head set on straight and would be a wonderful gute helper, for sure and certain."

Hope ducked her head so that he couldn't see her reaction. "What time should I be there?" she asked.

Had he said the wrong thing, telling her? Maybe she was worried about being too prideful. Aaron let it drop. "Mamm said to be to the store by eight. We open at nine, so that will give us an hour to show you around."

"Oh." She bit her lip. Worried? It wasn't the first time she'd done that.

Aaron thought quickly over what he'd said. "Do you need a ride?" he asked slowly.

She stopped biting that lip and tipped her head to consider him. "Maybe I could walk to your house and ride with you from there?" she asked. "I don't want to inconvenience you."

"I don't mind at all."

"I enjoy walking in these woods, and it's not far coming this way."

He could see by the stubborn tilt to her chin that she wasn't going to budge, so he gave in. "Be at our house fifteen minutes before eight."

"Denki, and please tell your mamm denki for me." She paused, seeming to consider him again. Then she shook her head, expression sort of befuddled. "Aaron Kanagy. Who knew you would be the answer to my prayers?"

Before he could respond, she turned and hurried away.

Aaron stood still and watched her go. "Mine, too, Hope," he murmured.

As she disappeared from view, the dark woods swallowed her up, and he had the strangest sense of wanting to follow to keep her safe. He even took a step or two off the bridge before he stopped himself.

What a foolish notion.

He shook his head at himself, then backed up over the bridge in the opposite direction to return to his own home. A notch in the wood on one of the main railing posts caught his attention and he stooped to squint in the fading light only to find the word HOPE carved into the grain.

He traced the letters, a small smile playing about his mouth.

Perhaps he could change her opinion of him. Being friends with Hope suddenly seemed like something he should want very much.

Chapter Four

✳

AN EARLY START was what Hope needed.

Or perhaps more to the point, her mind wouldn't let her sleep. Hope had lain in bed most of the long night, staring through the moonlit darkness at the ceiling in her and Hannah's bedroom. As soon as the Prices' rooster—a mean old thing that liked to chase her up to the front steps when she visited her friends—finally crowed at its terribly early time, she'd been up and about.

Rather than get dressed immediately, which might wake her sister early, she'd gone about the lower floor getting a few extra chores done. Fewer things to do when she returned from work today. No doubt close to suppertime.

Work.

She still couldn't believe she'd made that deal with Aaron.

Hope battled back a flock of nerves as she snuck back into her room to change at a decent hour.

"Are you already up?" Hannah murmured groggily from her bed.

"Only just," Hope whispered back.

"M'kay." Hannah rolled back over. Her sister, who was practically perfect in every other way, was not much of a morning person and never had been.

Dressed, Hope quickly pinned back her hair and got ready for the day. At first she'd refused to check the small mirror in the bathroom to be sure she at least appeared neat, determined not to think about what Aaron saw when he looked at her, or wanting to be at her best. Because that was a ridiculous, silly notion. Then common sense got hold of her and she'd reasoned that as an employee working in a store that dealt with the public—Amish and Englischers alike—she should at least appear presentable.

Except, looking in the mirror, she'd paused to wonder what Aaron didn't see, what had just been "okay, I guess." She wasn't as beautiful as Beth Schwartz, with her wide dark eyes and beautiful curls the color of a raven's wing, or even Hannah, whose complexion was like cream and whose hair was thick and golden and all but glowed in sunlight. Hope's hair, meanwhile, was untamable and bright as a new copper penny, but she'd always secretly liked it. It fit her personality. And her eyes were lovely, with long curling black lashes at odds with her hair color, and she had a nice mouth that tipped up at the corners.

"'Beauty's sister is vanity, and its daughter lust,'" Mammi quoted from right behind Hope, making her jump.

"Oh, help," Hope squeaked. "You scared me."

With a nod at the mirror, Mammi shook her head, her long salt-and-pepper braid falling off her shoulder. "Staring won't change whatever it is you're worried about."

Hope shook her head. "I'm not worried. I'd like to look neat for my first day in the—"

Mammi waved a hand at her, cutting off the next words, and Hope frowned her confusion. Until it occurred to her that Dat hadn't headed out to the fields yet. Guilt, despite having Mammi's blessing to go, dug a deeper pit in her heart, and she wrestled with herself over it. Maybe growing up had changed her into this anxious worrywart of a woman.

"What are we doing?" Hannah whispered as she crept down the hallway toward where they still stood, half in and half out of the bathroom.

"'Then you would trust, because there is hope; and you would look around and rest securely,'" Mammi quoted from the Book of Job.

Hannah didn't even blink, merely nodded like that made sense as an answer to her question. Mammi was always tossing out random bits of scripture. Though this time in on the secret, Hope suspected that perhaps the sayings might not be quite so random.

"I need to get the casserole out of the oven," Hope said and shooed them off.

"It smells edible, at least," Mammi mentioned ten minutes later as she entered the kitchen after dressing.

As Hope pulled the pan carefully out of the propane-powered oven, she tipped her head, studying the concoction she'd whipped up last night. Today was her turn to cook breakfast, and she'd chosen a casserole because she could get all the messiest parts of preparation done and cleaned up the night before, instead of this morning when she needed to be out the door as soon as she finished her chores.

Except the casserole didn't look quite right. *Did I miss an ingredient?*

Probably. She was always doing something like that. While she loved reading and drawing, and didn't mind cleaning or tending the garden, cooking was not a gift Gotte had blessed her with. More's the pity.

"You forgot the green onions," Hannah said, glancing over her shoulder as she gathered silverware to set the table.

"Oh, sis yuscht." Darn. Hope wrinkled her nose. That was the best part of the recipe. "Do you think if I sprinkled them over the top, it would be okay?"

"Here." Hannah gently took it from her, careful to use her apron to handle the hot dish and save herself a burn. She set it on the counter. As Hope watched, her older sister not only cut up green onions, but also minced some fresh dill and parsley from the garden, two herbs Hope had never thought of combining, and sprinkled them over the top like a fancy garnish. Then she popped it in the oven again and turned to find Hope shaking her head.

"What?"

"I don't know how you do that."

Hannah rolled her eyes as she wiped her hands on her apron. "I paid attention when Mamm taught us, and you didn't."

"If you aim at nothing, you're bound to hit it," Mammi piped up from where she'd finished setting the table.

But Hope *had* paid attention. Painful, careful attention. Not that it helped. The steps just wouldn't stick in her head. She'd worried that maybe she wasn't Amish enough, if she didn't care for cooking. What would her husband think of her after they married?

She shook off the worry. Time enough for that trouble, no need to go borrowing more for today. She had plenty to keep her busy.

In short order, they had the table laid and bread and butter with the last of the fig preserves set out. As they worked, Hope hummed a tune, eventually the words tumbling from her lips, sending the notes, most of them wrong, to Gotte's ears with joy.

Dat's feet on the back stairs thumped. He appeared—tall and slender, his horseshoe beard turning gray and silver at his temples, Levi Beiler had always been a handsome figure of a man. "Something smells wunderbaar."

"Denki," Hope said eagerly. "I made a bacon, egg, and potato casserole."

His eyebrows inched up and he glanced at Hannah, who gave a tiny nod that Hope pretended not to see. Dat did that every time it was her turn to cook, and she was certain Hannah was reassuring their father she was on top of it.

Not that Hope could blame them. Two weeks ago, she'd gotten ambitious and insisted on trying Hannah's French toast casserole recipe, but she'd remembered wrong and doubled the amount of eggs to put in. That had been a disaster. Like eating scrambled eggs covered in soggy bread and syrup with a praline crust, because the crunchy topping had sunk to the bottom.

"It'll be fine," she insisted now, trying not to let her feelings get hurt.

A year ago, Dat would've laughed and tapped her on her nose, making her laugh, too. Instead, Dat's expression didn't change, mistrust born from experience not entirely tempered by affection these days, and suddenly she missed her mother more than anything, the ache of it a hole inside her chest. With the French toast, she would've eaten the ruined food with every appearance of enjoyment. Instead, Dat had taken the dish to the hogs and the family had all eaten thick slices of Hannah's bread spread with creamy, sweet butter along with quickly boiled eggs.

"Handy that we raise chickens," Mammi had commented.

Thankfully, this time, the food came out smelling and looking exactly as it should, if a little extra green on top. After a silent time of prayer, they quickly ate, again mostly in silence.

"This is . . . well done, Hope," Dat said after a while, sending her a small smile.

The clouds lifted and Hope straightened to grin happily back, trying not to notice the way Dat blinked and dropped his gaze, almost like he'd doused a lantern behind his eyes.

"Hadn't you best be going, Levi?" Mammi prompted. "Those fields won't work themselves."

Hannah paused with her fork halfway to her mouth, giving Mammi a funny look. Their grandmother never spoke sharply to their father that way. At least, not since she'd come to live here. In fact, she usually tried to get him to talk more, not leave. No doubt she was doing it to get rid of him so Hope could rush through her chores to leave for the Kanagys'.

Hope kept her eyes on her own plate and continued to eat.

"I'll be planting in the north field today," Dat said as he got up from the table. "Hope, the garden is getting out of control."

She put her fork down and shared a glance with Hannah. All day yesterday she'd worked on the garden so that Mammi and her schwester wouldn't have that additional burden while she was working at the shop. She'd toiled until every growing plant could reach the sun and soil without weeds, and each row had been hand-tilled and turned to neat, blooming order. She'd even managed to plant her strawberries, looking forward to summer for her favorite fruit.

It wondered her how her father hadn't noticed on his way in yesterday evening or even this morning. The sun rose earlier each morning, lighting the world by six a.m. at the latest these days, and he'd had to walk past the garden from the barn after taking care of the animals.

"Yes, Dat."

"Gute girl."

With a kiss on the forehead for each of his dochders, and a kiss on the cheek for Mammi—a tradition that hadn't disappeared with her mother—Dat gathered his coat against the chill before the sun had time to warm the earth more, along with his straw hat and other belongings; took his lunch from Hannah, who had put it together last night; and left out the back door. Before Mamm, Dat would come up at lunchtime, but since, he'd taken his lunch with him and stayed out all day.

"Hannah," Mammi said almost casually as she dried dishes. "Hope will be working at A Thankful Heart gift shop for the Kanagys for the next few weeks."

Hannah, already elbows deep in the sink of dirty dishes, straightened abruptly, worry pinching her brow. "I know things are . . . tight," Hannah said after a minute's consideration. "But not so bad she should have to work for the Kanagys. Dat wouldn't like it."

Mammi flapped a hand. "Let me worry about your dat. I've given her my permission."

Hope, in the process of clearing the table, paused to glance over. Maybe she'd finally discover what the trouble had been between the families, but Mammi gave her the pinched-lipped stare she got anytime the subject of the Kanagys was raised.

With a resigned sigh, Hope explained. "I'm not doing it for money." *Not exactly*, she silently amended. "Aaron Kanagy and I made a trade. And it's a surprise, so please don't ask more questions. It should only be six weeks or so."

Hannah's brows only furrowed deeper as she glanced between Mammi and Hope. The trouble was, they needed Hannah in on the situation to a certain extent. She would notice Hope's absence each day, as well as needing to take on or divvy out some of Hope's chores. "I am *not* cleaning the bathrooms for you."

"I'll do them and as many of my other chores as I can in the morning before I leave. Denki, Hannah." Hope hugged her sister, thinking of how, in a few short months, they might not have her here in the mornings anymore. Not if Noah bought that house. Bittersweet, weddings were. Both beginnings and endings. "You'll thank me later, I promise."

That sent her sister's eyebrows sky-high, but Hannah said nothing further beyond a small smile. "You'd better hurry with those toilets if you want to walk to town before the store opens."

"I'm going to walk through the woods to the Kanagys' house and get a ride with them," Hope assured her.

Hannah's expression cleared, but not all the way. She shook her head slowly. "I still say Dat won't like it."

"If she was still with us, Mamm would've talked him around," Hope insisted with all the emotion of her name.

That, finally, pulled a real smile from Hannah, one that reached her blue eyes, though they darkened with sadness. "Yes. I think she would."

After that, they'd gotten down to the business of daily chores, chatting and singing as they worked, so that Hope hardly remembered she had elsewhere to be.

She'd just finished the last of the bathrooms when Mammi appeared in the doorway.

"You'd better fly, chickie," Mammi said, flapping her apron at Hope like she would the chickens in their coop.

A glance outside at the already bright blue sky told her she'd need to hurry. A quick kiss for Hannah and Mammi, just like Dat did every morning, then Hope grabbed her own lunch—she and Aaron hadn't talked about schedules, but she assumed she'd be in the shop during all business hours—and flew out the door, heading for her woods and the boy waiting for her on the other side.

AARON TRIED TO assure himself that he wasn't watching for Hope any more than he should be in order to be able to leave on time. She didn't like him enough to marry him, but he'd win her over. Not for marriage, or any such thing. But maybe they could see their way fit to being friends.

The horse blew a gusty sigh, and Aaron patted his soft neck.

He'd gotten up and done his chores like normal, helping Joshua feed and care for their various animals and milk the cows before coming in for breakfast, and thankful he hadn't had to sneak out of the house early to get to his workshop. Hope had saved him that, at least for a time. No need to bear the burden of his guilt as he worked, which he was impatient to get to now. Imagine a full day doing only woodworking.

What an unexpected gift.

After breakfast, he'd hitched up Frank, their reliable horse, though he was starting to get old. Mamm and Daniel already sat inside as they waited in the buggy. He peeked at his pocket watch, which he wore only during business hours, and glanced again at the corner of the house Hope would likely come around when she arrived.

"I am sorry for being late," a soft voice called from

behind him, and Aaron whirled to find Hope there, cheeks and nose bright red and puffing a little from her effort. A few stray curls had escaped her kapp to frame her face.

He grinned at the sight of her, telling himself that his heart lifted at the humor of her tousled appearance, as though she'd just escaped pirates or some other nonsense, and not at Hope herself. "Did you run all the way?"

Hope wrinkled her nose as she stopped in front of him. "Not *all* the way." Which for some odd reason made him want to laugh. Picturing her flying through the woods fit her. "I bet you stopped at the bridge, though," he teased.

The pink that rose in her cheeks told him he was right.

"Leave be embarrassing the girl, Aaron," his mother called from the buggy.

"Yes, Mamm." Aaron winked at Hope.

But instead of sharing his amusement, she frowned. Why? Because of innocent teasing? He hadn't meant to offend her. Maybe that was why she wouldn't marry him. Because she found him rude and unmannered.

Vowing to be the best-mannered man in the district around her, he cleared his throat, then led her to the buggy. Only Hope stopped when she realized his mother had sat in back with Daniel. "I should sit in back, shouldn't I?"

"Nonsense." Mamm waved Hope into the front beside Aaron. Reluctantly, Hope climbed in, not bothering to argue. Her reluctance stung, like she'd said the words all over again. She really had something against him.

"I'll be on time tomorrow," Hope turned to say to his mother.

Suddenly she smiled, dimples winking at him from his view of the side of her face, and Aaron snapped the reins a bit harder than he'd meant to, sending Frank into a jolting trot. Hope jerked sideways with a gasp, and he shot out a hand to steady her, though he retrieved it quickly when she scooted around to face forward, putting as much space between them on the bench seat as she could.

"Sorry," he muttered.

Thankfully, his mother treated Hope's presence like she would a guest and didn't rebuke him in front of her; otherwise his ears would be red from her sharp words.

"Anyway, I'll be earlier tomorrow," Hope said. "We had to explain things to Hannah but in a way that she wouldn't know what was going on."

"You're right on time," his mother assured her. "Isn't she, Aaron?"

He tried hard not to let his face show his thoughts. They'd waited ten minutes and Mamm had been fretting about opening the store late, though they'd get there with plenty of time to spare. What's more, Dat and Joshua were already there, having left directly after breakfast to walk down and deal with the extra inventory one of their vendors from Lampton would be dropping off early.

"Still, I'd rather be early yet," Hope insisted, winning a satisfied nod from his mother.

And why that should make Aaron anything but mystified about his mother's behavior, he didn't know.

This is ridiculous. We're trading services and that's all.

He shouldn't be noticing how Hope's slim hands pleated the bit of apron that peeped from beneath her sweater, or wanting to tuck those wayward curls back for her.

He liked girls. Had ever since he'd turned fourteen and sprouted and they'd given him a decent share of attention. He should be more humble, but he had to admit he liked that he was considered a decent catch in the district. He tried to be hardworking and faithful, and if the girls' attention was anything to go on, he was not too bad to look at. He also tried to be kind.

More than enough for any girl. Including Hope Beiler. Not that he wanted to catch her, but proving her wrong wouldn't hurt.

They started the ride in relative silence, but about halfway there, Mamm started explaining the store to Hope.

"We receive deliveries daily from various suppliers, all local of course, and Amish-made. In addition to learning our inventory system, what we sell, and helping shoppers find the right items, you'll help do things like adjusting displays, restocking shelves, and organizing in the back of the shop. Aaron will teach you."

Aaron sat up straighter and must've unconsciously tightened his grip on the reins because Frank suddenly slowed. He clucked softly at the horse, who settled back at a slightly faster pace. "I thought I'd get started on the—"

"Plenty of time to get started tomorrow," Mamm snapped.

"I'm a quick learner," Hope offered to him in a quiet, apologetic aside. "You won't have to spend much time with me."

Was she trying to get rid of him already? Hope was turning out to be hard on his self-esteem. Perhaps Gotte, in His wisdom, had sent her to teach Aaron a lesson in humility?

"I—"

Mamm, who had ears like a wolf, cut him off. "I'm sure you are, Hope. It will be a blessing to have a woman in the store with me. Someone to counteract these big, strapping men in my family."

Aaron tried not to wince as realization settled over him like a heavy, scratchy horse blanket. Mamm was serious about trying to matchmake him and Hope. No doubt of it now. Big and strapping indeed. Ach vell. Nothing he could do about it except ignore it. Mamm would get the idea sooner or later.

"Mamm," Daniel groaned behind him.

Hope glanced sideways at Aaron, he suspected with suppressed laughter. "Unlike your sons, I'm definitely *not* big and strapping," was all she said.

Jah. Definitely laughing at him.

"But such a hard worker for such a little thing," his mamm was quick to reply, probably worried she'd offended Hope.

"Denki. I will try to be helpful for you."

Thankfully, they'd reached the store. Aaron didn't have to direct Frank, who knew the way down the alley behind the storefronts that lined the main street of Charity Creek, narrower where his workshop now took up space. As their numbers grew and land became a scarce commodity, turning ever more costly as well as limited in availability, more and more Amish were leaving farming behind, with some starting small businesses. The Troyers, one of the first families with a storefront in town, had had the sense to purchase an open field that backed up behind the shops. All the other Amish owners would turn their horses out and park their buggies at one end of the field, for a small fee, during the day.

"Send Joshua out to take care of the horse," Mamm said as she got down.

"But—"

She cut him off with a firm stare. "I suggest if you want to have any time in your workshop today, you get started showing Hope what to do."

"Yes, Mamm." No use arguing when his mother got a bee in her bonnet.

Daniel sent him a look across Frank's back with his rather stoic version of a grin, earning a scowl from Aaron, who then turned to find Hope watching with her eyebrows raised and color rising in her cheeks. But she didn't comment.

Nothing he could say would make that better. "Follow me."

Meekly she trailed behind him into the store, where Joshua and Dat were already busy sorting through their new wares.

"Welcome to the shop, Hope," Joshua called as soon as she walked in. He even came forward to shake her hand. "Mamm's glad to have you helping."

No blush and no solemn little face for his younger brother. Taking his hand, she smiled easily. "Mammi said to thank you next time I bumped into you. Our horse's leg is much better since you helped us with it. That poultice worked a treat."

Joshua ran a hand round the back of his neck, almost embarrassed at her comment. Not that Aaron was in the least surprised. His brother would honestly rather be a horse than a human, probably, as much as he loved working with the animals. "That's gute," Joshua said. "I'm glad."

"When did you work on the Beilers' horse?" Dat asked from the corner he hadn't left, where he was unpacking boxes.

Dat had not been too happy about the situation with Hope, mostly concerned with Levi Beiler's response and not wanting to stir up more trouble with the man. Aaron had no idea what Mamm had said to Dat behind closed doors, but he'd come down before breakfast this morning resigned to Hope's helping, if not exactly agreeable.

Hope cast a nervous glance in his direction now, no doubt thanks to his gruffly voiced question. Of course,

Joseph Kanagy, who'd given his boys his height and broad shoulders, managed to appear imposing even when he smiled, thanks to his piercing dark eyes.

"After singeon last week," Joshua said. Oblivious as usual. "He threw a shoe and was a bit tender after I helped walk him home."

That's where Joshua had disappeared to last Sunday evening? How had Aaron not known that? And why was his younger bruder still holding Hope's hand? "Mamm wants you to take care of Frank," Aaron said.

Joshua cast him a questioning glance, probably at the tone of voice he used, but at least dropped Hope's hand, though he grinned at her as he went to handle the chore.

Hope hid a smile in the face of their father's stern demeanor, but Aaron still caught it. That was one smile for Daniel and two for Joshua and none so far for Aaron. Not that he was keeping track.

"What did your fater say about working for us?" his dat asked next.

"Ach vell, Mammi gave me permission and said she would talk to him."

Hope didn't blush or stammer or even shift on her feet as she said the words. Maybe that's why he noticed . . . the fact that she went so still.

"He's a stubborn man, for sure and certain." His dat nodded as if that put paid to the matter.

Rather than get angry or defensive, Hope laughed, the joyfully amused sound filling the small room. "A quality I would pray for, if I didn't first need to pray for my own stubbornness so I could remove the log from my own eye before helping him with the splinter in his," she said, quoting the Book of Matthew.

His dat blinked a couple times, probably as bowled over

by the way her face lit up with her laughter as Aaron was. Then he threw his head back and roared with laughter. No one ever talked back to him like that, but Hope did it with such a sweet innocence, just as she did everything, that he couldn't be mad about it.

"Jah," Dat finally said, wiping his eyes. "True of us all."

Hope turned to Aaron, smile fading. "What do we do first?"

Chapter Five

❋

AARON MUST BE eager to be rid of her. He started his tour of the business not in the storage and office areas in back, but in the storefront. Hope had been in the shop often through the years, but had only paid attention to the particular items she was interested in. Now she paused to take in the full room with all its different displays and wares.

The Kanagys had done a lovely job with it. Long and narrow, as part of Charity Creek's downtown historic main street buildings, they'd set it up similar to an old-fashioned general store. Honey-colored wood—polished to a high sheen but still obviously original based on the wear—lined the floors, and the walls were the original stone with the beams showing through, giving a rustic feel. As though the building itself could tell its story of the various people who'd owned it or passed through the doors.

The walls were lined with whitewashed freestanding shelving units. Each unit displayed a different set of goods. Meanwhile, down the center of the store were several tables with more displays and one long, old-fashioned wagon filled to the brim with barrels of different candies that customers could scoop into cellophane bags however they wanted.

Given Aaron's penchant for woodworking, Hope wondered if he'd had a hand in making all the display cases and tables. Probably not. The store hadn't changed much through the years that she could recall.

She almost stumbled into him as he stopped at the first display to wave at a wall of beautifully designed and hand-stitched quilts.

"These are the quilts."

Hope stifled the giggle that wanted to rise up.

Her expression must've given her away, because Aaron paused then chuckled. "Obviously. We get them from many different ladies across both counties, including the Millers' quilting circle. No schedule for deliveries and they set the prices based on the intricacy of the design. We take a percentage."

He moved to the next display, which contained a large variety of canned foods by, again, women around both counties. Talking in rapid-fire bursts, he moved on before she even had a chance to nod. Then came goat's milk soap by Milk and Honey, leather goods from Bontrager's Harnesses, handbags by Galena's Hand Crafts, pottery and cutting boards by Zachary Treber, baskets by Dinah Schrock, wooden toys by Aaron himself, honey and beeswax products from his brother Daniel, straw hats by Benton Hats, iron crafts by Elam Wegler and Mervin Stutzman, and the list continued on and on.

By the time they'd finished the tour of the front, Hope's head was spinning with the sheer number of items and craftsmen's products they carried. She was trying her best to soak in every detail, regretting she hadn't brought a pad of paper to write this all down.

"Any questions?"

Where did she start? "Um . . . prices?"

Aaron opened his mouth, then closed it again with a grimace. "Sorry." He picked up the nearest item, a purple candle that smelled of lavender. Made by . . . Hope searched her brain but couldn't come up with it.

"The maker of the individual items sets the prices. Other than the quilts, which are priced by design and size individually, most of the pricing is set beforehand. The supplier will discuss it with Dat or Mamm and agree on what would work best. Prices are either stickers on the bottom." He tilted the candle to show her. "Or attached with a string and tag."

She nodded. At least she wouldn't have to remember the prices.

"After you've sold enough stuff and had to ring them up or answer questions a few thousand times, you'll just remember. Until then, either check the sticker or don't be shy to ask."

Hope nodded again. She was doing a lot of nodding. *Please let me remember this.* Not like what happened with recipes. "What does 'ring them up' mean?"

"Ach vell, we have a computerized cash register, which you will need to learn."

A computer? Nerves knotted in her stomach faster than when Rachel, who was all thumbs, tried to sew. Hope had never done more than use the basic computer in the library to search for the location of a book. Was she going to be expected to learn this one?

Aaron led her over behind the checkout counter to show her. "We started with an old-fashioned cash register, but almost none of the Englischers pay in cash anymore, only credit cards. The bishop gave us special permission to use one for the business only."

Tapping a button, he turned on the screen, and Hope had to stuff her doubts way down to her toes. Only Aaron didn't say anything for a long beat, so she lifted her gaze to find him staring down at her, amusement playing around the corners of his mouth.

Not like he was laughing at her exactly.

"What's that look for?" he asked.

"I don't know what you mean."

"You looked ready to run a mile, rather than use this."

Hope bit her lip. Had she been that obvious? No use but to fess up. "With so many buttons and key combinations, I just know I'm going to ruin something." Like the way she ruined anything she cooked.

Aaron chuckled and she tried not to scowl. Tried and failed. "Don't laugh at me, Aaron Kanagy."

He sobered quickly. "I'm not laughing *at* you, Hope. More like with you," he said, so sincerely she believed him, and forgave him immediately.

"You're not?"

He shook his head. "I'm laughing at the deerich notion of you ruining anything. You were one of the schmaert girls in school, if I remember right. Wonderful gute at maths."

She wouldn't have said she was smart. Was she being foolish with her worries? But Dat's expression anytime her turn in the kitchen came around popped into her head. "You should try my cooking," she muttered.

A twinkle returned to his dark eyes, one that dared her to join in his fun, but he didn't laugh again. "I have."

Her mouth dropped open. "You have?"

He shrugged. "When your family hosted Gmay and singeon last year."

Of course. She deflated, like the balloon Mamm had surprised her with for her fifth birthday. Hope had seen a young Englischer girl with one and had begged for months for her own. When the thing lost its air and drooped to the floor after only a few days, it had felt exactly like this. "That was Hannah's cooking."

Aaron shook his head. "I happened to come inside as your mater and schwester were discussing where to put *your* cookies."

Hope's face immediately heated. With her pale skin and strawberry blond hair, her blush had been her curse since childhood, but she found it coming and going with frustrating regularity around Aaron. "They didn't serve them."

How had they gotten on this topic again?

"But I snuck one anyway." That twinkle really was fun, even when she was cringing inside.

She might've smiled in commiseration if she weren't mortified to find out he'd sampled her terrible cooking. "I burned the bottoms."

"I like my cookies a little on the burned side," he insisted.

"And put in too much cinnamon. I got the amount mixed up with the sugar."

He grinned. "That must be why I liked them. I love cinnamon."

If she hadn't heard with her own ears his talking about how she was just "okay, I guess," Hope would be tempted to think of Aaron as the nicest man in the county.

Except she *had* heard, the hurt pinching any pleasure she might have taken from his words now. "Ach vell, you'd best show me how this thing works."

The twinkle disappeared, which sent a twinge of regret through her.

"I can show her," Joshua offered.

Hiding a wince, Hope turned to find Aaron's younger brother standing behind them. When had he snuck up? And more important, did he overhear about her terrible cooking? It'd be all over the district before she got home from her first day of work at this rate. So would her working in the store. Thankfully, her fater only got out of the house for church these days.

"I've got it," Aaron insisted.

"Dat needs help with Mr. Bontrager's delivery."

Aaron only grunted as an answer, but he left Hope standing by the counter to head to the back room.

Joshua stepped up to take his place. "Aaron's terrible with the cash register and Mamm tries to keep him away from it," he quietly explained.

Such a notion surprised a laugh from Hope. So, Aaron wasn't perfect either. Somehow, that made her soften a tiny bit toward him.

She also relaxed now that he was gone. Having to keep herself together around him left her muscles as tight as a drying line.

"Here. Let me show you," Joshua said.

JOSHUA HAD GOTTEN her laughing in seconds, which made Aaron want to growl like a hungry bear in the winter. *What am I doing wrong?*

People, girls in particular, smiled and laughed around him. Aaron enjoyed it, other people's pleasure feeding his own joy. So far, though, Hope had been completely immune to him, or he managed to stick his foot so far into his mouth he could untie the laces with his tonsils.

"I hope you're being nice to Hope," Mamm said as he passed her on his way outside.

"I'm always nice to Hope," he said.

Which was true. And again begged the question . . . why didn't she like him? He managed not to think too hard on the other question of why that bothered him as much as it did.

Outside Dat stood with Mr. Bontrager beside a wagon piled high with boxes. "Aaron, did you approve the addition of these new tool belts from Eli?"

"Jah. While you were in Nappanee with Daniel a few weeks ago." He took the beautifully crafted leather belt with pockets and loops for all sorts of carpentry tools. Attached to the belt was a leather suspender system, which would allow for more weight in the belt without it slipping off a man's hips. "In three different sizes, starting at two hundred dollars. Mamm agreed."

Eli Bontrager, his long white beard covering the top buttons of his shirt, nodded solemnly.

Aaron's dat nodded as well. "Do you think these will sell?" he asked next, eyeing the large pile.

"I only brought six belts. Two in each size," Eli assured him. "The rest is my usual delivery."

"I see. That's fine then. Aaron can take care of unloading while we settle up from last month's sales." So saying, he led Eli inside, leaving Aaron to the heavy lifting, kindly saving the older man's back. Eli had a large extended family but had refused to move in with his oldest daughter five years ago, after his wife died. He hadn't wanted to leave his tanning setup, though Aaron understood Eli to be in search of an apprentice. Perhaps then he'd move in with family.

Moving quickly, though he had to pause to make space on the racks in back beside the few remaining inventory items from Eli, Aaron unloaded the cart and had it all stacked away before Eli and his father finished.

Then, with only one longing glance at his workshop, he

hustled back to the front of the store to find Joshua and Hope, heads close together as Joshua went through how to use the register and computer. Hope's face was all squished up with concentration.

"What do you think?" Joshua prompted.

"How's it coming?" Aaron asked at the same time, and Hope jumped back to face him.

"I think I'll get it. Hopefully before I stop working in the shop," she replied with dry humor.

"You will," he said, confident. "Any other questions about the storefront before I show you the back?"

Hope visibly gulped at the mention of more, then drew her shoulders back, as though she'd told herself she'd could handle it. Except she glanced around, almost like she was determined to have at least one question. After a second, she shook her head.

"Don't worry," Joshua assured her in a loud whisper meant to be heard. "If Aaron can learn how to work in this shop, anyone can."

Hope did laugh at that, sliding Aaron a sidelong glance brimming with laughter. "That does make me feel a little better," she teased.

Still no smile meant for him, but better than the serious side she seemed determined to treat him to.

"Joshua Kanagy, manners," Mamm snapped as she came in from the back room. "In front of Hope, no less— you can help me open the store and work the front while Aaron teaches her about the back."

"What about Daniel?" Joshua wheedled.

Aaron ushered Hope away before she could get embroiled in the argument he knew was coming. Joshua usually liked working the front of the shop, unlike Daniel, but less so if he had to with Mamm, because she made him do more than work the cash register.

"Your bruder has gone home to tend to his bees since he will be away two days with your dat soon. And Dat left with him, before you ask."

The rest of the conversation turned muffled as Aaron closed the black curtain that hung between the front of the store and the back room. The quiet filled the space between them, and he paused, looking down at Hope, who looked back with a wide, expectant gaze.

Suddenly, he found himself without words. Something that never happened to him, as he was an admitted talker. Or as Mamm would say, he could talk to drying paint and be entertained.

"Your eyes are gray." He said the first thing that popped into his head.

The front of the store they lit with electricity, yet another allowance for the business, though they tried to supplement with oil lamps. The constant hum of electricity was more noticeable probably to Amish ears, as their homes were deeply quiet, the soft tick of a clock and the rustle of the breeze through the open windows the sounds they lived with. Aaron didn't care for the buzzing sound of electric power, no matter how low.

In the back of the store, however, where they worked without customers, they followed the Ordnung and did without. Yet in the dimmer lighting, helped by a set of three small windows toward the top of the wall facing the alley, the color of her eyes caught his attention now.

This time she didn't blush. Instead, she tipped up her chin. "You've known me since we were children and you just now noticed the color of my eyes?"

He shook his head. "Nae. I thought they were more a pale blue, but up close, I see I was mistaken."

"Oh." She glanced away, long dark lashes hiding her eyes from him.

Aaron cleared his throat and started talking about the shelving system and how they handled inventory. The system they had for noting when they took merchandise to the front of the store, and the rolling ladder he'd built that attached to the shelves, making it easier and safer to retrieve or put away items higher up.

Mamm came in at the tail end of that, knocking—which she'd never done before—and poking her head through the curtain, her expectant expression turning disappointed. What did she expect to find? Them holding hands or him down on one knee?

Not even Gotte, with all His amazing miracles, could move that fast.

Aaron made a mental note to put Mamm off this idea of matchmaking right quick tonight. After supper at home. She was always happier after supper was done and the kitchen cleaned, when they could sit down together to enjoy the rest of their evening in peace.

Mamm straightened. "All done with showing Hope the back?"

Aaron nodded.

"Gute. I'd like you to work the front of the store today. Hope can follow you and see how it's done, maybe have her do the cash register while you help."

"I was going to start on the—"

Mamm flapped a hand. "Plenty of time for that tomorrow."

"I still have to get the wood I'll need to make the bed frame. I was going to borrow Eli Bontrager's wagon while he's in town."

"Oh, help," his mother muttered. The look she tossed his way clearly said he was not holding up his end by trying hard to spend time alone with Hope. Maters could be as silly as chickens when it came to marrying off their kinder, it seemed.

"Go do that now," she said. "I'll have her follow me until you get back."

Aaron spared a quick glance at Hope, who'd watched this exchange in silence. "Any kind of wood you have in mind?"

She shook her head. "Whatever you think would be best."

Aaron snapped up his hat and tipped it at her like a cowboy. "Yes, ma'am," he drawled.

Her lips twitched, but that's the closest he got to a smile before he headed out the back door. He'd figure out how to make her smile—really smile—at him eventually.

Chapter Six

✳

PART OF HOPE wanted Aaron to set his horse to a faster clip, to get home sooner and see how Mammi and Hannah had fared without her. See if Dat had commented on her absence. The other part struggled with dread that was trying to grow into a boulder in her stomach, pinning her to the ground so she couldn't move.

I'm not doing this to hurt Dat, I am doing this for Hannah, she reasoned, sitting straighter in her seat with the thought.

At least she hadn't ruined anything in the store. She'd had to ask for help with the computer every time, but she'd enjoyed talking to the customers and arranging one of the table displays to Ruth Kanagy's specifications. The shop itself felt warm and welcoming, a small ray of delight to each person who entered. If it weren't for Aaron and the way he tied her stomach into knots, she could see herself enjoying working in the store forever.

Not that that was an option. This was a temporary bargain only.

Joshua hopped out as Aaron pulled up to the house. Immediately, he started unhitching the horse, crooning to Frank in low tones and promising him a warm blanket and food.

"Aaron, please walk Hope home," Ruth insisted.

Hope glanced at the still bright sky. They closed the shop at six, but they worked another hour to seven in order to restock shelves, use their inventory system to determine what orders to place, and tally the sales for the day.

Still, sunset wasn't for another hour and Hope would've preferred to go alone. She didn't need any more knots in her stomach, compliments of Aaron Kanagy. But neither of them argued, simply headed around the side of the house to the small path in the back that led into their woods.

They didn't speak for the first little bit, and Hope actually found her shoulders easing as birdsong and the gurgle of the stream, still out of sight, soothed and lulled her into a sense of peace. As they neared her bridge, Aaron cleared his throat. "Hope, do you not like me?"

Just like that, her peace shattered, tension coiling in her muscles even more than what she'd let go mere moments ago. Oh, help! He did *not* ask her that, putting her on the spot. As if she could ever tell him she'd overheard those mortifying words that night and how much they had hurt her, even if she hadn't wanted to let them. She hadn't even repeated those words to Hannah . . . or Mamm or Mammi.

"What a question." She quickened her steps.

"It's just that I . . ."

He trailed off as though he might give up the topic. No such luck. "You don't seem easy with me."

A hand on her arm, warm and solid and steady, stopped her on his side of the bridge, turning her to face him. As soon as she did, he dropped his hand to his side. His earnest expression, like a puppy begging for scraps with those big brown eyes, told her he wasn't going to let this go.

She stared at him, willing her panicked mind to come up with some kind of suitable response. "I don't know what to say to such silliness," she said. "*Everyone* likes you."

Maybe that's why it had hurt so much. She had been part of the everyone who liked him.

Only his expression didn't lighten. "I would like us to be friends, Hope."

Ach du lieva. Surprise held her tongue for a long moment. Friends with the boy who thought she was only just "okay, I guess." Could she see her way past her own pride to try? Scripture came to mind from the Book of James. A passage Mamm would quote to Dat from time to time.

"But he giveth more grace. Wherefore he saith, God resisteth the proud, but giveth grace unto the humble."

Gotte would want her to truly forgive in her heart and show that by deed. After all, she'd been no better the other day, blurting out that she couldn't marry him.

But can I forget the hurt? Maybe I'm more like Dat than I realized.

Thinking over his own situation, realization settled over her softly. Thirty years of not liking the Kanagys hadn't made his life any better. For sure and certain.

Hope drew her shoulders back, a pleased light filling her up, lifting her as she came to a decision. "You don't even know me," she teased gently. "What if I'm actually a troll who lives under this bridge? I caught an enchantress and made her turn me human so I could come out and terrorize the first boy who wanted to be friends."

Aaron's eyes widened with each word. When she'd finished, he threw his head back and laughed. "I forgot how you used to make up stories on the way to school," he said.

He remembered that? "Hannah's shoes were too small that year and hurt her feet. I made up the stories to distract her."

She hadn't thought of that in years and years.

He crossed his arms and nodded. "Like a loving *schwester* should." Then he held out a hand. "So . . . friends?"

This was the second time they'd shaken hands in almost as many days. Only this time felt . . . bigger, more important somehow. Which was ridiculous. Aaron was one of those people who wanted to be liked by everyone, and she had kept her distance. He didn't mean anything by it much.

Hope slipped her hand into his and got a hearty shake that tugged her off her feet a bit.

Aaron's grin could light up the dimness of the trees whose tall canopies blocked out the setting sun. "Are you going to change back into a troll when we go over your bridge and eat me?"

She glanced around as though checking for spies and leaned closer to loudly whisper. "You better not risk it and stay over on your side."

Only Aaron shook his head. "*Mamm* would tan my backside if she thought I didn't walk you all the way home."

Aaron blinked at what must've been a look of horror to cross her face.

"Maybe not all the way." The words popped out of her mouth before she could think them through.

Dat would likely be getting home about the same time, and what would he say to see her walking out of the woods with a Kanagy boy?

Aaron's brows beetled in a way she could tell would be in use when he became a father, chasing his *kinder* around the house and laying down the law. The picture was so clear in her head, her breath stuck in her throat.

"Why not all the way?" he demanded in a voice gone gruff.

Hope thought fast. "Mammi knows all about our deal, of course. But it's a surprise for Hannah."

He didn't need to know that Hannah was aware of her working in the shop. Except the hole of hiding the truth she was digging around herself kept getting deeper and darker. This had started out as such an innocent plan to do something nice for her sister. Maybe she should end it here before things got complicated.

"Ach vell, I'll just walk you to the edge of the woods then," he said before she could speak up.

Trying to hide her worry, Hope led the way over her bridge, not even pausing to stop and enjoy the melody of the stream or the whisper of the breeze in the trees as she went.

Only her heart wouldn't let the matter drop, and at the edge of the woods, she turned sharply to Aaron, her nose colliding with his chest. "I lied. I'm a liar and a terrible person and you shouldn't want to be friends with me." The words tumbled out.

Rather than shock or horror, Aaron cocked his head, amusement dancing in his eyes. "Is this the troll showing?"

Hope scrunched up her face at him. "I'm being serious, Aaron."

He managed to remove the smile from his lips, though they still twitched. "I can see that you are. What is this terrible lie?"

Hope opened her mouth to tell him, then shut it, not sure of the words. *Help me, Gotte*. She sent the quick, silent prayer out.

"I don't want my dat to see you. Mammi gave me permission to work in the shop, but he doesn't know yet, and he won't like it."

The sparkle did leave his eyes at that. "I see," he said slowly.

Did he? Clearly the Kanagys were aware her father didn't care for them. Hope dropped her gaze to her feet. "Maybe we should stop this now," she mumbled.

"I already bought all the lumber for the bed."

She flinched. "Oh, help."

He ducked his head, searching her out, only straightening after he caught her eye. "I don't like keeping things from your dat," he said solemnly.

Hope bit her lip and nodded. Now she'd pulled Aaron into her web of deceit. Maybe she was more like a spider than a troll, even if a good-intentioned one.

"You promise your grossmammi gave you permission?"

She blinked and nodded again. But determined to be truthful with him from now on, added, "Although her words were more along the lines of better to ask forgiveness than permission."

Aaron made a sound that might've been a laugh or a huff. She wasn't sure.

"Fine. I will go along with your mammi on this. But no more sneaking around, and if he is angry when he finds out, make sure it's not with my family."

A gasp parted her lips, her heart turning as light as one of Hannah's butter cookies. "I promise."

Aaron paused, tipping his head to the side as he stared at her uplifted face, sort of taking her in, that small smile playing around his mouth. Then seemed to give himself a shake. "Now, let's get you home."

Hope hesitated only a moment before following him out of the woods and up to the house. She'd promised no more sneaking around. If Dat discovered her with Aaron, they'd tell him the truth. This was much better than the way she'd been handling things.

"That rosebush looks like it's seen better days," Aaron commented as they passed it on the way up the stairs to the front porch.

"Jah. I've been asking Dat to dig it up, but . . ." Hope paused at the top of the stairs and bit her lip, not wanting to share Dat's troubles with anyone outside the family. He especially wouldn't care for a Kanagy to know. "He hasn't had time," she finished lamely.

"With no boys to help," Aaron said, "it must be difficult running the farm by himself."

That he understood—in fact, the kind way he'd handled her entire confession—melted away some of that old pain even more than his wanting to be friends had. She'd been holding that grudge for too long. It wasn't Aaron's fault that she wasn't his type, beyond friendship. There were boys who held no interest for her beyond friendship yet.

Gotte, help me to be a better friend to him than I have been.

"Noah will help take much of the burden after he and Hannah are married."

Aaron smiled. "Gute."

Then he stuck his hands in his pockets and rocked back on his heels, like he wasn't quite sure what to do with himself.

He opened his mouth, but before a sound came out, Mammi opened the door and shoved a pie at him.

AARON WASN'T SURE what surprised him most. The fact that he found himself holding a pie hot enough that he could tell it hadn't finished cooling and was in danger of blistering his palms, or the fact that Hope smiled at him. Finally.

Joshua had earned fifteen of her smiles, Daniel nine, and Mamm six. Even Dat had gotten a few. But not a single one for him until now. Only it didn't really count, did it? This one was because of her mammi.

"That pie is in thanks for helping my Hope," her grandmother said. Then flapped her apron at him. As though he were a pesky bird, come to snatch a treat from her fingers. "Now shoo."

Aaron glanced at Hope, whose gray eyes were lit with mirth, then adjusted his grip to the edges of the dish, which were slightly cooler. "Chocolate pie always was my favorite," he said. "Denki."

Then he headed down the stairs and across the newly spring green expanse of lawn to the woods. He chuckled as he crossed the bridge, thinking of Hope as a troll underneath, lurking there to torment unsuspecting boys. He used to try to time his and his bruder's walk to school so that he could trail behind her and listen to whatever story she made up that day. Not that it happened often.

"She baked you a pie that quick?" Mamm asked when he stepped inside.

"Nae." He shook his head as he deposited the treat on the counter. "Her grossmammi gave it to me."

Mamm brightened visibly at that. "Ach vell, it will be lovely to have after supper."

"Jah." Aaron debated how to bring up what he wanted to say. "Mamm . . ."

"Hmmm?" She had her back to him now, pulling their own supper from the oven. A pot pie by the looks of the flaky golden topping. She must've made it last night. Mamm did that a lot. With only boys and the entire family working at the shop, Mamm had kept most of the cooking, divvying up much of the cleaning among the boys.

"About Hope . . ."

She straightened at that. "What about Hope? What did you do to make her so serious around you?"

As though this were all his fault. He had no idea what he'd done to Hope, though maybe things would get better now that they'd agreed to be friends. "Nothing."

"Uh-huh." Squinty eyes told him Mamm didn't believe him.

"Hope and I are just friends, Mamm. You realize that, right?"

She sniffed. "Friends can become more."

Not when Hope didn't want to marry him. Ever. He didn't say so, though. "In this case, I don't think so."

She eyed him closely. "For you or for her?"

"For her."

That brought out a glower. "Why on earth not? You'd make a wunderbaar mann, and any girl would be lucky to marry you."

"I think Hope is too busy helping at home to worry about husbands."

The glower softened, worry darkening the eyes he'd inherited from his mother. "Maybe we can help," she said.

Aaron had had the same thought. "I'll see what I can do."

She patted his cheek.

A second ago she assumed he'd been the one to offend Hope. Now he was a good boy? He'd never understand his mater.

"Just promise me no more throwing us together or matchmaking?"

"Jah. Jah." She turned back to her meal and waved a vague hand at him. Not exactly a promise, but probably the best he'd get.

"Maybe Joshua will have more sense to snap that girl up," she said as Aaron retreated. He paused, booted foot on the bottom stair of the back steps.

What now?

A glance over his shoulder found Mamm watching his retreat with a challenging light in her eyes, arms crossed. "They got on quite well today." She nodded to herself, as though this idea were excellent.

Aaron had to swallow back a growl of frustration. "I'm sure Joshua and Hope can figure that out without help."

His mother's derisive snort followed him as he took the stairs two at a time. "Everyone needs a push when it comes to love." Her voice floated up to him.

"What was that about?" Joshua poked his head out of his room, eyebrows raised.

"Mamm has her heart set on marrying Hope Beiler off to one of us. Apparently, it doesn't matter which one."

Joshua barked a laugh.

And Aaron grinned, crossing his arms. "Don't laugh. You're in the line of fire along with me."

That sobered his bruder up right quick. "We'll see what Dat has to say about that. A Kanagy marrying a Beiler. Even if she did make him laugh today."

True enough. And given Hope's confession about her dat, Levi Beiler would be even more against such a union than their own dat.

"Mamm just wants dochders," Joshua said.

"Jah. And boppli to dote after. For sure and certain."

"Who wants dochders?" Daniel asked as he appeared at the top of the stairs.

"Mamm."

The oldest of the three of them raised his eyebrows, then just shrugged. "Who can blame her with all the big, strapping men in this house."

Aaron choked on a laugh.

"She called us big, strapping men?" Joshua asked, glancing between them.

Daniel chuckled. "To Hope in the buggy this morning. At least she called us men instead of boys."

"Boys can't be as big or as strapping." Joshua grinned. "Did Hope look impressed?"

"Not even a little," Aaron said.

Amused at his expense? Yes. Impressed? Not as much.

"Still . . ." Joshua got a look on his face Aaron hadn't trusted since childhood. One that usually came right before Aaron ended up in a heap of trouble while Joshua managed to escape any punishment, like water off a duck's back.

Like the time Joshua organized all the boys who lived closest to their house to swap chores. The idea had been brilliant. Using chores like money. If you didn't want to mend a fence, swap that for something else, or even a few something elses, that another boy didn't want to do.

It had worked a treat until Mamm found Micah Miller weeding her herb garden. For Aaron. He'd gotten an earful, along with a month of weeding every day by himself as punishment. Never mind that he'd already finished mending that darn fence for Micah as payment.

He crossed his arms, eyeing Joshua warily. "What?"

Joshua shrugged. "Hope is a sweet girl. Hardworking. Faithful. Kind. *One* of us could do worse."

"Oh, jah?" He tried to keep from scowling.

"Maybe I'll ask her to drive home after singeon on Sunday." His brother fingered his chin like he had a full-grown beard.

Aaron did scowl at that.

Why did the image of Hope standing in front of the gmay with Joshua, saying her vows to be united with him, mann and fraa, drive a nail through Aaron's gut?

"Shows what you know," he said. "She hasn't been to singeon in months."

"Oh?" Joshua gave him a suspiciously innocent look. "I'm surprised you noticed, seeing as you're just friends and all."

Aaron clenched his teeth so hard, he might've cracked a tooth. "We have chores, and supper will be served soon."

Then he spun on his heel and tromped away, refusing to get drawn into further conversation about Hope. Between Mamm and now Joshua, he might well regret making this deal with her.

The sound of Daniel's quiet chuckle joined Joshua's louder laughter and followed him down the front stairs and out of the house.

Chapter Seven

HOPE HUMMED A tune to herself and circled the display she'd been working on all afternoon. A rainy day apparently resulted in fewer customers dropping in, so she had the time. With spring in full bloom, assuming they didn't have another late frost, she'd received permission to take one entire table up front and combine whichever products she felt would sell best related to her spring theme.

A small test, perhaps, but one she'd enjoyed. Maybe she'd gone a little too far?

In the center of the table, she'd arranged a few packaging boxes of varying heights, which she'd gotten from the back room, and laid a handmade tablecloth in spring green over them. On each box went a different featured item. The sweetest bunny and lamb dolls, Daniel's honey, and a dried flower display from one of the store's newest artisans. Hope made a mental note to ask who'd made it.

Tilting her head to the side, she finally declared herself satisfied, right as Aaron's mother appeared from the back.

"That's lovely, dear. Better than I even expected." Ruth Kanagy beamed. She picked up a jar of the honey with a fond smile. "Daniel does love those bees," she murmured, more to herself than to Hope.

Putting the jar down, Ruth glanced around the shop, then cast a frown outside at the gray, drizzly day. The kind that set the cold deeper into your bones. Not even sitting close to the fire at home this evening would thaw Hope all the way.

"We'll close early today," Ruth declared. "We haven't had a customer in several hours."

Hope nodded, already thinking of the extra chores she could help Mammi and Hannah with. "I'll start counting out the cash drawer."

"No, no." Ruth shook her head. "Joshua can balance the register and do a quick inventory check. You go tell Aaron we'll be leaving in thirty minutes. That boy might need prodding." She paused to mutter to herself again. "Doesn't know when to quit."

"Jah," Hope agreed. "For sure and certain."

She shared a commiserating smile with Aaron's mother before Ruth returned to the back room. The woman wasn't exaggerating. Hope had worked in the shop for a week now, and the man had to be dragged from his workshop each day. He had a passion for his craft and a strong work ethic, traits she admired about him.

"Here comes trouble," Joshua said suddenly from where he stood behind the counter. His gaze was directed over Hope's shoulder.

She turned in time to recognize Joy Yoder with her dark hair, bright yellow dress, and perpetual laughter. Only a year younger than Hope, the youngest daughter of Anna and Mervin Yoder was a sweetheart if a tiny bit wild.

"What do you have against Joy?" she demanded.

Face pressed up against the window, Joy cupped her eyes to peer inside. Her gaze landed on Joshua and she broke into a grin and waved.

"Against her?" he asked as Joy headed to the door. "Nothing. We've been friends since before we could walk. But she has a tendency to drag me into messes."

"You've dragged me into just as many," Joy declared as she came inside, her smile tilted at a challenging angle. The bell over the door tinkled as the girl in question closed it behind her. "Joshua Kanagy, I have something I wish to discuss with you," she said as she navigated around the displays, making a beeline for him.

"Oh." She paused and turned back to Hope. "Hello. Terrible weather, isn't it? Don't you hate drizzle? I'd much rather be outside enjoying the sun. But we needed the rain, too, I guess. Spring and all that."

Before Hope had a chance to reply to any of that, Joy was back to her mission, stalking Joshua, who glanced to his right and left as though an escape route could be found in one of those directions.

"I'll leave you to it," Hope said.

"Hey!" Joshua's protest followed her out the door along with the ring of the bell. Hurrying, because the drizzle would only make her hair frizz worse, Hope scooted around the corner to the small alley that led back to Aaron's workshop. Why they hadn't built it so that he could walk in and out of it from the back door of the shop, she wasn't sure.

She stepped inside, out of the mist, and brushed droplets off her sweater, only to shiver more. If anything, the workshop was colder than the gift shop. Aaron stood with his back to her, sanding a long length of wood. Based on the shape, she'd guess it would become a post for the bed eventually. As he sanded by hand, the muscles under his shirt bunched with each forceful slide, his hands capable and strong on the wood.

Hope turned away sharply. *What kind of girl are you to be noticing his muscles?*

Instead her gaze landed on the little chair that had caught her attention the day she'd come up with the plan that had landed her here. Had it only been a week ago? She wandered over to squat down and admire the work up close. Made of solid oak, the rocker featured cutouts in the arms that sort of swooped and had a heart cutout in the top back panel.

Such a sweet yet simple design.

She reached out a hand to trace the wood grain, sanded so smooth it slid softly under her fingertips.

"Hope?" Aaron's voice made her jump.

Awkwardly she pushed to her feet to face him.

"Can I do something for you?" he asked.

"Your mamm said to tell you we're closing up and going home early."

He nodded and made to turn back to his project but paused when she didn't also turn to leave him be. "Anything else?"

"Why did you take the chair out of the store?" She pointed at it, lonely on the floor.

"It wasn't selling." He shrugged.

"That's because of where you had it by the toys."

Aaron's eyebrows shot up. "Mamm put it there because most of the other woodworking pieces are in that section."

That made sense. "Only most of those toys are for boys. Toy trains, and a marble machine, and a monkey ladder. Not that girls can't enjoy them, too, but still."

Aaron crossed his arms, a doubt pursing his lips. "I

know you're headed somewhere with this, Hope, but I'm not following."

"This chair, with its heart cutout, is one little girls would love. I think if you put it over with the dolls, it might sell faster. Maybe if you made a matching one and set up a display of dolls, *both* chairs would sell right quick. Oh!" She bounced on her toes as another idea struck. "And if you were to paint flowers on them, even better."

His brow puckered as he stared at the chair, and immediately, Hope reconsidered her words. Perhaps painting flowers was too much? Too ornate a decoration. Amish-made toys tended to be simpler. Basic wood with maybe one or two colors, if any. Beautiful because of the simplicity, allowing kinder's imaginations to supply all the details. "Never mind—"

"I think I like that," he said slowly.

Oh. A small glow of warmth lit inside her, like an oil lamp in a window. Aaron liked her idea.

"I'll definitely put it by the dolls," he said. "Only I can't paint." His eyes crinkled at the corners when he smiled. Why did she like that about him?

Maybe because, while he smiled often, he also took important things seriously. A gute way to walk through life, it seemed to her. What would it be like to walk through life with him that way?

She gave herself a shake. No use getting stuck in her head about it. Aaron, at best, thought of her as a friend who worked in his family's shop. Which was perfectly fine. "Maybe I can paint it for you?"

The words popped out of her mouth before she realized they were even in her head. She wanted to reel them back in like her dat reeled in a fish. What a deerich thing to offer. She was already busy in the shop.

Slowly, Aaron's eyebrows rose practically to his hairline. No doubt he was having the same thoughts.

She flapped a hand. "Don't answer that. I'm being silly. Of course you don't—"

"Your drawing is beautiful, but have you ever painted furniture?"

"No," she said slowly, her gaze sliding to the chair. She considered if it would be more difficult. Probably. Smoother than paper and less able to soak up the paints thanks to Aaron's diligent sanding, and the curvature would make it tricky.

"Kumme." He moved to one of the tables in the room. "Why don't you try it on one of my scraps of wood."

Hope didn't move, blinking at his back. Was he serious?

When she didn't step up beside him, Aaron paused to glance over his shoulder at her. "Hope?"

She still didn't move. "I don't have any paints."

Again, his eyes crinkled, though his lips remained neutral, like he didn't want to offend her with his amusement. "You don't carry them everywhere with you?" He tutted teasingly. "Don't fret. I do. For when I work on the toys, but I only paint them one color, or maybe two, so it's easier."

Her curiosity, not to mention the sudden urge to bring color to life under her brush, got the better of her and she moved to stand beside him.

"Here." He brought out a small, rectangular piece of wood. "This size should do, except . . ." He searched around and grabbed sanding paper, setting to work on it. "Just give me a minute."

Once again, she found herself mesmerized by his skill, the surety of his hands as he worked, the strength in each sweep over the wood.

For the second time since she'd entered the workshop,

she found herself having to turn away. "Where are the paints?" she asked in a tight voice. "I'll get them out."

Anything to keep her gaze off Aaron. Temptation came in surprising ways, didn't it?

He barely took the time to stop and tipped his chin at a spot across the room. "In those drawers."

Vague, but apparently he wouldn't have a problem with her snooping around. In short order she found the paints, along with brushes of several sizes and cups obviously used previously to hold each color, as well as one for water to dip her brushes in.

As soon as she'd brought everything over, Aaron finished his sanding and grabbed the water cup. "Here. You get started, and I'll fill this."

Before she could say anything, he disappeared. Hope turned back to the wood, tipping her head to the side and staring at it, debating what to try.

Then she glanced at the chair. If the idea was to paint the chair, probably best to try what she'd do for that. Something a little girl would like, but still simple, perhaps, to complement the design of the chair itself. Glancing out the window to the field behind the shops where the buggy horses grazed in a field of green, Hope brightened. Small, pink flowers with tiny vines and a few spring green leaves would be beautiful.

Nodding to herself, she got to work, starting with the flowers. She became so absorbed in the work, she didn't realize when Aaron came back until she reflexively dipped her brush in the cup of water only to finally notice he'd put it there.

"Oh." She snapped up her head to find him standing beside her, watching in rapt silence. "I didn't hear you come back in."

Aaron's chuckle was the nicest kind, deep and rolling. "I know. I said your name, but you didn't even twitch a muscle. I get like that, too."

She couldn't help smiling back. "You get lost in what you see in your head and trying to make it match?"

"Ach jah. Exactly."

"Mamm always said the world could be crashing down around my ears, and if I was painting, I wouldn't notice."

She paused and waited for the dull ache of her loss to settle over her, but it didn't this time. Instead, the warmth of that memory seemed to keep out the chill. Hope wasn't sure if she should feel relieved, grateful, or guilty about that.

"Don't stop on my account," Aaron urged.

This time, with him there watching over her shoulder, it took Hope longer to get lost in her world of colors, but she did, working on the vines and leaves next. Then she went back over it with darker and lighter hues to add shading and details. Finally, she was satisfied with her work. "What do you think of this?"

Aaron didn't say anything for long enough that she lifted her gaze to find him staring at the simple floral design she'd created. His expression gave away nothing.

Biting her lip, Hope looked back at it, trying to figure out what he might be thinking. "You don't like it. Is it too childish?"

"It's beautiful." No mistaking the sincerity in his voice.

She raised her head to find him staring at her now, the corners of his mouth drawn up and his dark eyes kind and warm. An answering warmth started in the region of her chest, spreading out through her like forks in a river, filling her up.

Because Aaron Kanagy liked her painted flowers.

Only she couldn't find her resentment of him anywhere. Just happiness that he'd liked it. "Denki."

His mouth tipped up more, but he didn't look away, almost as though seeing her properly for the first time. The warmth from his enjoyment of her simple design spread up into her cheeks, which no doubt turned blotchy and red. Only she couldn't make herself look away either.

"Joshua has the buggy hitched and we're ready to go. What is taking you two so long?" Ruth's words preceded her into the shop.

HIS MOTHER'S APPEARANCE jerked Aaron out of the strangest sense that he didn't want to look away from Hope, as though an invisible string tied him to her, tangling them together.

Hope, too, apparently, because she yanked her shoulders back, spine going stiff, and spun away from him— snapping that delicate string—to pick up the small wood piece she'd been working on. "Sorry, Ruth. I'm afraid we got distracted."

Distracted was right. What had he been doing, staring at Hope that way?

Only, he'd found himself drawn in by the way the small flowers had come to life under her hands. The painting was nothing overly complicated, and yet it seemed like if he reached out even now, he could feel the softness of the pink petals under his fingertips or watch the small leaves lift and sway in the spring breeze.

She had a gift, for sure and certain.

But what had truly captured his attention had been Hope. The pleasure in her expression, the peace as she'd worked. A glow that had made him want to step closer, become a part of the creation.

"Distracted by what?" his mother demanded.

Aaron stepped back to give her space as she came over and peered at the wood block Hope held. "Oh! How *precious*. I know my son couldn't have painted that. Did you?"

Hope lowered her gaze, not looking over Ruth's shoulder at Aaron. If anything, he got the impression she was avoiding his gaze. And why not? After the way he'd behaved. He'd probably embarrassed her.

What would he do if she ever looked at him with more than vague friendliness?

The initial sting to his pride, thanks to her words about never marrying him, still lingered, but now another emotion joined it. Heavier, laced with an ache more like . . . longing.

She might not ever want to marry him, but Aaron knew he wanted to be her friend. As though having her in his life, and her letting him into a small part of hers, had become important somehow.

Fanciful thinking, but real all the same.

"I'm going to have her paint it on the child's chair I made and put it by the dolls," he said. Thankfully, his voice came out normal.

"That will be nice." His mother's expression changed to a familiar one. Impatience. "But not today. Today we are ready to go home, and Frank is already tossing his head."

"Sorry, Mamm." Aaron offered the apology contritely.

Hope's gaze flicked to his, and he winked over his mother's shoulder. In response, she shot him a look his teacher had often given him when he'd been a scholar in grade school. Amusement-tinged exasperation, plain and simple.

"We'll get these paints cleaned up right quick and be with you."

His mother gave a sharp nod. "If you're not in the buggy

in ten minutes, we're leaving without you, and you can walk home in this rain."

Not an idle threat, Aaron knew from experience.

As his mother went back outside, he and Hope hurried to clean up, not speaking to each other. Then they circled around through the front. Hope's step slowed as they neared the door and she lifted a hand in a wave of greeting. Aaron followed the direction she was looking in to find Luke Raber waving back.

Luke Raber? Aaron glanced between the two, catching a hint of Hope's smile directed at the other boy.

Luke's family owned the café and were one of the more well-off families in the district, though they did what they could not to gather too much wealth, as was the Amish way. But Aaron had yet to see Luke work there much. Granted, he could be at home managing the chores, swapping them the way Aaron's own family did, but the Rabers had sold all their land and moved into a small home near town years ago. They didn't even keep a garden. Aaron often saw Luke meandering around Charity Creek, and hadn't quite figured out what, exactly, Luke did with his time.

Not that it was his place to judge. Gotte, in His wisdom, would determine the worth of a life. And Luke's behavior never bothered Aaron. Not really. Until this moment.

Hope deserved a man who would work hard to provide for her and to make her life happy. That wasn't Luke.

"You're friends with Luke?" he asked as he ushered her into the store, locking the door behind him.

Hurrying to the back of the store to grab their coats, she didn't even glance his way. "Of course," was all she said.

Then they were rushing outside and hopping in the back of the buggy and the moment passed to ask her more.

Mamm was already up front by Joshua. The back of the

buggy had the benches facing each other, and Aaron had no choice but to sit beside Hope. With Dat and Daniel on the bench across, and all three of them tall, he had nowhere to put his legs except to swing them sideways, pressing him up against her.

"Sorry," he muttered.

She shook her head.

His mother turned in her seat to address her. "Hope, we'll drop you off first, so you don't have to walk in the rain."

Only because he was pressed up against her did he notice how Hope stiffened at the words. And no wonder.

"Oh, I couldn't let you do that, Ruth," she said. He could practically hear her mind spinning to produce a reason why not.

"Of course you can," Mamm insisted.

Dat, meanwhile, narrowed his eyes.

"It will delay all of you in your chores and supper," Hope tried next, a thread of anxiousness in her voice now.

"How about I take Hope after we drop everyone else off?" Aaron found himself offering.

She turned her head to blink up at him, with that little lost owl look that made him want to comfort her. A colorful owl, with her coppery hair, soft eyes, and determined chin, but all the same, he had to sit on his hands to keep from reaching for her.

His mother, no doubt pleased with that idea even more than her first suggestion, given her matchmaking goals, brightened. "That's a wonderful gute idea."

Hope cleared her throat. "Denki, Aaron."

His dat relaxed, shoulders dropping and his gaze moving away from Hope's face, though not entirely at ease. Aaron could tell by the set of his jaw. Given his concern for

Levi Beiler's daughter working for them in the first place, no doubt he was on alert for any hint of trouble.

Hope didn't speak the rest of the ride home, her gaze lowered, probably trying to pretend she was invisible. An impossible task, as far as Aaron was concerned. A bluebird stood out among the brush, even when quieting its song to hide from a nearby predator.

After dropping off his parents and bruders, he and Hope both moved to the front seat and he turned Frank's head—who wasn't too happy about another journey when he'd been anticipating the warm barn and food in his belly—back down to the lane that would take them to Hope's house.

"I can drop you not too far from the house," he said.

Hope shook her head. "Nae. That would be too much like willful deceit. If Dat sees, then I'll just have to explain to him."

And probably stop working at the shop, except she now owed Aaron for the wood and his time. A notion that had him gripping the reins tighter. He hated to put her under such an obligation when she'd made it plain that her family was struggling for money.

"Maybe you could say that you couldn't walk home from the shops because of the rain and I offered you a ride."

She nodded slowly, though her anxious expression didn't lift, lips pinched and flat.

Aaron didn't say any more, a quiet falling between them that was oddly just as comfortable as talking. Usually he didn't like silence, finding it awkward. But this was different. Like they were both aware of each other's thoughts and giving the other the space to dwell there without judgment or need to fill the silence with idle conversation. Frank's hooves set a gentle *clop, clop, clop* rhythm that, along with the light dripping of rain against the roof of the buggy, lulled him even more into a sense of serenity.

As he pulled around the looped drive in front of her house so that Hope only had to hop down and run right to the stairs leading up to her porch, he eyed that dead rose-bush that still needed digging up. It wondered him that Hope's dat hadn't gotten round to it yet. He must be busy with planting, working alone as he did.

Aaron drew Frank to a stop, the buggy rocking a bit as he did, and Hope turned to him with the polite smile of a well-mothered child. He didn't count that one either. "Denki, Aaron—"

He shook his head. "No need for thanks. I'd feel terrible thinking of you cold and wet walking home through the woods."

Her blue eyes lit up with appreciation though she didn't exactly smile.

He'd have to try harder. "You're peaceful to be with, Hope."

That made her wrinkle her nose. "You mean boring."

He laughed. "'Boring' is never a word I would use for you."

An expression flitted across her face that he had a hard time pinning down. Disappointment maybe, or disbelief and a hint of hurt. Why hurt?

Instinct to assure her had him reaching out to put a hand over hers, delicate in his grasp, her skin soft but cold thanks to the weather. "I mean it," he said soberly. "Peaceful is a fine thing. I like it. And I'm never bored with you."

Her eyes went wide, and she studied his face, as though searching for the truth behind the words. "Denki," she finally said slowly.

Her hand twitched under his, and with a reluctance that surprised him, Aaron released her. But he still wanted her to believe him, which he had the sneaking suspicion she didn't.

"I *like* you, Hope, for sure and certain."

Her mouth dropped open and she stared at him with wide eyes. Then smiled—really and truly smiled—and the breath whooshed from his lungs as though Frank had kicked him in the gut, only to be followed with a burst of happiness, like the sun breaking through thick clouds.

Making Hope smile like that could become a weakness of his. A need.

"I'll see you tomorrow," she said. And was gone, hopping to the ground and shutting the buggy door behind her before running to get out of the rain.

He should have walked her to the door but doubted Hope would have appreciated the gesture. Simply delivering her here was already worry enough for her. Instead, he waited until she was inside, then clucked to Frank, who was only too eager to get to his warm, dry stable.

All the way home, Aaron pondered Hope Beiler and the strange reactions he was having around her. Like his common sense had deserted him in favor of the urge to truly win her friendship.

Or more.

Chapter Eight

✳

AARON STOMPED DOWN on the shovel head, burying it deeper under the rosebush in front of the Beilers' house.

The rain from a few days prior had cleared to reveal a land turned lushly green and skies as brightly colored as blue jays. Gotte had certainly worked a miracle when He'd made this gute earth, for sure and certain.

He'd also softened the ground for Aaron's efforts, though the weather had turned warmer. A bead of sweat wandered lazily down his spine as he worked, making his shirt stick to his skin, especially where his suspenders touched. With each chunk of dirt and roots removed around the bush, he called himself all kinds of fool. Today was supposed to be his day at home to do his share of chores. Since all his family worked in the shop, they each took a day away weekly to split the work that still needed attending to at home.

Today was his day. Chores still waited.

But instead of tilling the garden for Mamm and repair-

ing the bathroom door, which kept getting stuck closed—
and which he would get to, he'd assured himself—he was
at the Beilers' house digging up this darn bush. Hope's dat
was already off in the fields; he'd made sure of that before
coming over. Hope herself was at the shop with the rest of
his family. He had yet to see anyone else.

"Aaron Kanagy, what on earth do you think you are
doing?"

He about dropped the shovel as he jerked up to find Rebecca Beiler, Hope's grossmammi, standing on the porch.
He hadn't had much interaction with her since she'd moved
in with the Beilers. Curling white hair escaped her kapp
every which way, reminding him of Hope as she stood
there, hands on her hips and watching him with interest.

At least interest fared better than irritation.

Stuffing down his embarrassment at being caught, and
trying his best to ignore the heat climbing up his neck like
weeds climbed Mamm's garden trellises, he cleared his
throat. "Helping?"

"Is that a question?"

"Er . . . No. I'm helping." *I hope*, he silently tacked on.

Rebecca Beiler narrowed her eyes as though assessing
both the truth and the need for such a thing, then gave a
sharp nod. "That bush has been a terrible sight to see for
quite a time. I'll get you a drink and kumme help you."

Aaron opened his mouth to protest, but the front door
closed before he could make a sound. Hope's grandmother
was fast on her feet. With a shake of his head, he went back
to digging.

Then jumped again when Rebecca showed up beside
him without his being aware she'd come back out yet.
"Lemonade?" she asked, holding out a tray.

Only the concoction appeared more like water than lemonade to him. Still, with the sun heating his back, he could use it.

"Denki." He picked up the glass and took a big swig. Then paused and wished he hadn't.

This wasn't lemonade. It was lemon juice in water with no sugar. More lemon than water, too, at a guess, and so sour, he had to bite down on the inside of his cheek to keep his face from puckering. Aaron hid a cough as he managed to swallow it down.

"It's . . . gute," he said, voice slightly strained as he tipped the glass to her in a gesture of thanks. He couldn't get more words than that out, his throat constricting around the amount of lemon he'd forced down it.

Rebecca watched all of this closely. At his words, she grinned as though she approved—of what, he had no idea—and went back up to the porch, only to return with a canvas folding chair and her own glass.

"Hold this." She shoved the glass at him. Then set herself up close enough to be slightly in the way. She held out her hand for her lemonade and took a long gulp. How she could stand the sourness, he had no idea. With a sigh of contentment, she lowered her drink.

"Well . . . get going." She waved at the bush.

He hid a snort of laughter and did as she said.

"Tell me about yourself, Aaron," came her next request. "I don't know much about you, I'm shamed to say."

He opened his mouth to speak, only to close it again when she kept going.

"I mean, I know your mamm and dat, of course, and your bruders. Also knew your grossdawdi when I was a girl. And I've seen you at Gmay, though we haven't ever really talked much."

True enough. The tension between the families had

caused that rift, more so than with other families in the district.

"Though I do recall the time you brought me a blanket when worship was held in the Yoders' drafty barn in January." She rolled her eyes. "Someone wasn't thinking that schedule through."

"I remember." He'd been given a stack of blankets by his mother and instructed to pass them out among the elders first. Aaron had forgotten all about that. Rebecca hadn't apparently.

She propped her chin in her hand. "And I'm familiar with the shop. Do you like working there?"

Aaron took his time answering. Partly because the answer wasn't straightforward, and partly because he waited to see if she would keep talking. When she raised her eyebrows in obvious impatience, he answered. "The shop provides well for our family and Mamm loves it."

Based on the way her eyes narrowed, he had an idea that Rebecca saw through that piece of whitewashing.

"But you love to work with wood," she said next, confirming his suspicions.

"I do," he replied cautiously.

"What do you like about it? Not the splinters, I'd imagine."

He chuckled at that. "No, not those." Then he gave her question the consideration it deserved. Maybe because he got the impression that she truly cared to hear the answer. "I like to make things that are useful. To bring out of wood the best parts that a tree, no longer gracing this earth with its leaves and shade and splendor, can become instead."

"You have a poet's soul. For sure and certain. It's no wonder my Hope likes you."

For the second time since she'd appeared, Aaron about dropped the shovel on his foot. Mid-dig at that. He tried not to let her see his reaction, setting the thing on the ground more carefully and wiping his palms on his pants, pretending it had slipped, thanks to sweat. "That's nice," was all he said in return.

And received a snort for his trouble. "You wanted to ask me if she really does like you. Am I right?"

Aaron paused and leaned on the shovel to give her his full attention. Her blue eyes, several shades darker than Hope's soft gray, sparkled at him with an infectious amusement he couldn't help but return. "Jah," he finally agreed. "I'm surprised to hear you say she does. I got the . . . idea that she doesn't like me much."

Rebecca tipped back in her chair alarmingly, balancing precariously on the skinny, unstable wooden legs. "Ach vell, I shouldn't have said anything anyway."

Disappointment settled over him and he rubbed at a spot in the center of his chest like it might ease the sensation. "I wouldn't want you to betray a confidence."

"Oh, she hasn't said anything to me." She waved him off as though shooing a buzzing bee away.

He paused at that. "Then how do you know?"

She grinned. "With my Hope, I can tell."

He went back to shoveling, trying not to take Rebecca too seriously. Clearly Hope's grossmammi danced to her own tune.

"You like her, too? Jah?"

Aaron blew out a long breath. He was never going to get the rosebush dug up at this rate. At the same time, he couldn't deny an interest in the topic of conversation she'd landed on. He finished scooping the dirt into the pile he was making and turned to her. "Jah. I like her very much."

The two legs off the ground dropped with a thump. "Well, of course you do. Any boy willing to dig up an old rosebush must like the girl he's doing it for."

Aaron opened his mouth to spout off about neighborly kindness. He didn't want Rebecca getting the entirely wrong idea. Otherwise, between her and his mother, he and Hope would be married off come next Gmay. Something he was well aware Hope didn't want.

Not with him at least.

Except the words wouldn't come out. Because, truth be told, he *was* doing this for Hope. And if he searched deep enough into his heart, he was doing this because he more than liked her.

"That's what I thought." Rebecca's expression turned alarmingly satisfied. "You'll have a time of it with her dat, though. My son holds a grudge the same way a beaver builds a dam. It would take Noah's flood to break it." She shook her head.

Given Hope's behavior up till now, he'd figured that out for himself.

Rebecca suddenly stood up, thrusting her glass of lemon water at him again so she could fold up her chair. Taking both, she walked away. "Carry on," she tossed over her shoulder at him.

She managed to scooch her way inside the house, the front door closing behind her with a thump.

Aaron stared after her then shook his head. He had no idea if Rebecca Beiler approved of his liking Hope or not, but it seemed, at least to him, that he had her on his side.

The question was, what, if anything, did he do with that?

Was it duller outside today? Hope glanced out the front store window at the cloudless blue sky and the sun shining down on the droves of people milling about, many wandering inside through the doors propped wide open, and crossed the weather off as a reason why the day had lost its color and time slowed to a crawl.

Usually, she was so busy in the shop, she hardly had a second to herself to even notice the passing of the day, always slightly surprised when Ruth turned over the sign to CLOSED and locked the door, declaring the day finished.

But not today.

Not because Aaron isn't here, she told herself for what had to be the third time in less than an hour.

Why did it matter if he was or wasn't? Most days he was in his workshop and she hardly caught sight of him. Why should knowing that he wasn't close by make any kind of difference? It had to be because of the item she was in the process of ringing up. He should be here for this.

With a satisfying *pring*, the cash drawer opened at the touch of a button. Careful not to show exactly how tickled she was that Aaron's small chair, with her painted flowers, had sold so quickly, she put the bills from the customer in the right slots. Aaron would be thrilled.

Hope counted out the change. Handing it over, she smiled at the kind face across the counter. This customer was an Englischer. Many came here to shop. Hope was getting more used to their stares and occasional questions. So far, none meant any harm.

"Do you mind if I take your picture, dear?" the woman asked.

A not uncommon question. Tourists had once asked as she'd been coming out of a store and loading her buggy with groceries if she'd pose with her horse for them. Hope understood. Her way of life and dress were different from most. The Amish way was to live in the world, but not be of the world, as Gotte willed it. But still, she found the question thoughtlessly rude. What would those same Englischers think if she approached them in the middle of their daily life and asked to take a picture?

People didn't think before speaking sometimes.

Now, as she had that day with the groceries, she offered a kind smile. "I am sorry, but nae. We believe that pictures are graven images, which the Bible forbids."

"Oh, really?" The woman turned flushed, her free hand fluttering at her side. "I'm so sorry for asking. Oh my goodness, I've taken so many pictures. What those people must have thought of me."

Hope chuckled. This woman was perfectly nice, just not aware. "Not at all. Especially these days, with cell phone cameras, we can't do much about it. And some Amish don't mind as much as others." A few, like the more traditionally minded groups of Swartzentruber Amish, minded more, though. "But it does go against our beliefs. In fact, the dolls we make also don't have faces for a similar reason." She moved around the counter to the display of children's toys and picked one up, turning it to face the woman, whose color had returned to normal. "See."

"Oh! I wondered about that."

Hope nodded. "I imagine you follow traditions and beliefs that would be different to me, yet."

That earned her a grateful smile and the lady's hand stopped flapping. "I guess you're right. Thank you for being kind about explaining it to me."

"For sure and certain."

"Charlie," the lady called out. Her husband's balding head popped up from the back near Eli Bontrager's leatherwork. "Are you ready?"

"Yes." He loped over to his wife. "That leather stuff is dang expensive, Martha," he said. Only to be shushed.

Ignoring his comment, Hope kept her smile pinned in place. "I hope you enjoy the chair."

"Oh, it is just perfect for my granddaughter."

With a wave, the customers exited the shop, leaving it empty except for Hope. She stared after them, shaking her head.

"You have a knack for the customers, I'll give you that."

Hope swung around to find Aaron's fater standing at the door that led to the back room. "Denki," she said, ducking her head, and moved back to the register to finalize the sale.

Joseph Kanagy didn't spend much time in the shop, usually out finding new items to display and sell instead. When he was in, he stayed in the back dealing primarily with inventory. Which meant she hadn't gotten to spend too much time with him.

"You have a gentle way about you, Hope. I wasn't expecting that."

She lowered her gaze at the compliment, wanting to accept it humbly while at the same time debating approaching that telling comment head-on. "Because I'm a Beiler, you mean?"

She lifted her gaze to his. Rather than frown, which she half expected, Joseph's lips tipped in a lopsided grin that reminded her starkly of Aaron. "Gentle but forthright. An effective combination. And jah, because of that."

She blinked, not expecting either the compliment or the admission.

Hand on her hip, she tipped her head to regard him closer. "I do not know why you and Dat have this tension between you. He doesn't speak of it."

Joseph's expression gave nothing away. "I don't either. It happened a long time ago."

In other words, she wouldn't get the story from him. Amish were a people who practiced Gotte's forgiveness, the power of which the outside world often didn't understand. But they were also still human, with all the flaws and struggles that came with that.

"Maybe . . ." No, the words even sounded presumptuous in her head. She'd been going to say that maybe Gotte had brought her to the shop to start a healing between their families. But that smacked of pride, as though she were special or above the anger. And she was not.

Joseph raised his eyebrows in question, but she shook her head. "I hope you and Dat can both find a way to forgive each other someday and come together as friends."

She received a narrow-eyed stare, as though he was well aware she'd thought to say something else. But after she returned his look with a questioning one of her own, Joseph shook his head and ran a hand over his beard. "If it is Gotte's will . . . I pray for such a time. Levi's allowing you to work here with us is a first step."

"Oh. Mm-hmm." Hope turned away to fix the pillowcase arrangement, hiding her wince at his words. "I'll pray for many more steps."

She surreptitiously glanced heavenward, sending silent, heartfelt words to Gotte. As she did, an image of Aaron, confident and solid and easy, filled her mind and the anxiousness lifted a skosh. A glimpse of the intrepid, positive girl she had once been took over, turning her thoughts. Things would turn out all right in the end.

"Ach vell, leave the poor girl alone, Joseph Kanagy." Aaron's mother came in, flapping a dish towel at him. "The sins of the father are not the sins of the child."

Oh, help. Hope hid another wince. Her father might be

lost right now, and yes, holding on to this particular grudge was sinful, but he was a gute man and a gute fater.

Ruth came over and patted her shoulder. "We are glad to have you. I hope you know that."

"I've been happy here," she said. Only to still as realization followed softly on the heels of the words.

I am happy here.

Happier than at home? What a thing to think. She had been blessed with a loving home and life. She should be more grateful.

"Wunderbaar." Ruth beamed. "And you sold Aaron's chair. He will be pleased. Maybe, after Aaron is done with your schwester's gift, we can come to a new arrangement."

Hope had no idea what to say to that. There was no way she could keep this from Dat long term, and she wouldn't want to. She couldn't see how working beyond this short time would ever be possible. Instead, she gave the other woman a noncommittal nod.

That seemed to satisfy, because Ruth clapped her hands, turning away. "Now . . . I was thinking I would like to re-arrange the center of the store. You have an excellent eye. Would you be interested?"

Hope paused, trying to catch up with the change of topic, then turned to face the displays down the center. "What were you thinking?"

"To start, I would like to move the wagon of candy nearer the middle, so that maters can keep an eye on their kinder while shopping."

Hope nodded along. "And it will make people come farther into the store."

"Yes! I thought that, too."

"What would you want up front?"

"I was thinking I'd leave that to you."

Oh. Ruth trusted her that much? All she'd done was that honey and bees display so far. "All right."

Already her mind was spinning with possibilities. Perhaps a display of any new items recently added to the shop? Or seasonal items would be lovely. The end of spring had so many possibilities and the small display she'd done was selling well. Maybe a larger version would catch the eye of people passing by.

"Such a big move will take time and disrupt the store," Ruth said, interrupting her thoughts.

"For sure and certain."

"What if we closed the shop an hour early one evening? Instead of working during the day, you could come in a little before that and do all the changes in the evening?"

Hope paused, her mind swiftly doing its best to solve the problem of what to tell her dat and family. The wedding preparations were increasing the closer they got to the day. But Mammi and Hannah seemed to have them well in hand. Rachel and Sarah Price had been a great help, too. Still, how could she explain being away in the evening without outright lying?

I'll figure something out. "I think that would work."

Ruth nodded, but her forehead crinkled at the same time. "I'd stay and help you, but I'm feeling a bit off."

Hope peered closer but couldn't detect anything wrong. Though come to think of it, Ruth had been coughing a lot lately. "Are you well?"

Ruth waved off the question. "Just a small headache and a cough."

"Well . . . Maybe you could get the boys to move the tables before you leave when we do this? When I'm done rearranging, I can close up the shop."

"I can move the tables," Joseph's voice called from the back.

Annoyance flashing in her eyes, Ruth turned to call back. "You have to go visit the blacksmith in Skokegan again, don't you?"

"Ach jah. I forgot about that."

Ruth gave a sharp nod, her expression oddly satisfied as she turned back to Hope. "I'll have Aaron stay and help you with anything you might need and lock up after. He can drive you home yet. It'll be after dark and I would worry about you otherwise."

Hope refused to acknowledge how her stomach did a happy flip at the thought. For no reason. No doubt Aaron would move the tables, then probably go back to his workshop while she finished arranging things. Nothing to get excited over.

"When were you thinking?" she asked.

Chapter Nine

✳

In the soft glow of the oil lamps he'd placed around the store—they'd shut off the electricity feeding the front as soon as they turned the sign to Closed—he had to admit that Hope was possibly the prettiest girl he knew. Prettier to him tonight than she'd ever been for some strange reason.

He'd always found her vibrant with her strawberry blond hair and her cream-colored skin made more interesting thanks to a smattering of freckles, and a smile that could light up those around her, as though sending rays of sunshine straight to their hearts. But now he found her . . . entrancing. He couldn't take his eyes off her, didn't want to.

What had changed?

Hope glanced his way for the umpteenth time, her expression saying as clear as day that she was confused by his continued help with the display . . . and his staring.

If his mother would've asked him to do this before Hope, he would've had a difficult time keeping a positive attitude about it. Rearranging displays was not his favorite task. If he had his way, he'd lump everything on a table and let the customers figure it out. Luckily for him, his mother was better with the shop than that, and he did admit her displays were eye-catching.

Hope's, too.

He never would've thought to do a spring-related display up front. All pastel colors, flowers, gardening, raincoats and umbrellas, and other more practical items for the season.

"Are you sure you wouldn't rather be working in your shop?" she asked. For the third time.

Aaron ducked his head, pretending to focus on putting all the buckets of candy back on the wagon in the right order with the right signs after having moved it, hiding the consternation no doubt written on his face. Maybe he *should* go to his shop. "Would you rather work alone?" he asked back. "Am I in your way?"

"No . . ." she said, drawing the word out.

He lifted his head and grinned. "You don't sound sure."

Hope bit her lip. Holding back her thoughts again, no doubt.

Ach vell, if she kicked him out, that would put him in his place.

Aaron crossed his arms and lifted a single eyebrow. "I can see you have something on your mind. Out with it."

That drew a chuckle. If she was laughing, that had to be gute. Right?

"It's just that I know you don't enjoy organizing the displays."

He grunted. "Now how do you know that?"

"Because when Ruth asks you to, you make a face like this . . ." She gave an exaggerated pout that he'd put up against a toddler throwing a tantrum any day.

"I do not." He deliberately pitched horror into his voice.

Just like he'd hoped, she tipped her head back and laughed, the sound washing over him like warmth on a summer day after swimming in the river and climbing up onto the rocks to dry.

"Do too," she shot back. "And usually you can't wait to run off to your shop. I don't want to make you—"

He held up a hand, cutting her off in mid-thought. "I'm at a stopping point for the day on the bed frame and figured you could use the help. Doing all these by yourself will take a long time."

"Hmmm . . ." A vague sound of agreement. Or maybe she was still holding back, though he doubted that. She considered him, a glitter in her eyes that he hadn't seen in some time. Maybe since her mamm had passed away.

"It's up to you," he said. "What's easiest?"

Hope pursed her lips. "I wouldn't mind the help," she said softly. Then turned back to the display she was working on.

She wanted him to stay. Aaron wanted to punch a fist in the air, but he didn't want to push his luck, so he managed to control himself and simply went back to work.

They fell into silence. Not that awkward kind like with other people. This was the easy, companionable kind he found around her, as though they'd been doing this for years together.

After about ten minutes, she started to hum softly to herself, totally off tune, and Aaron grinned. She did that a lot, especially when she was concentrating. Any second now she'd change from humming to singing.

Sure enough, perhaps ten minutes later, words were put to the odd tune. Quietly, Aaron worked and listened, finally able, by the words, to identify the song. Ach du lieva, Hope could not sing at all. Had she been a bird, she would've been kicked out of the nest early. But the delight she obviously derived from the act gave Aaron an odd sense of joy in return.

Still singing merrily along, she walked past him to grab an item from the food section of the store, coming back with her arms full of glass jars of a bright green substance.

Curious, Aaron followed. Helping her set them down carefully, he turned one over to read the label. "Mint jelly?"

"Dorcas Miller assures me that it's served with lamb."

Mint jelly and lamb? People did that? "Sounds, ummm . . ."

Hope's laugh warmed him through and through. "Sounds awful. Jah?"

"I didn't want to say so."

She took the jar from his hands, her fingers brushing his, and Aaron tried not to stiffen. How could he be so aware of another person like this? As though each gesture and where she was in the room and the things she said mattered.

They do matter. Hope matters.

He almost frowned over his thoughts, trying to make sense of them. This felt like more than wanting to prove himself to her.

"I know," she said. For an agonizing second, Aaron wondered if he'd spoken his thoughts aloud and she was agreeing. But she continued. "My family certainly never had mint jelly, but we don't eat lamb."

"Nae. Us either."

"Dorcas was so proud of having found a recipe for it and using the herbs she'd grown herself. I didn't have the heart to say no when she brought it in. But it's not selling."

"It wonders me why not," he managed to say with a straight face, only to be rewarded with a twitch of her lips.

"Did you know the green is not real? It's from food coloring." She held the jar up to one of the lanterns, letting the light shine through. "Without it, the jelly is actually a golden color. Or so Dorcas said. She apparently hired a car to take her all the way to Walmart just to try it with the recipe."

Aaron stuffed his hands in his pockets, regarding the jar. "Why? Wouldn't it sell better a more natural color?"

"I guess green looks more minty? Or better on the lamb?" She pursed her lips as if giving that some thought. Then shrugged. "Maybe placed up front it will get more attention and we'll sell at least one."

"Maybe." He tried not to let his doubt that anyone would want the stuff creep into his voice. That would be unkind to Dorcas Miller.

Apparently, he didn't do a great job because Hope snickered. "Maybe not. I'm tempted to buy a jar. To make Dorcas happy, but also just to try it."

"With lamb?"

She scrunched up her nose then shook her head. "Maybe with peanut butter?"

Aaron snorted. "That sounds even worse."

That earned him her hands plonked on her hips, even as amusement danced in her eyes. "What would you try it with?"

"I wouldn't try it."

She made a clucking sound like a chicken.

"Are you calling me a chicken?"

She opened her eyes wide, blinking at him in apparent innocence. "Who, me?" She glanced around the store as though he might be talking to someone else, then made the sound again as she tweaked a hand towel positioned on the table.

Rather than argue, Aaron walked over to the till and rang up a jar of jelly. Pulling out cash from his pocket, he made change for himself, then went to the back room, emerging with two spoons.

Holding one out to her, he waggled his eyebrows. "Are you up for it?"

"We should finish the store—"

Aaron imitated her chicken clucking.

Hope shot him a narrow-eyed glare. "You are trouble, Aaron Kanagy."

"You started it, Hope Beiler." He grinned and reached for the jar, twisting the top off. "Only the gute kind of trouble yet." He held out the jar to her.

With an expression akin to one she'd make if she'd smelled a skunk, she dipped her spoon in then quickly shoveled it into her mouth. Pursing her lips, she smacked the jelly around, thinking hard.

"Well?" he asked.

"Sweet and tangy and minty all at the same time. It's . . . different. Try it."

Aaron copied her, rolling the jelly around over his tongue, the flavor bright, and she was right, oddly sweet and minty at the same time. "I'm not sure I'd like it on lamb," he said.

"Or with peanut butter," she added. "Maybe on a buttery biscuit?"

Aaron straightened. "Mamm made some the other night. I'll bring a few with me tomorrow and we can try it when we eat lunch."

She smiled.

Aaron smiled back. Was it possible to fall in love with a girl over a jar of mint jelly?

"We'd better get back to work," she said, waving a hand at the half-finished tables.

"Jah." Turning away, he put the lid back on his jelly jar and set it on the checkout counter.

She went back to arranging her display, scattering the remaining jars—which admittedly did have a beautiful, though unusual, color to them—throughout her display.

It took Hope closer to twenty minutes to return to singing this time, after she had to stop and give him directions on the third table display. Aaron found himself humming along under his breath. Only because she'd picked one of his favorite songs.

Abruptly the sound ended, leaving a yawning silence, as Hope stepped back, hands on her hips, and tilted her head to one side then the other, considering her work. Then she scrunched up her face, and Aaron paused, one of the new leather tool belts from Eli Bontrager hovering in midair as he forgot to finish setting it down. What about that moment caught him like a fish on a line, he had no idea. Just a sudden desire to be able to see her like this—totally herself, in the midst of her work, and happy—and to do things like try mint jelly together, every day.

As though that would ever be an option. Oh, sis yuscht. He wasn't trouble, *Hope* was. And he was hooked, for sure and certain.

With a satisfied hum, oblivious to the fact that his plain world had upended, she glanced up. "I think I'm all done. How are you coming?"

It took a second for Aaron's brain to engage, processing the words so slowly that she raised her eyebrows.

"Just a few more things," he managed to say in a normal-sounding voice. "But you might want to make changes."

Hope made her way over to stand beside him, observing his work. He waited for her to do what his mother always did, immediately rearranging everything to her own satisfaction. But Hope simply smiled up at him. "You've done a wonderful gute job, Aaron."

Really? He turned to face the table with a critical eye. She wasn't just saying that? "I guess Mamm's nagging and making me redo things finally sank in."

He hadn't realized he'd muttered out loud until Hope laughed. "My mamm was the same way. Only she got on me about my cooking and the lessons didn't help, I'm sad to say."

Knowing about her cooking—those cookies he'd tried the one time *had* been burned to a crisp, even if he did like his cookies on the toasty side—he chuckled.

Then he glanced at the clock that hung at the back of the shop and blinked. "Speaking of cooking, Mamm will have already cleaned up from supper by now."

Following his gaze, Hope put her hand to her mouth. "Mammi and Hannah will have cleaned up as well."

Aaron stepped closer, dipping his head to catch her gaze. "Is your dat going to be angry?"

She shook her head, lowering her hand. "Mammi said she'd take care of explaining where I was and not to worry about the time."

"But you're worried anyway?"

Sadness. Not worry. Stark in her soft gray gaze now. As though she'd drawn back the curtains, allowing him to glimpse inside. "No. Dat may not even notice my absence, to be honest."

Then she slapped her hand over her mouth. "Please forget I said that?"

As much as he wanted to make the pain in her eyes go away, Aaron forced himself to stick a finger in his ear and jiggle it, like he was getting water out. "Huh? What'd you say?" he teased.

An act that earned a giggle that went straight to his heart. "Denki, Aaron."

He sobered and nodded. "Sometimes, when I've worked late in the workshop, I have supper at Raber's Café."

She stared back, obviously not understanding his meaning.

"My treat?" he offered.

"Oh." Hope glanced around the shop as though searching for an answer, which escaped her. "That would be nice. Denki."

Aaron couldn't stop his wide smile even if he wanted to. For once, she wasn't trying to get away from him. "Let's clean up here first."

He'd hardly finished speaking before Hope spun away, doing just that. To get the cleanup over with or to get to supper quickly and get that over with, he wasn't sure which. He hoped it was the first option.

HOPE REALIZED HER mistake, allowing Aaron to take her to supper at Raber's Café, when Dinah Raber, Luke's sister only two years younger than Hope, seated them and gave them *that* look.

One filled with eager speculation, followed by the words, "Just you two? No . . . other family will be joining?"

Dinah glanced out the window as though searching for other members of their party.

Aaron appeared completely oblivious and waved off the question. "Just us, denki."

That earned Hope a quick once-over of further speculation, one edged in feminine suspicion.

"Right this way," Dinah murmured, and even those words had Hope gritting her teeth around her smile until her jaw ached.

This was a deerich idea. Of course being seen together would cause speculation. What if it reached Dat's ears? She needed to nip this in the bud immediately. But how? If she turned and ran out, that would only cause worse gossip.

So . . . what to do?

"Denki again, Aaron, for suggesting a meal after we finished helping your parents," she said as forcefully as she dared. "I didn't realize we'd worked so late." She picked up her menu to hide behind more than read.

"Why are you talking so loud?" Aaron asked, much more quietly than she'd been.

She cleared her throat and didn't lower the menu. "I'm not."

A big hand came over the top to pull it down slowly. Doing her best to stare back into his searching gaze with innocent curiosity, she waited for him to speak first.

"Are you embarrassed to be seen with me?" he asked, his expression so serious her heart reached out to him.

Making him feel bad had not been her intention. "Of course not."

His expression didn't change in the slightest. Hope leaned nearer, as close as the table between them would let her, and lowered her voice to a whisper. "My dat."

Immediately Aaron's expression cleared. "Oh, sis yuscht. I forgot about that." He glanced around and finally seemed to comprehend that the few Amish in the café found them of interest.

He leaned back. "It was wonderful nice of you to help out, Hope," he boomed. "With Mamm not feeling herself, someone needed to organize those displays and us boys are hopeless at it."

The ridiculousness of the situation suddenly hit her funny bone hard and Hope shoved the menu back up in front of her face, trying not to give in to the fit of giggles that wanted to escape. "Happy to," she managed to choke out.

"Don't laugh," Aaron half hissed, half whispered at her through the menu barricade. "If you laugh, I'll laugh."

A giggle made it out in the form of a snort-grunt. "Shhhh."

"I'm serious." The vibration of suppressed hilarity in his voice only set her shoulders shaking.

"This isn't funny," she managed to shoot back.

A sound like sucking in had her curling one corner of her menu over to peek at him, only to find Aaron sitting straight and serious, but with his dark eyes lit by laughter. As though stars had been thrown into the night sky, sparkling at her.

Forcing her brows into a consternated frown her mamm would've been proud of, she shook her head at him. "You're as bad as kinder at Gmay." Growing up, Hope and Hannah were terrible about giggling when it got quiet, much to the dismay of Mamm and Dat. Even Mammi had sent them cross-eyed stares from time to time. They'd learned to sit quietly . . . eventually. Hannah much sooner than Hope.

He crossed his arms. "Ach vell, the last thing I want to be to you is a child."

He wanted to be something to her? Hope ruthlessly corralled her jumping heart with a hand to her chest before it hopped right out of her. He had offered to be friends, so that had to be what he meant. "Then you'd better behave. Or I'll tell your mamm."

His expression of horror was so comical, she had to jerk the menu back up or she'd laugh loudly at his antics.

"You sure are taking a long time deciding," he said next.

The boy was a tease, for sure and certain. Primly she folded the menu and placed it to the side, not having seen a single word. "I suddenly feel sorry for your mother."

He cocked his head in question.

"I bet you were mischief and mayhem to raise."

Aaron affected an offended scowl. "I don't know what you're talking about. I was a perfect angel."

She shook her head. "I remember you in school. Always playing pranks on the girls and wrestling with the boys." Always the center of attention. Not that Hope minded attention herself. She just didn't clown for it.

"I never pranked you, though," he said, as though she should praise him for it.

Only to her, it had been a clear indicator that she was insignificant in his eyes, though he was perfectly nice. "No. You didn't."

Aaron sat forward, studying her. "But you wanted me to?"

How had he seen that?

"What a thing to ask." She paused, needing to put a stop to his teasing, and the look in his eyes, and the way her breathing constricted, and how everyone was still watching. "So . . . what do you usually get here?"

To her relief, Aaron picked up the menu, only to cluck once like a chicken, softly. Which had her biting her lip around her laughter yet again, even as heat surged into her cheeks.

"Ready to order?" Dinah popped up beside their table like a jackrabbit, directing the question to Aaron.

Aaron kindly raised his eyebrows, deferring to Hope with the proper manners his mamm no doubt insisted on.

"I think so," Hope said.

Only Dinah was still staring at Aaron, hardly paying Hope any attention. For his part, Aaron sent her a polite but distant smile, then kept his gaze on his menu as he ordered.

"The pot roast is particularly tasty tonight," Dinah offered when he paused.

"Um . . . I'll have the baked chicken, I think," he said.

Dinah noted it on her pad, then, not even looking her way, tossed a "What about you, Hope?" in her general direction.

"Same." Probably easier. Given the focus Dinah had on her dining companion, ordering something else might get confusing for the girl.

Dinah stood there, watching Aaron until he finally lifted his gaze to her. Then she jumped as though realizing what she'd been doing. "Anything else?"

"Nae, denki," Aaron said.

Cheeks red, Dinah hurried away.

The second Aaron turned his gaze her way, Hope widened her eyes at him.

"What?" he asked.

"Nothing." She shook her head. She'd just never been on the observing side of what it was like to be Aaron around girls. Did they all act like that around him?

Thinking back over the years, she realized that they probably had. Taller than many of the other boys, not too bad to look at, a hard worker, and seemingly talented at everything he did, Aaron also had a knack for making everyone around him comfortable. More than kindness, she thought of it like a heat lamp, radiating warmth the closer you got.

Even Hope was not unaffected, despite those horrible words he'd said.

Maybe that had been the biggest shock, thinking he sincerely liked her, even if as a friend, only to hear that he considered her just okay. Maybe not even that.

"I'm not that person, Hope."

The serious way he said that, his dark eyes intent on her face, suddenly they weren't joking anymore. "What person?"

"The boy that flirts with all the girls and can't be serious or dependable."

Oh, help. Despite their joking and teasing, which another girl might take as flirting, Hope believed him. "I know."

"And I'm a trustworthy friend."

Was he worried that she didn't think so? "I can see that about you."

The sudden intensity in his gaze eased and his mouth relaxed into his usual half smile. "I'm glad."

"Hope?"

At the sound of her name, she glanced over to find Luke Raber standing beside their table. "Oh, hi, Luke," she said. "Nice to see you."

He glanced at Aaron and nodded, then turned his focus back to her. "I haven't seen you in here since—"

Obviously about to say since her mamm died, he cut himself off.

"We've been so busy getting ready for the wedding." Hope hurried to cover for him, receiving a crooked smile for her effort.

She and Luke had always looked out for each other.

"Of course," he said. "Vell, I better get back to the kitchen."

"You work in the kitchen?" Aaron asked, the words shooting from him.

Hope frowned across the table at him. Of course Luke worked in his family café. What was wrong with him?

"Jah," Luke said slowly, obviously thinking the same thing. He didn't explain more. "See you around, Hope."

"Bye," she said to Luke's retreating back.

Aaron watched him go with a frown.

"He does the short order cooking," she said. "Anything that has to be grilled or seared."

That pulled Aaron's attention back to her. "So . . . you and Luke are . . ."

"Friends?" She supplied the word he didn't seem to want to speak. "Jah. Of course. I grew up with him, same as you."

Aaron grunted at that and didn't talk much more until the food was served. Between his sudden reticence and the speculation aimed in their direction—speculation she could feel, like the wind against her face on a stormy day, practically another presence in the room—Hope inhaled her food.

"Ready?" she asked as she laid down her fork and knife.

Aaron paused, own fork midway to his mouth. "Um. You eat fast," he blurted.

Heat crawled up her neck, but Hope ignored it. "My family are probably waiting for me," she said by way of explanation. "But you finish first. I can wait."

"No, it's fine." He waved Dinah over, asking for a box for his food. "I had a big lunch anyway. I'll put this in the shop fridge and finish it tomorrow."

As they waited for Dinah to bring the box and the check, Aaron picked up his untouched biscuit then grinned. "You know what would go great with this?" He jiggled the golden pastry at her.

Hope could see the answer coming a mile away. "Mint jelly?" she asked with a grin she couldn't hold back.

"Exactly what I was thinking." He leaned closer. "Are you a mind reader, Hope?"

Unfortunately, Dinah appeared right then. Clearly catching their exchange, she cast Hope another one of those speculative looks that made Hope want to chuck something. Mostly at Aaron's head.

This was sure to get back to Dat, and then what was she going to say?

Aaron insisted on paying for them both, even though this wasn't a date. At least he loudly proclaimed that her meal was "on the shop, since they were working." Hope thanked him nicely. As she tried to follow him out the door, Dinah grabbed her by the hand, pulling her to a stop.

"Are you and Aaron Kanagy sweethearts?" She squeaked the question.

Hope did her best to appear unruffled. "No. I'm helping in the gift shop for a few weeks and we had to finish changing out the displays tonight. It took longer than we thought."

"Oh!" Dinah's look of delight at least might help things a bit.

"He's waiting for me. Bye, Dinah." Hope hurried out into the evening, the brisk air making her shiver. She'd left her coat in the shop earlier.

"What was that about?" Aaron asked.

Not wanting to embarrass the other girl, Hope shrugged.

"Was it about me?" Now he sounded worried.

"Don't worry. I set her straight."

Aaron's groan had her doing a double take. "What?"

"Dinah Raber . . ." He cut off his own muttering.

Hope ducked her head, knowing exactly what he was thinking and finding his reluctance to embarrass Dinah by talking about her crush on him sort of . . . sweet.

Why did he say what he did about you, then? an insidious little voice asked. Why hadn't he been reluctant to talk about his disinterest in Hope?

She brushed it off. "Sorry. I'd let her think we were sweethearts if it wouldn't get back to Dat, but that would, for sure and certain."

Maybe even before Gmay next Sunday, despite the way her dat avoided people the rest of the week.

Aaron tossed her a strange glance. One she had trouble

interpreting. "I understand," he said. But the words sounded off to her. Like he was holding back or distracted by his own thoughts.

Hope didn't push. They were friends, he understood the situation with Dat, and as soon as he was done with the bed, her life could go back to normal.

Why the night suddenly grew a shade duller at the thought, she wasn't willing to explore.

Chapter Ten

✳

STANDING AT THE sink Sunday morning washing up after breakfast, Hope glanced out the window that faced over the backyard and garden and the chicken coop beyond. Mammi had sent Hannah out to gather eggs. The Hostetlers were hosting Gmay, and Anna Hostetler was one of Mammi's oldest and dearest friends. She'd promised to bring a dish and they wanted to get there early to help set up.

Mammi sidled up beside Hope, taking a dish towel to dry the dishes. "What is this about you eating supper at Raber's Café with Aaron Kanagy Friday night?"

Hope lost her grip on the soapy bowl she held, and it dropped into the water with a splash that covered the apron across her chest. She whipped the apron off before the wetness could sink through to her nice mint green dress, which she did *not* wear with Aaron in mind. Grabbing a different apron from the back of the pantry door, she returned to the sink and snatched the offending bowl right out. All this Mammi watched with eyebrows sky-high.

"It was nothing," Hope muttered.

"Nothing?" Mammi's tone of voice said she clearly expected more than that.

Hope wrinkled her nose. "We finished arranging the displays in the store too late to make it home for supper, so he suggested we eat there."

Mammi put down the dish she was drying with a thump. "That's not what I heard."

Oh, help. "What *did* you hear?"

"Exactly what you think I heard."

Hope slumped over the sink with a groan. "But I tried to make it clear we weren't there as courting sweethearts. Dinah Raber even asked me straight out and I said no."

"Your dat isn't going to like it when this reaches his ears."

Aaron was only halfway finished with his work on the bed for Hannah and Noah. This was a disaster. Hope lifted her eyes up, sending a prayer of apology to Gotte for her lies to her dat and at the same time begging Him to hold off just a little longer. Not wanting to break the commandment to honor her parent, just . . . bend it a bit.

Or maybe she should just confess.

"I'll tell Dat before we leave for Gmay," she said, disappointment settling in the words like silt settled in a river. "Better he learn it from me than through idle gossip."

Mammi turned and leaned a hip against the counter, nodding slowly. "That's one way to go."

Hope paused, not entirely trusting what that twinkle in her grossmammi's eyes meant. "But?"

"But there's a way to divert the talk, show for sure you and Aaron aren't sweethearts, so that your dat won't believe it anyway."

Now she knew that twinkle wasn't to be trusted, for sure

and certain. What bee had Mammi got in her bonnet now? "It's better to fess up and finish this, don't you think?"

"Is the bed ready?"

Hope bit her lip and shook her head.

"Then you haven't worked off your debt to the Kanagys. No going back now."

As usual, Mammi did have a point. Hope would feel terrible leaving Aaron with a bed half done, all the materials paid for and bought, and no one to sell it to. That would be a shame. Not to mention no one to help in the shop, forcing him to work all hours. The image of his sleep-strained face had her biting her lip.

"What do you suggest?" Hope asked slowly, cringing inwardly at whatever advice was about to come her way.

Except this was Mammi, and Dat was her son. She wouldn't steer Hope wrong. A little off center, maybe, but never wrong.

"A distraction, of course!" Mammi grinned as though she'd solved all the world's problems.

An hour later, Dat pulled the buggy up to the Hostetlers' house. A boy ran out to take charge of the horse, and Hope and Hannah followed Mammi into the house while Dat joined the men standing outside the barn. She refused to look around for Aaron. Doubtful he'd be here yet anyway, since her family was there early to offer help.

Inside, she joined the women bustling around, doing what she could as more and more people arrived. Then folks started to separate out into the groups they sat with during the service. The older women gathered in one part of the house, with the young mothers and babies in another. She and Hannah went to join the older unmarried girls. On the way, Hope waved at Ruth Kanagy, who sent her a beaming smile despite appearing slightly pale. Hope would have

liked to ask if her cough was getting any better, but the painfully aware sensation crawling down her neck at the few
stares already conjured kept her feet moving in the other
direction.

Mammi's plan would be . . . effective . . . if she could
make it to tonight without anyone saying something to Dat.
A risk she'd decided to take.

She paused at the top of the stairs. What a horrible dochder she had become.

Except Mammi had pointed out that, had Mamm still
been alive, she would have insisted Hope do what she was
doing, working off a fair trade with Aaron and his family
for Hannah's sake. Mamm would have smoothed things
over with Dat. Hope took a determined step forward at a
sharp glance from Hannah.

She'd have to trust in Mammi and the rightness of her
intentions.

Per the tradition that provided a sense of steadiness and
something solid to grasp on to in a world that seemed ever-
changing, the congregation filed in order by age and gender
into the barn, where the backless benches sat already set
up, men facing the women across the way. All a form of
Gelassenheit—each one having his or her place.

Normally the quiet practice settled Hope into the service, peace falling over her as she prepared to worship with
people whom she'd known all her life. Singing the songs
and reciting prayers that she knew by heart and yet found
surprising newness in each time she formed the words.

Not today.

Today Mammi's plan swam in her head like the swirling
torrents of a creek swollen with rain. The thoughts coiled
through her, blocking out everything else, including when

one of the men called out the hymn number. Hannah dug a discreet elbow into her side, and Hope jerked her spine straight, then realized everyone was opening the small black book with *Ausbund* on the spine to the hymn number. Hannah flashed the page at her, and Hope found it in her own copy, joining in the slow, solemn singing.

The hymn was as familiar as Mammi's hugs. Sung by generations, the German words were drawn out, slow and steady, sliding between notes in unison, blending together. Only Hope barely mouthed the words. By rote, she moved with the others into the second hymn, the *Loblied*, a praise hymn asking Gotte to bless the preachers and make the worshippers receptive to Gotte's message.

She lifted her gaze across the way, only to collide with intent dark eyes directly opposite where she sat. Aaron. His expression didn't change, but still, somehow, she caught the question in his eyes. As though he were silently asking her if she was well. Blatant concern that sent warmth of affection rushing through her, joining the rest of the confusing torrent of emotions.

Unable to answer him, even if they'd been the only people in the room, Hope deliberately lowered her lashes, determined to keep her gaze focused on her lap. A feat she managed to accomplish through the rest of the almost three-hour service, doing her best to listen attentively to the opening sermon reminding the congregation why they had gathered and calling members to humble themselves before Gotte.

Am I sinning with my actions?

Was that why her stomach was a mass of nerves and her mind was jumping everywhere other than where it should be?

After prayer and the reading of scripture came the message. Only that didn't help her either. As was said in the Book of John, "And this is the condemnation, that light is come into the world, and men loved darkness rather than light, because their deeds were evil."

The words only piled on to her own growing guilt. Was she willfully turning away from the light to go forward with her own plans? Were her deeds evil?

She flicked a glance at Hannah, whose expression rested in serene beauty as she listened quietly, obediently attentive. The decisions that had led Hope here had come from a place of light. Could evil come from light?

Gotte, what am I to do? Your will be done. Show me the right way.

"'Therefore,'" the minister continued, quoting Colossians now, "'as God's chosen people, holy and dearly loved, clothe yourselves with compassion, kindness, humility, gentleness, and patience. Bear with each other and forgive whatever grievances you may have against one another. Forgive as the Lord forgave you.'"

Hope lifted her gaze to her fater, seated toward the right. Suddenly the knots unwound inside her, tranquility easing through her body and soul. Right or wrong, she had taken this path with loving intentions. Mammi was right—she did still owe a debt to the Kanagys. And Dat would forgive her when all was said and done. Mamm would have seen to it that there would be no need for forgiveness, giving her permission had she been here. She had to believe that.

No matter the path that had brought her to this place in life, she had to see it through to the end and pray that Gotte, in His wisdom, would lead her the rest of the way.

Starting with Mammi's plan tonight.

* * *

"OH, LOOK. HOPE came," Daniel murmured in Aaron's ear.

For once, Aaron didn't try to dismiss the quickening of his pulse, his heart thudding against the inside of his chest like a trapped bird, as he turned to see Hope stepping down from the Prices' buggy with Sarah and Rachel. If she wasn't with her sister, she was with the Prices, and that had been true since they'd been children.

Hope turned suddenly, facing his way.

He'd always thought her lovely, but something about her now stole his breath, leaving his chest tight. The way she moved, like a dance, and the beauty of her kind smile as she greeted others.

She won't think of marrying me because of her dat.

The thought that had been beating at him since Friday night, when the realization struck with all the power of a bolt of lightning, flitted through his thoughts yet again.

That *had* to be why she'd said what she had when she hadn't known he'd been listening. She couldn't let herself consider him because of their families, but Aaron surely hoped to change her mind about that.

Aaron plucked a cookie off the table without seeing what he was grabbing and shoved it in his mouth, only to immediately stop chewing as the taste hit him. What had he eaten? Holding his mouth closed but still not chewing the oddly salty and sweet concoction, he glanced at the table. Mary Gingrich's thumbprint cookies, that's what he'd grabbed. She made them every Sunday.

Spitting it out would only hurt her feelings if she'd seen. Forcing himself, he managed to finish chewing and swallow it down.

He didn't dare glance at his bruders, the wall of silence behind him giving him a decent idea that they had to be staring and wondering at his behavior.

The thing was . . . Had Hope always been this way for him? The girl who stood out above the rest?

The feelings pouring over him, growing like spring flowers brought forth by rain and sun, in these short weeks of spending more time with her had to be rooted in something longer lasting than that short amount of time.

In the middle of Gmay, when he should've been focused on Gotte, he'd found himself watching her. At one point, a crease between her brows had given her an almost sad expression, and he'd had to physically stop himself from crossing the room, in front of Gotte, her fater, and everyone else, to make sure she was all right.

Only, other than the one brief glance when he'd sworn she could see his heart in his eyes, she hadn't looked his way again.

Three hours spent anxious for her thoughts, but even after the service was over and the congregation had transitioned to the meal, he couldn't approach her.

Her dat. Maybe I should talk to him. Ask his permission to court her.

Now, surrounded by the other girls her age, she talked and laughed, her usual light glowing from her and touching everyone around her, making them smile with her. Just like in church, he willed her to look his way. To cross the yard to where he stood and show the others that she wasn't afraid to be his friend.

Only you want more. The small voice whispering ideas in his mind wouldn't leave him alone.

Aaron straightened, tension seizing him, as she turned

her head suddenly. As though she'd heard him. Her gaze wandered over to the tables of food, where he stood with his bruders. Had she stilled when she saw him?

Aaron had the strangest urge to cross to her side and take her hand, walk with her quietly in the night, letting the coolness of the dry air and the sounds of the woods fill the silence. No need for words. Not between them.

He could see it so clearly, a future with her like that—her working in the shop, him on his furniture, evenings filled with family and time together, walking to her bridge in the cool of the evenings, just the two of them.

Am I falling for Hope?

The question filled his head softly, as if the idea had always been there, whispering to him until he could finally hear. He wasn't sure of the answer yet, but that future in his mind seemed so . . . real.

He didn't cross to her. Of course he didn't.

This would probably only end in heartbreak, because nothing had changed as far as her dat was concerned.

Was it worth the risk to find out how deep his feelings went? *I'll ask her to drive home tonight.*

The decision that had been hovering at the back of his mind solidified with her presence here tonight after she'd skipped so many Sunday evenings.

He took two steps toward her, only to stop as Hope turned away, the move sharp and, he had the sense, deliberate. As he watched, she crossed the yard to where a few of die youngie were setting up a volleyball net to play. Including Luke Raber, who grinned widely then laughed as Hope spoke to him.

Luke. Raber.

Oh, sis yuscht.

A low whistle sounded in his left ear. "I've never seen you stare without blinking before," Joshua muttered. "That's quite a trick."

Aaron jerked his gaze away, trying to play it off. "I was lost in thought, trying to remember if I closed Frank's stall when we left."

"Oh, jah?" Joshua snickered.

Aaron ignored him.

"Luke has been interested in Hope for years," Daniel pointed out. At least he bothered to lower his voice, keeping this between themselves.

Trying hard not to glance over at the couple, Aaron shrugged. "Who she—" He paused over the word. He was going to say "allows to court her," but that gave too much of his own desires away. "Talks to . . . is up to Hope. She's a kind girl, nice to everyone."

Not now, though, Gotte. Before I have a chance. Please?

"Want to join in?" Joshua asked, already walking in the direction of the volleyball players as they got set to start a game.

"Jah," Aaron found himself saying before making the decision and following his bruder over.

As he got nearer, Hope glanced over and shot him an instant glower, though she quickly cleared her expression to neutral.

Pain snagged in the region of his heart, like a blackberry bush snagging at his shirt in the woods. Followed swiftly by the burn of irritation.

What? He wasn't allowed to play volleyball now? Granted, he usually didn't. But neither did Hope.

By luck of the draw, he ended up on the opposite side, directly across from her to start. Once again, she refused to look at him. Now he was sure the move was deliberate.

And that's how the rest of the night went. Hope avoiding him. Hope not looking at him. And finally, Hope driving away in Luke Raber's buggy, taking a raw chunk of Aaron's heart with her as she went without a backward glance.

Chapter Eleven

✳

LUKE HAD SET his horse to the slowest possible pace. Ever. And Hope was trying her hardest not to jiggle her leg in impatience to get this ride over with. Her other option was wringing her hands in her lap to keep from glancing over her shoulder and looking for Aaron, even though they'd long since left the Hostetlers' house behind.

"Okay, Hope Beiler, do you want to explain what all that was about?" He hitched a thumb over his shoulder.

She jumped at Luke's demand, suddenly loud in the otherwise hushed interior of the buggy. Then she sighed and didn't bother to hide it.

The first thing Sarah and Rachel Price had asked her tonight when they'd picked her up on the way here was if she and Aaron were courting. They hadn't been the only ones. At least the questions had slowed after she'd made a show of speaking to Luke instead. Feeling foolish the entire time.

And for the first time ever, she'd accepted Luke's offer

of a drive home. After all, Mammi had said to create a diversion for the gossip. As distractions went, it served as a big one.

And a safe one, but even Mammi didn't know that.

Luke had lived one house over for all of Hope's life. As kinder, they'd played together, though her parents stopped letting her go over to his house after she'd turned five. She was well aware most people didn't like Luke all that much. He'd gone a bit wild in his earlier Rumspringa years . . . maybe even still. He had a reputation of chasing the girls, and the boys saw him as lazy.

Despite all that, he'd always been kind to Hope, even when he was at his worst. Even when it looked as though he was going to travel the same road as his father.

She also knew something about him others only suspected. A secret they shared.

Abram Raber, his father, was a known bully and apt to get physical. But when the man publicly confessed his sins, the community extended forgiveness—over and over. The Amish way. They trusted Gotte to make the judgments in the end. Even for one such as Abram.

The Amish took a vow against violence. But they were as human as anyone else, with real feelings like anger. Violence, like all other sins, was part of the human condition. Violence, disobedience, hate.

Otherwise, humanity wouldn't have needed Jesus's sacrifice on the cross.

Abram Raber more than most. Only the community didn't seem to know that Abram's bullying had been directed at his own family. He'd never confessed that particular sin.

One day, on the way to school, Hope happened to see Luke hiding in the bushes, his face a bloody mess. Concerned, she'd sent Hannah on without her, not mentioning what she'd seen, then ran back to her house for ice and wet rags. When she returned, she'd managed to find him, still hidden off the road. It was a cold, misty day that made the chill seep into one's bones. He must've been desperate to hide outdoors in such conditions.

Hope hadn't asked questions. Simply cleaned him up, ignoring how he acted like a skittish wild animal, glowering at her at first. Then she'd showed him the secret way into her parents' basement, where he could stay the rest of the day out of the weather. She'd brought him food—nothing fancy: an apple, homemade cheese, and water—an oil lamp, and a book to read, as well as a blanket. That basement was always cold, even in summer.

"Why are you being so nice to me?" Luke had asked. Not with his usual sneer or mean sort of teasing. Almost as though he'd lost his way. And perhaps he had.

She opened her mouth.

"And don't say because it's what a gute Christian would do." *There* was the sneer.

Hope shook her head. "I wasn't going to."

Skepticism crawled across his face like a spider.

She ignored it. For some odd reason, Luke had never frightened her like he did a few of the younger kinder. "I'm being nice because you've always been nice to me."

He'd blinked several times, then scowled. "No, I haven't. I teased you about your hair."

True. But more boys than Luke Raber had called her names like carrot top. It never really bothered her because she liked her hair. "That's just teasing, not actual meanness," she reasoned.

"I don't want your pity," he muttered.

Pride. Every human struggled with it, apparently. "Pity

the biggest, strongest boy in school?" she said. "There would be no point."

He'd glanced away, his sullen expression easing. Or she thought so. Hard to tell under the swelling quickly closing up his eye.

"Anytime you need to have . . . time alone . . . you can come here. No one ever comes down except when Mamm's canning," she'd told him.

Mamm used the basement as storage otherwise.

Luke hadn't responded, still not looking at her. So she'd headed to school, where she'd told the teacher he'd gone home sick. After she'd gotten back that afternoon, she'd snuck down to the basement to find the blanket folded neatly on the floor beside the lamp, turned off, and dishes washed clean. She wasn't sure how he'd managed that part.

She also wasn't sure if he'd ever taken her up on her of-fer of using the basement as a place to escape. But she'd left the lamp, blanket, and book down there, just in case. They never moved spots.

To their mutual shock, Luke had a chance to repay her kindness four years later.

When she'd first entered her Rumspringa years, the idea of a boy asking to drive her home and having to reject that boy got into her silly head. Not that she was shy of boys or didn't want to be asked. But she hated the thought of hurt-ing someone's feelings. Her first singeon, Luke had found her alone on the porch, trying to avoid being alone with a boy. To her surprise, since he'd all but ignored her since that day in the basement, he had stopped to ask what was wrong. Even more surprising, she'd found herself confess-ing her worry.

First, he'd hooted with laughter. Then he'd grinned. A real, honest grin. Not one filled with spite or resentment, like usual. "I guess the nicest girl in our district would have to worry about something like that."

"It's stupid to worry about, I know."

He shook his head, eyes still laughing at her. "I tell you what, Hope. I'll make a show of asking to drive you home each Sunday. That way, if someone else asks, you can say you already agreed to go with me. Deal?"

He'd held out a hand to shake. The perfect solution, and she'd been grateful, so they'd shaken on it. He'd asked every Sunday. Every Sunday she'd said no, usually earning a wink and a teasing remark.

Who knew Luke Raber would become a true friend?

As the buggy made its steady way down the road, she still hadn't answered his question. "I don't know—"

"Don't you dare say you don't know what I'm talking about; Aaron Kanagy about took my head off with that volleyball. A couple times. And you've never had to take me up on our deal before."

"No one has asked me."

"That's not true. Amos Lambright asked you a few months ago. And before that, I know Gideon Miller did, too."

How did he know that? She let it go as fast as her mind asked the question. It didn't matter.

Hope sighed again. She hadn't wanted to drag Luke further into her mess than she had to. "I did something deerich."

"Doesn't take a genius to figure that out." He softened his words with a grin.

"It's a long story."

"That's why we're going slow." He waggled his eyebrows. "That and so that Aaron has longer to stew over us."

A laugh punched from her before she could push it back down. "You're enjoying this too much."

He shrugged, but she still caught his grin. He could be a handsome boy, with his blue eyes and nice smile, if he just stopped glowering or smirking all the time.

Hope shook her head. "Ach vell . . . it started with a chair."

And before she knew it, the entire story poured from her. Luke, for the most part, listened quietly, asking only a handful of clarifying questions.

He pulled the buggy up to her house as she finished. It rocked as he brought his horse to a stop.

Uncharacteristically, Luke said nothing for a long moment.

"Well?" she pushed.

He shook his head. "That is quite a situation you've got yourself into."

"I already know that," she huffed.

"Do you like him?"

She frowned. "Who?"

"Aaron."

More than she should. "We're just friends."

Luke snorted at that. "That volleyball game was *not* friendly."

"Oh, help. I honestly don't know what that was about. I haven't seen him since Friday. They gave me Saturday off and keep the shop closed on Sundays. Maybe he had a bad day."

"One he aimed at my head."

She grimaced. "Sorry."

Luke laughed and bumped her with his shoulder. Then he lowered his voice, suddenly gruff. "I'm just glad you finally said yes to driving home with me."

Hope couldn't hide the shock in eyes gone wide. Did he really say that?

Luke sniggered. "You should see your face. I meant because my reputation was starting to suffer after all those rejections."

Hope rolled her eyes. "Someday, Luke Raber, you'll find a girl who'll take your particular kind of teasing seriously, and then where will you end up?"

He heaved a dramatic sigh. "As a tired, old bachelor, I imagine."

"What would your mother say?"

Something flashed in his eyes, an emotion gone so quick she couldn't be sure she'd seen it. Pain. He glanced away. "Mamm does want boppli to cuddle and coo over."

None of the Rabers had married. Luke, at twenty-three, was the oldest. Plenty of time yet.

"I thought you didn't like Aaron?" he suddenly asked.

For a brief second, Hope considered sharing with Luke the story of overhearing Aaron that night last year. But decided against it, feeling disloyal to Aaron, who'd been kind otherwise. Especially lately. No need to burden Luke for an action she'd forgiven, if not exactly forgotten.

Besides . . . insults aside, she liked Aaron fine. More than fine if the strange awareness she experienced around him was any indication.

But she was also still irritated with him for tonight. He knew . . . *he knew* . . . she was worried about her dat. His behavior almost ruined everything with her plan to have Luke drive her home and deflect the rumors.

Guilt piled higher. Like the compost heap in the backyard and with just as bad a schtinke.

"Luke Raber, is that you?" Mammi's voice, slightly muffed, had them both swinging their heads to find her standing on the porch, hands on her hips, bent over to peer in the window.

Luke slid the door up and helped Hope out, nodding at Mammi.

"Won't you come in for a bit?" her grossmammi invited.

His gaze slid to Hope, who had to bite back a grin. For once, Luke appeared at a loss for words. At a kind offer? Maybe he didn't get enough of those.

"Nae, denki," he finally said. "I'd best be getting home. Mamm will have waited up."

Something in his tone struck her as off, but Hope couldn't put her finger on what. Before Mammi could argue, he was already gone, back in his buggy and setting his horse to clop steadily down the lane at a faster pace than they'd arrived.

Hope watched after him. Luke had acted almost . . . happy . . . tonight. *I hope things have gotten easier at home.* He'd outgrown his father by quite a bit years ago, towering over him yet. Abram Raber might think twice about coming at Luke now.

Maybe that helped.

Slowly, she made her way up the stairs, only to pause at the one that usually creaked and bent as though getting ready to snap. Not only did it not creak, it didn't even wiggle. She gave an experimental bounce. Solid. She stepped back and leaned over to inspect it, her mouth falling open.

Someone had fixed it.

Like the dead rosebush being dug up. Maybe Dat was finally coming out of the terrible sadness that had consumed him since Mamm's passing.

"Stop dawdling, miss," Mammi insisted, waving her inside.

"Did I hear right that Luke Raber drove you home tonight?" Dat asked as she followed her grandmother inside. As usual, he was sitting in his chair in front of the fireplace—

not lit tonight because there'd been no need for the extra warmth—his Bible in his lap.

"Jah, Dat. He kindly offered me a ride."

The lines on his forehead folded over on themselves. "Are you sure he's the kind of boy—"

"We're only friends, Dat," she rushed to assure him.

The frown didn't clear up. "Kumme." He beckoned her closer with a shade of his old self and a pat on the couch beside his chair. Something he hadn't done since Mamm took sick.

Eagerness hurried her steps as she crossed to him, taking a seat on the couch and resting her hands in her lap. As he had when she was a child, Dat reached out and tugged at her kapp a bit and probably set it wonky, but Hope didn't mind.

"You always did have a soft heart. All the broken things you brought home for us to fix. Ach du lieva. Like that baby bird that fell out of its nest. You cried and cried. Or when the barn cat had a litter and rejected the runt. You nursed that thing for weeks."

Hope chuckled. "He turned into the best mouser we have."

"True." Dat's eyes crinkled at the corners, the memory clear and sweet. Then he sobered. "Your mamm had the same kind of heart. Brave . . . but sometimes too kind, to the point that she put herself in harm's way."

"Jah," she whispered. "I miss her." Then she held her breath. Dat never talked about Mamm anymore.

His gaze drifted far away over the top of her head. "When I was courting her, she almost married another man, though she didn't love him. One she had befriended when his parents passed away. She thought of accepting his proposal because he was left alone and that broke her tender heart."

Hope straightened, eyes wide. Mamm had almost married another? "But she loved you so much, Dat."

The corners of his lips drew up a tiny bit. "We loved each other very much, and she admitted later that she would have regretted marrying him. Not because he wasn't worthy, but because she'd given me her heart."

"Why are you telling me this?"

"Because you are of an age where you'll be choosing a young man to marry soon, and my Hope deserves to find someone who'll take care of her." He glanced out the window, and Hope realized what her dat wasn't saying.

He was warning her that Luke Raber wasn't for her.

"That's what I want, too," she said. "Only . . . what if I fall in love with a boy you don't approve of?"

Aaron's dark eyes stole into her thoughts. The sound of his voice. The way he made her laugh. How hard he worked at everything he did.

"Why wouldn't I approve?" her father asked, lines appearing on his brow again.

Hope shrugged one shoulder. "Maybe you wouldn't like his family, or he lives far away, or any kind of thing."

Usually the one of her parents to think through each situation, to consider all the angles quietly—unless it involved Joseph Kanagy—her dat stared at her long and hard, as though trying to plumb the depths of her thoughts for himself.

"I would pray to Gotte that His will would be done," he said slowly. "And I would expect you to honor my decision if I had to tell you no."

Disappointment clogged her throat, as though swelling her airways shut. "But you would spend time with the boy, getting to know him first, jah? Trusting that you and Mamm had raised me right to choose wisely."

Again he studied her upturned face.

"Jah. I would try to consider everything I could first."

At least there was that.

"As long as I could be assured that my dochder would be safe, cared for, and provided for, led by a strong Amish mann who seeks Gotte in all things, that is all I could ask for."

Safe? He'd emphasized the word. Was he thinking of Luke Raber's dat? A shiver skated down her spine. She wished she could assure him that he had no need to worry in that regard. But she couldn't. Not without ruining the effect of the distraction that Luke created.

Guilt, the churn of it turning into her constant companion of late, rested so heavily on her shoulders, she sagged beneath the weight of it, her stomach clenching and unclenching. *No more keeping things from people I love ever again after this is over.*

She might be brave sometimes . . . she knew that girl still lurked inside her somewhere . . . but hurting others hurt her more.

Hope patted her fater's knee, not even sure herself why those words meant so much. "Denki."

He laid a hand on top of hers, and they sat that way in comfortable silence for a long while, enjoying each other, both lost in their thoughts.

Chapter Twelve

❊

AARON STARED AT the ceiling, the wood grain familiar after twenty-two years of staring at it. In the other twin bed across the room, not quite close enough to reach over and touch, Joshua snored lightly.

They'd shared this room since they were toddlers, as soon as Joshua started sleeping in his crib, though Aaron had only been two at the time. As far as he was concerned, Joshua had always been there. Not always a good thing. Bruders could be wonderful annoying. When he'd been ten, they'd agreed they needed to marry off Daniel quickly. As the oldest, he had a bedroom all to himself. If he married, he could move away, and they could each get their own bedroom.

Twelve years later, that plan hadn't exactly held up as the brightest or easiest to carry out.

They'd given up on that idea almost as soon as Daniel started Rumspringa and it became obvious that no girls in the district interested him. Or perhaps more accurate, his deliberate nature kept him heart-whole, despite the way girls tried to catch his attention. Aaron had secretly thought maybe Faith Kemp had caught his bruder's eye, but then she'd followed her sister Mercy and jumped the fence.

Not that he was thinking of Daniel's girl troubles tonight. He had his own.

Hope's face imposed itself in the darkness every time he closed his eyes. Hope frowning at him. Hope laughing at him. Hope riding away with Luke Raber at the slow pace a boy would set if he wanted extra time with that certain special girl.

Outside his open window, an owl's soft hoot floated on the currents of the lazy breeze.

With a low sigh, Aaron quietly threw back his quilt and shivered, but didn't lie back down. Sleep was not coming. Maybe he could use work to bleed off this anxious energy gripping his body. As quickly and silently as he could, he gathered his clothes and snuck out of the room. He dressed in the bathroom he shared with Daniel and Joshua, then made his way out of the house.

He had every intention of heading to the small workspace in the barn where he often did whittling work on smaller toys, or anything else he could do without the bigger tools located in his workshop in town. Only his feet seemed to have developed minds of their own, turning him toward the path that led into the woods. He tried to convince himself he was simply wandering. But secretly he knew better. He was going to Hope's bridge, using the bare light of the moon to guide him there in the dark.

As soon as he rounded the bend in the path that opened up a clear view of the bridge, he stopped, afraid that what he was seeing were his own thoughts come to life. A spirit sent to torment him.

Not a troll under the bridge, but an angel above.

Hope sat in the center of her bridge, legs drawn up, arms wrapped around them, chin resting on her knees. Her bare toes peeped out from the bottom of her dress. The soft glow of the lantern she'd set on the rail above cast her in an almost ethereal light. Beautiful . . . and remote.

He blinked several times, but she didn't disappear. Hope was real and there. With him. Though she had yet to glance up. Delight buzzed through him, filling him with anticipation, and pleasure, and . . . new wonderings.

"Are you not cold?" he called out softly.

A soft gasp escaped her lips as she straightened, eyes wide, then just as fast and jerky, she blew out a sharp breath, shaking her head at him. Before he could say anything, Hope grinned—wide and beautiful and sincere—and that smile shot straight through him.

"You scared me," she accused, the soft burble of the creek trying to steal her words from this far away.

"That's what you get, sitting in the dark woods all alone," he said.

Her doubtful snort made him grin.

"It's never been a problem before," she said.

"I could go," he offered, waving over his shoulder in the direction he'd come from.

Hope shook her head. "I don't mind company. I couldn't sleep."

Because of Luke Raber? Did he kiss her? Did he do something inappropriate or scare her? Aaron wasn't sure which sent a burn of concern through him more. But he did know that what he was feeling was wrong. Jealousy. A sin. Coveting was a sin. He should be satisfied as long as Hope was happy.

So he buried the dark emotion deep, making a note to pray about it when he got back home.

"Me neither," he said as he approached the bridge. "Mind if I sit?" he asked.

She scooted to the side, giving him room. Only with the way the bridge curved, and because of his bulk, he tipped sideways once he managed to squeeze himself down there, which meant his crossed legs, knees jackknifing up on either side, wanted to come all undone.

After he'd shifted several times, Hope's giggle stopped him.

"Here," she said. Instead of sitting sideways on the bridge, facing the stream, she scooted her body around to face him. Aaron did the same, which was a tiny bit better. At least he wasn't tipping over.

"Remind me to bring a chair out here next time," he muttered.

"My dad made this bridge for a little girl, not a . . ." She paused, pinching her lips together around obvious laughter. "What did your mater call you? A big, strapping man?" She made a muscle with her arm, lowering her voice as she said it.

Aaron groaned and ran a hand over his face. "Maters can be so embarrassing."

"Jah." Only the word came out quietly.

Was she remembering her own? Of course she was. Without thinking, Aaron reached across the space between their knees and hooked his pinkie finger around hers in a silent show of comfort. The most he could dare.

She didn't pull away.

"Do you miss her?" he asked.

"Jah," she murmured. "Every single day."

He nodded slowly, his gaze focused on their fingers. That small touch connected them in a way he hadn't expected. As though her soul and his soul communicated through that tiny contact.

"What is your favorite memory of her?" he asked, lifting

his gaze to find her watching him with an expression that appeared oddly . . . content.

Content was promising. Wasn't it?

Or was he seeing only what he wished to see? No. The emotions he truly wished to see in Hope's eyes went way beyond contentment.

"Mamm used to have special days with each of her girls," she said, the words coming out slowly at first. Her expression brightened. "Once a month, on our own special day, she'd take one of us in the buggy to do something, just the two of us. Picnics, or going into Charity Creek, or going to visit friends or family."

A special day for each child set aside. Aaron tried to picture it.

"Now that I'm older, I realize how deliberate that time was for her," she said, her gaze focused on the past, on memories he couldn't see.

"What do you mean?"

She blinked and shrugged. "You know running a farm is hard work, and my parents only had girls. Their days were filled with nonstop chores and things to do. These days Dat barely keeps on top of it, even with our help, and we're no longer small kinder to care for."

Again, in only so many words, Hope alluded to the farm being too much for the Beiler family. Only he couldn't think of a way to help change that circumstance for them. He wasn't a farmer. His family had owned the shop for generations.

Most of his friends and even their fathers now worked in factories nearby. Either that or, like his family, had become merchants with shops of varying kinds. Maybe Noah would become the answer to the Beilers' problems once he and Hannah married.

That had to be it. What the family was waiting for.

"She sounds very special."

Hope dropped her gaze. Was she staring at their linked fingers? Did she like the way her hand looked in his? Felt against his? He did. Like they fit together. Or was he being deerich?

Hope's shoulders rose and fell in a deep, silent breath. "She was." Her voice came out choked, and immediately Aaron wanted to wrap his arms around her and hold her until the pain subsided.

"I shouldn't have asked. It makes you sad to talk about. I'm sorry—"

She gave her head a vehement shake. "It's nice to be able to talk about her. We don't at home much . . . Ever." Even in the dim lighting he could see the way her eyes darkened. "I guess it hurts too much for Dat. But sometimes, it's like her memory is fading in the silence."

Aaron twisted his hand to take hers fully in his, giving it a squeeze. "You can talk to me about her anytime you want."

She stared into his eyes, a small smile hovering around her mouth. "You are a gute man, Aaron Kanagy."

He grinned. "You should tell my mamm. She's not sure they got it right with me yet."

At his wink she laughed, as he'd intended.

"What's your favorite memory of *your* mother?" Hope asked suddenly.

Aaron thought for a moment. "I love that Mamm tries to be strict, but is a secret marshmallow, all soft and gooey on the inside. We boys got away with a lot growing up."

"Still do," Hope teased.

He shrugged. "I expect that's true. But I think my favorite is the way she bakes our favorite desserts for any special occasions. Mamm doesn't like baking and cooking much."

Hope straightened. "She doesn't?"

Remembering her dismay over her own efforts, Aaron chuckled. "Yes. And she's still an upstanding Amish wife and mother and woman. So don't you fret, Hope Beiler."

"Hmmm."

"Anyway . . . Since she doesn't like to bake, it makes her efforts that much more special. You see what I mean?"

"I do. It's a bigger effort to get it right."

"Exactly." Aaron smiled at the thought of the shortbread cookies he loved so much. He'd asked to help make them only once. What a lot of work for such small things. But such pleasure, too, as though Gotte blessed the act and the results.

"'And whatsoever ye do in word or deed, do all in the name of the Lord Jesus, giving thanks to God and the Father by him,'" Hope murmured, so quiet he had to lean forward to catch the words.

"Colossians," he said automatically.

She lifted her head on a nod.

He stared into those soft gray eyes, the connection so strong, it wound around his heart. A sense of rightness settled over him, like this was how they should be for always.

"Hope . . . will you marry me?"

The shock that sent her eyes wide reflected his own and sent fear shooting through him and Aaron scrambling to his feet. With hands trembling slightly, he reached down, needing to face her and try not to mess this up more. Blurting it out like that. He wasn't even sure he was ready for that step. He'd only just decided to court her tonight. What had he been thinking?

This was not the way to start a proposal.

Hope appeared to be in a daze as she hesitated briefly before she put her hands in his and allowed him to gently lift her to her feet. Aaron kept hold of her, almost as though he knew if he let her go, she'd run off.

He opened his mouth to speak, to convince her, only the words wouldn't come out, lodging in his throat like his grandmother's dry wheat bread that was so hard to swallow.

What do I say?

She would never believe him. It had been only a month, though they'd known each other for years. He hadn't been courting her or shown other signs of his interest. Because he was a coward.

Oh, sis yuscht. She'd let Luke Raber drive her home only tonight. What if they were courting? What if he was too late?

"Aaron?" Hope prodded when he stood there, mouth open, panic sending the words swirling in his head like a tornado picked up debris and flung it every other direction.

The sound of her voice, shaky and yet still so sweet, galvanized him. "I know this seems . . . fast."

Despite the doubts visible in her eyes, her lips quirked. "For sure and certain."

"But it makes total sense if you think about it."

Her brows, darker than her strawberry blond curls, lowered over her eyes. "Makes sense?"

He nodded eagerly. Now that he'd hit on an argument he thought would convince her without scaring her off, he was ready to talk her into this. *Needed* her to say yes. "Think about it. It's as though Gotte has brought us together. Put us in each other's paths."

Confusion reflected back at him, her head tipping to the side almost as if she was assessing the state of his health.

"If we married, we could make the perfect partnership," he said.

"Partnership?" she repeated, confusion lowering her voice, slowing the word.

He nodded again. This had to work. "You love working in the shop, don't you?"

"Yes," she replied, drawing the word out.

"And I love what I'm doing in my workshop. I think I could make it into a fine business."

Hope blinked. "It would be wonderful gute business, Aaron. You are talented and hardworking. But how does this mean we should marry?"

Should. Not want. But this was a perfect plan, now that he was sorting it out in his head. They got on well. The connection he could sense couldn't merely be his own wishful thinking. This was right.

"If we married, we could both continue with those roles. You in the shop and me with the furniture."

"I see."

Did she? Based on the ominous note in her voice, Aaron wasn't so sure. She was slipping away from him, despite still holding her hands in his. He let go of one to run his through his hair. "I'm not explaining this right."

She tugged her other hand free as well. "I think I understand. I would make a convenient partner and our marriage would allow you to keep doing exactly what *you* want to do."

That was what she'd heard?

"No."

"No?" she challenged, her expression so guarded, his throat started closing up.

"It isn't just about me. This is for you, too. You love working in the shop, and as my wife, we would help your family as well. Think of the things we could do to help the farm. I mean if you wanted."

"I don't need you to marry me for charity, Aaron Kanagy." She took a faltering step back.

"That's so far from what I'm thinking, Hope." He tried to move closer, but she backed up, so he held up both hands. "Please hear me out."

"Nae."

Nae. The word dropped like a boulder onto his shoulders, making him want to double over with the weight and the pain.

"I couldn't marry you, Aaron," she continued. Only the words trailed off and she glanced away, unable to even stand the sight of him, apparently.

"Why?" But before she could answer, he figured it out. The biggest reason she'd reject him, of course. Their families. Aaron still hadn't figured out the best way to approach Levi Beiler for his blessing. There had to be a way, though. "Because of your dat?"

She jerked her head around. "That's not—"

"I know there's still . . . er . . . tension there. But if I talked to him, told him how I would take care of you. And if it would make you happy, too, don't you think we could earn his blessing?"

"It's not about Dat," Hope said, louder.

Aaron stuttered to a stop. "Then why?" he asked again. Begged.

"Because . . ." She paused, shaking her head, though more at herself than him, it appeared. "Because I overheard you at singeon last year."

Confusion tumbled through his panic. Overheard him? Doing what? Saying what?

"At the Prices' house in July. I was standing outside on the porch cooling off, and you and a bunch of boys came out, but couldn't see me around the corner. You were talking about different girls and who you were interested in. Joking around, mostly, teasing one another."

Aaron frowned, trying to think back over that night. But it blended together with the other weekly singeons and other gatherings of die youngie all year long.

"One of the boys mentioned my name and asked you what you thought about me. Do you remember what you said?"

Vaguely the moment was coming back to him, though his exact words escaped him. Aaron shook his head, a sense of dread adding to the weight trying to bury him.

"You said . . . 'Hope Beiler is okay, I guess.'"

Her voice cracked on the last word, and that small sign of the pain his words must've caused yanked the breath from his lungs.

He'd done that. To Hope.

The shaking in his hands from adrenaline and dreams for his future turned to shaking due to weakness and regret and the desperate need to take it back.

This was why she'd said she'd never consider marrying him.

Not because of her father, but because I hurt her.

He'd said words that had made her feel small and unwanted. He remembered that night now. Luke Raber had been the one to bring up Hope, and Aaron, aware that the other boy had a habit of going after girls that other boys showed an interest in, had played it cool.

Aaron *had* been interested in Hope. He just didn't want Luke to know. "Hope, I didn't mean—"

"Please." She backed off the bridge, eyes glittering in the dim glow of the moonlight in the woods. Tears. "I shouldn't have let it bother me. I forgave you, or at least I tried to."

That she had to forgive him for anything shattered

Aaron's heart, embedding the shards in his lungs, making breathing painful.

"And now you want to marry me because it's . . ." Her hands raised then fell to her sides. "Convenient. And that might hurt more."

"Nae. Hope—" Aaron reached out, as though he could pull her back, pull her into his arms to soothe away her pain.

Only she jerked back, his comfort, his coming near, clearly unwelcome.

"Let's just . . . forget this happened. Jah?"

"Hope—"

But she'd already turned to run through the woods. Run home. Run away from him.

Aaron slowly lowered his hands to his sides. As she disappeared around a bend into the trees, a soft breeze ruffled his hair. The creek below him gurgled softly.

And he'd never been so miserably alone.

Chapter Thirteen

❋

HOPE HAD TO fight with herself every step away from the man who'd proposed marriage, torn, bewildered, and heart-broken. Confusion swarmed around her like gnats on a summer evening. Part of her needed to get away. To hide her pain from his searching gaze. Her skin burned with mortification, and she wished with all her might that she could forget what had happened and go on as they had been. Friends.

Making their lives easier so they could do what they wished was no reason to marry. Not when there wasn't love.

Only the tears, cold against her cheeks, kept coming. All the way home, where she had to sneak into her bedroom, avoiding the third step from the top, which had a tendency to creak loudly, forgetting Aaron had fixed it. At least she assumed it was Aaron when Dat hadn't known what she was talking about. Same as the rosebush. The tears didn't stop when she got to her bed, soaking her pillow.

Only the emotions pulling them from her weren't for the pain his words had caused.

An ache so deep it seeped into her bones came from the fact that she wished her answer could have been different. She wished, with all her might, that she could have said yes to Aaron. That he had made a different kind of proposal altogether.

But to wish that meant that she was in love with him. That she *wanted* him to want to marry *her*.

But she would always be "just okay" to him and a wife who conveniently let him do what he wanted in life. And just okay wasn't enough for her. She wanted what her parents had had.

I shouldn't have told him. It only served to hurt us both. Wasn't my forgiveness enough?

It should have been. Except she couldn't have him thinking that her father's continued bitterness toward his family was the reason . . . the only reason . . . she had to say no. It wouldn't be fair to Dat to do that.

Still, the last thing she remembered before the restless oblivion of sleep finally dragged her under was Aaron's eyes, dark and swirling and full of regret.

Daylight came too soon, and she pulled herself out of the momentary break from her thoughts to blink in the sunlight streaming through the window. She'd forgotten to close her curtains when she'd finally come to bed.

Groggily, she peeled tear-swollen eyes open to stare at the white ceiling overhead. Then everything hit her again and she wanted to close them and go back into that bliss of sleep where she didn't have to face the day.

No one else knew what had happened. They would all expect her to do what she'd done every day these last few weeks. Not that Dat would notice either way. How was she going to face Aaron this morning?

But you will.

Avoiding waking Hannah, who still slept, she made herself get out of bed and dress and brush her teeth and wash her face, holding the damp cloth to her eyes and willing away the bags and swelling. She ate a quick breakfast, said goodbye to Hannah, and kissed Mammi on the cheek.

"Are you feeling well, liebling?" Mammi whispered.

"I might be coming down with a cold, but I'm fine."

Age-clouded eyes, once the same bright blue as Hannah's, studied her face. Then Mammi held a hand to her forehead. "I don't think you have a fever."

Hope shook her head. "A small cold. I'm sure I'll feel better by tomorrow."

Grabbing her lunch from the propane-powered refrigerator, she left the house a tiny bit on the late side, hoping to make it in time to get right into the Kanagys' buggy and not have to talk to Aaron.

On the path through the woods, she almost expected to see him coming to meet her. Only he didn't, and suddenly the woods—her woods that had been her friend, her place of comfort all her life—became too lonely to bear. Hurrying her steps, even over her bridge, she emerged behind the Kanagys' house. Still no sign of Aaron. She braced herself, coming around the side of the house, to see him standing watch, like the first morning. But he wasn't there either. He already sat in the buggy, driving today, ready to go.

Daniel was the one waiting to slide the door up and help her in, taking a seat beside her in the back. This was Joshua's day home for chores.

"Where's Joseph?" she asked.

"He took the smaller buggy to visit the blacksmith in Skokegan again." Ruth dismissed it lightly. "Your nose looks a little pink this morning." She inspected Hope's face with a concerned gaze. "I hope you're not catching my cold, too. Aaron also looks pale."

"I'm fine, Mamm," he muttered from the front seat.

Hope pasted a smile on her face. "Me, too. I was running late and rushing, so maybe I am flushed."

Ruth nodded happily, accepting that explanation.

As soon as they arrived at the store, she hurried inside with Ruth and began the usual morning routine to get the store ready to open for customers. Aaron stayed outside and took care of the horse and buggy then, as far as Hope could tell, went straight to his workshop.

Great. Easier to pretend everything was fine when he wasn't there watching or listening. Granted, the hours dragged by, the only consolation being the mere trickle of customers. The hands on the clock in the front crawled their way around the face.

"I'll take over here."

Hope jumped at the sound of Ruth's voice and realized she'd been standing in the middle of the floor staring out the front window for who knew how long. Lost in her thoughts. Maybe she should stop working in the shop and figure out a way to pay for Aaron's time and materials to finish the bed separately?

Only she couldn't make the math add up, no matter which way she came at it. Her family didn't have the money and he didn't have the time without help to take over for him in the shop.

"You go eat your lunch now." Ruth waved her away.

Hope made to go but paused to peer closer at Ruth's face. Granted, the days had become warm, but certainly not enough to make Ruth sweat. Her skin had an underlying gray pallor that had Hope crossing to the older woman, concern pulling her along.

"You don't look well," she said, and, like Mammi had to her only this morning, lifted a hand to Ruth's forehead.

She gasped at the heat radiating from the woman. "You are burning up."

"It's nothing." Ruth tried to shoo her away.

But Hope took her by the hand and led her into the back. Daniel raised his brows at Hope in question when they walked past the curtain separating the front from the back and she gave a tiny shake of her head. "Daniel, can you go out front for a bit, please? I think your mother is sick."

To his credit, Daniel took one glance at Ruth and moved quickly to the front of the store, no questions asked.

"We should get you home," Hope insisted.

But Ruth tugged on her hand, shaking her head. "No. I'll go home when we all do. No need for a special trip. It's only a few more hours yet."

Hope bit her lip. Oh, help. "All right, but you're not working anymore. You need to rest. Agreed?"

Ruth nodded, her body seeming to droop in front of Hope's eyes. More alarmed than she wanted to let on, Hope led her to the small table in the kitchenette and sat her down. There she brought out one of the older quilts that had yet to sell and wrapped it around her. "I'll be right back."

The tiny kitchenette did not lend itself to cooking, and she doubted her sandwich brought from home would help Ruth feel any better. Instead she ran to Raber's Café and ordered chicken noodle soup to go.

"Hope?" Luke appeared from the back as she waited. "Everything all right?"

How had he known she was out here? She pasted a smile over her worry and nodded. "Just on a lunch break."

A small fib because Ruth wouldn't want it put about that she was ill. Luke accepted that with a nod and handed over the soup. Parting with the last of her pocket money was worth it.

Back at the shop, she sat beside Ruth and opened the soup up. "This will help."

"You didn't have to do that. I'm not *that* sick." Ruth managed a wan smile, the effort appearing to cost her.

To Hope's critical eye, she looked even worse. For a woman who never stopped moving, she hadn't scooted so much as an inch while Hope had been gone. Rightly so, Hope ignored the protest and got out a spoon.

"I can feed myself. You go check that Daniel is okay."

"I saw him on my way in. There are several customers in the store and he's handling them."

The *pring* of the doorbell announced even more customers.

"Hope." The edge to Daniel's call immediately put a lie to her words. Ruth lifted an eyebrow as if to say, "I told you so." Not that Hope should've been surprised. Daniel didn't exactly love the front of the store. He was much happier dealing with inventory or moving larger displays around. The happiest she saw him was on his home chore days when he got to care for his bees.

"I'll be right back." She patted Ruth's hand and hustled back into the shop, and immediately had to hide a chuckle.

No wonder Daniel had sounded semi-urgent. The new customers were five girls from their gmay. Five unmarried girls, several of whom had their eye on Daniel. And who wouldn't? The Kanagy boys were handsome, to be sure, but more important, they were upstanding Amish men, hard-working, kind, and faithful.

She gave him a wink as she sailed by, his grumble following her the rest of the way.

"I'm happy to see you," she greeted, and accepted a quick hug from Sarah and Rachel Price. With them were Joy Yoder and Alice Lehman. "Can I help you with anything?"

"We wanted to look at material for dresses," Rachel said, rather loudly. Then she dropped her voice to a whisper. "Sarah noticed Daniel was working the counter and wanted to come in."

"I did *not* say that," Sarah hissed. "I only pointed out that he usually doesn't work the front alone."

"Oh?" Rachel's grin widened as she plonked her hands on her hips. "And how often have you peeked in here to notice such a thing?"

Sarah's face turned candy apple red. "Oh, shush," she finally said.

All five girls giggled, and Hope joined them. Poor Daniel. He would hate feeling as though he worked in a fishbowl. "The materials are over here." She ushered them over. "We got in a lovely new pale green."

Amish clothing was plain, limited in various ways by their rules, even more so in some districts. Something Hope had never minded. Imagine having to try to stand out and preen like a peacock rather than have a boy love you for who you were? In their district they at least had the choice of colors.

"Is Joshua here?" Joy asked. "I wanted to ask him about a colt Dat's having trouble breaking."

The Yoders owned a horse ranch, training them not only for Amish work and use, but for Englischers as well. Joshua seemed to spend a lot of time at the Yoders' helping with the horses.

Hope shook her head. "He's working at home today."

"Oh." Joy wrinkled her nose. "I guess I'll run over to their house tonight instead."

Being the Kanagys' closest neighbor, Hope knew that wasn't unusual for Joy.

As the girls debated about the materials, Hope glanced over her shoulder, wondering how Ruth was faring. Not that she could tell if anyone was moving around in the back of the store. Maybe she should fetch Aaron.

Except Ruth wouldn't want that.

"This would be beautiful against Sarah's hair," Rachel murmured, and held up a swath of pale pink cotton beside her schwester's face.

"Yours, too," Sarah pointed out in her usual good-natured way. The two could be mistaken for twins, though Rachel was a few years older.

"So handy that we also wear the same size." Rachel smiled. Then turned to Hope. "Where is Aaron today?"

Especially around her friends, Hope had to be extra careful. She managed what she hoped was a pleasantly un-interested expression. "Oh, he's always in his workshop. I hardly see him."

"Well, he certainly wasn't happy about Luke Raber driving you home last night."

Not if it messed up his plans of nabbing such a convenient wife. Not rolling her eyes was a monumental feat. "Oh?" She managed to imbue the single word with a world of disinterest.

Rachel tipped her head, not saying any more, but certainly thinking more. Hope trusted her friend to keep whatever her thoughts were to herself. She might get an earful later, but not here in the gift shop.

Sarah didn't take the hint, though. "Ach jah. I thought he

was going to give Luke a black eye with that volleyball. Then when you left, he stared after you. Like this." She straightened and stared into the distance, her face arranged so forlornly, Hope had to laugh. At the same time, she didn't dare glance in Daniel's direction. What a terrible place to have this conversation.

"He was probably caught in thought and happened to be looking in our direction," she insisted.

"Maybe," Sarah said, though doubt lined the word. "But not with this face." She pulled it again. If Hope squinted, she might be able to see a lovelorn boy in the act, but she already knew good and well that would be wasteful, wishful thinking.

"You look ill," she teased. "Maybe he had a stomachache."

"After eating Mary Gingrich's thumbprint cookies, it would be no wonder," Joy said.

"Joy Yoder," Alice scolded. "Where is your Christian spirit?" Her scandalized face had Hope buttoning her lips to keep from laughing and making it worse.

"Now, now," Hope said once she felt confident she wouldn't giggle. Always quick to defend anyone else's cooking efforts. "I loved Mary's cookies." Granted, they had been extra sweet, so she'd eaten only one.

"You're so nice to everyone, Hope." Joy's face turned almost as forlorn as Sarah's impression of Aaron last night.

Not to everyone. Not to Aaron last night.

"And you're so fun to be with," Hope said back. "We all have our gifts."

"I guess I'm still figuring out mine," Joy muttered.

"Speaking of kindness, though," Hope said. "Could I ask a favor?"

Five sets of eyebrows shot up. "Of course," Rachel said. Waving them closer, Hope lowered her voice to a whisper. Quickly she explained about Ruth, who was obviously ill. "Did any of you come in a buggy today?"

They all shook their heads. "We walked," Alice said quietly.

Disappointment tugged at Hope. "Oh, help."

"Why do you need a buggy?" a deep voice demanded from directly behind her.

Hope jumped and gave a wholly inelegant squeak as she spun to face Aaron. When had he even come in? She didn't hear the bell.

Stepping closer, she lowered her voice. "Your mamm is sick but doesn't want to be taken home. She says she can wait until closing, but she's got a worsening fever, Aaron."

His brows beetled over his eyes as she spoke and he shot a glance at Daniel, who was busy helping another customer with the canned goods selection. "Why didn't you come get me?"

The bite to his words felt like a slap to the face, and Hope stepped back then scowled in return. "She didn't want me to, and it's all happened so fast."

"I see." He grimaced. "Mamm can be pretty stubborn. You stay here and help Daniel. I'll go check on her."

Before she could murmur her agreement, he spun on his heel and marched away.

"Maybe he did have a stomachache last night," Sarah whispered behind her.

AARON TOOK ONE glance at Mamm's slumped shoulders and ashen face and knew she needed to be home immediately. She glanced up as he entered the kitchenette, only to wince. "I told Hope not to bother you."

"She didn't. I came in to get my lunch. I'm getting the buggy."

She tried to push up from the table, and Aaron immediately hurried to her side and sat her right back down with a gentle hand to her shoulder. "Daniel and Hope can take care of the store. I'll send Joshua back in the buggy to join them."

His mother stared back at him, indecision written across her pinched face. She'd always been one to hate being a bother, especially when interrupting the work that needed to be done. Though that was an Amish attitude in general. "Hope can take me home," she finally said. "As much as I love you boys, she might be a better caregiver. I'll send Joshua back."

He had no doubt Hope would take wonderful gute care of Mamm. He nodded and strode back into the store, straight to the woman whose kind sweetness he'd smashed with his thoughtless words, ruining his chance with her long before he had the courage to take it.

Beyond a slight widening of her eyes and a quick glance at the girls she was helping, she gave no other indication of even remembering their conversation last night. Although his mother had been right this morning, not about the pink nose, but with a reason to look more closely, Aaron could see how her eyes were slightly puffy and red.

Oh, sis yuscht. He'd made Hope cry.

If Aaron could take back anything, it would be that. Hurting her felt like when he missed with the chisel once and scraped it over the back of his hand instead of the wood. "Mamm has agreed to be taken home."

"Ach vell, I'm glad you were able to convince her to go."

Hope went to turn away, but he put out a hand, grasping her wrist, delicate in his grasp. Hope dropped her gaze to his hand on her arm. Self-consciously—he had no right to touch her—he dropped his hold. "She'd like you to go with her and send Joshua back with the buggy."

She blinked for a second. "Of course. I'd be more than happy to help Ruth."

"We need to go anyway," Rachel Price murmured behind her. "Nice to see you, Hope." She moved her gaze to Aaron. "Please let your mamm know we're thinking of her and will check in."

"Denki. I will."

The next ten minutes happened in a flurry of getting Frank hitched to the buggy and helping Mamm into it before fetching Hope. Aaron paused, taking in her sweet face as she picked up the reins. "You're sure you'll be fine without help?"

She sent him a reassuring smile that warmed him from the toes up. "I'll take care of your mamm. Don't you worry."

Without a thought beyond wanting to extend his thanks, Aaron reached out and squeezed her hand. The soft hitch of her breath hit him like the pound of a hammer. But she didn't pull away or frown like before. If anything, her gaze reflected words he was sure were his own hopeful thinking. A sort of sad wanting. Regret, if he didn't know better.

"Denki," he managed in a voice that sounded like sandpaper to his own ears. He forced himself to take his hand away, shut the buggy door, and step back.

Shortly after Aaron returned to the shop to help Daniel, the customers cleared out. No doubt because of the lunch hour.

"How's Mamm?" Daniel asked as he folded a quilt to hang it back up.

"You know Mamm. It's hard to tell with her because she doesn't like to be a burden."

"Jah. She didn't look too well yet."

Worry for his mater niggled at him. "Nae. She didn't. But Hope will make sure she gets the rest she needs."

Daniel nodded. "Did something happen with Hope?"

Aaron did his best mildly surprised eyebrow raise, even as his gut tripped over itself. "What do you mean?"

"She's been crying, Aaron. I know you noticed it."

Aaron winced but didn't deny it. "Jah."

"And you know why, don't you?" Daniel regarded him with dark eyes so like his own. Their dat's eyes. His bruder noticed everything.

He should remember that better by now, but still managed to be surprised from time to time. "Jah. I know why. It's because of me."

Daniel didn't even bother to look startled. Likely he expected something along those lines. Which brought frustration simmering to the surface.

"You could act like it's not automatically my fault."

He got a grin for all his frustration. "I could."

Aaron growled low in his throat. "What made you think so anyway?"

"Because of the way she looks at you."

Wait. What? "What do you mean? How does she look at me?" Now he sounded eager, like a puppy tripping over its feet for a pat.

Daniel finished with the quilt, which hung haphazardly on the rung despite his efforts, and moved around to the canned goods, rearranging the shelves to be in precise order the way Mamm taught them. "She looks at you the same way you look at her."

Aaron's heart did a backflip. Only Daniel couldn't be right. "You must be seeing things."

"Nae. Two people dancing around each other in the way

you two do." Daniel rolled his eyes. "Gotte save me from love if that's what it does."

Love? "She doesn't . . ." He shook his head. "That's not how she feels."

But what about me? He'd pictured their future so clearly. A future making a home and a life together. But he also thought what he'd said last night, about being good partners, was true, even if it wasn't romantic. Not that any of it mattered. He'd lost his chance with her last year without even knowing it.

Daniel ran a hand over his jaw. "I don't think she knows it yet."

His bruder had to be wrong. After what Hope had overheard that night at singeon, no wonder she had told Rachel and Sarah Price that she'd never consider marrying him. Who would love a boy that said such things? Especially to other boys.

Only she doesn't know why I said it. Maybe that could make her feel better at least. Heal a small part of the wound I inflicted.

"You're mistaken, about Hope," he finally said. *Though maybe not about me.* But he couldn't focus on that while Mamm was sick.

Daniel simply shook his head. He didn't say another word but his unspoken "we will see" hung in the air between them all the same.

Chapter Fourteen

✳

AARON SILENTLY URGED Joshua to set the horse to a faster clip. The anxious pit in his stomach had grown into a gnawing monster as the rest of the hours had crawled by. As though time understood he'd rather be somewhere else and deliberately slowed to a creep. Much like the pace Joshua had set to get home.

He shifted in his seat, unable to find a comfortable angle for his legs.

Joshua cast an annoyed glance over his shoulder. "Have something to say?"

"About what?" Aaron asked.

A shrug answered that. "I don't know. My driving. The warmer weather. Mary Gingrich's terrible thumbprint cookies. Whatever's bothering you and making you squirm like a toddler in Sunday service."

The second time he'd been called out by one of his brothers today.

"I want to check on Mamm," he said.

Not an outright lie. The gray tone underlying her already pale skin had him more concerned than usual for a simple cold.

"Jah. We all do. You should've seen her when Hope and I helped her out of the buggy and to her room. Her legs were shaking so bad, she could hardly get up the stairs."

Aaron frowned. "Then she was worse by the time she got home. What did Hope say?"

"Mamm shushed her before she could say anything and insisted that being tucked into bed and having a nice long sleep was all she needed."

Daniel echoed Aaron's grunt of disdain. Mamm could be a stubborn one, for sure and certain, and she hated being sick.

"Jah. That's what I thought," Joshua agreed.

As he pulled up their lane and around to the barn, Frank moving faster in his eagerness to be in his warm, dry stall with food in his belly, Aaron caught the twitch of a curtain at an upstairs window. Hope, no doubt. Had she been watching for them? Not a good sign.

A sense of foreboding spread over Aaron like a film of filth. He turned to his bruders, mouth open to tell them, but Daniel beat him to it.

"Go," he said. Joshua nodded. They'd take care of the horse and buggy first.

Running across the yard and in through the back door of the house, Aaron still paused to remove his boots in the mudroom. It had rained recently, leaving the yard soft and clumpy, and Mamm would take a switch to him if he got mud all over her nice clean floors.

"Mamm?" he called as he hit the bottom of the stairs.

"Shhhh . . ." He looked up to find Hope leaning over the banister, her lovely face creased with worry as she held a finger to her lips.

Moving more carefully—difficult on wood floors given his size, even in his sock-covered feet—he hurried up to where she waited.

"I'm so glad you're home," Hope murmured as she waved him all the way up.

Home. As though they were married and he'd returned from a day of work. Her next words knocked that image clean out of his head.

"Ruth's asleep and I'm worried." She leaned close to whisper, her flowery scent curling around him. Only he couldn't see beyond her eyes, darkened to stormy gray with her concern, reflecting the skies outside.

"That's helpful, isn't it?" he asked.

She bit her lip. "Usually. But this feels different. Deeper and not deep enough at the same time."

"Let's go see her." Capturing Hope's hand in his like it was the most natural thing for him to do, he led her back to his parents' room. Together, they stood at the head of the bed, leaning over Mamm.

"Her fever is worsening and she's restless," Hope whispered. "I've tried cold compresses without much effect. I haven't had any luck getting any food or water into her either."

Aaron reached out with his free hand and laid the back of it against his mother's forehead. Oh, sis yuscht. Hope was right, the fever was worse. "I'll send Joshua to bring Amity Lambright. If it gets much worse, we'll go to town and call a driver to take us to the hospital in Lowton."

"Okay." She nodded. "Gute."

Almost at the same time, they both seemed to realize they were still holding hands. With a silent gasp, her lips forming a perfect O, Hope let go and stepped back, tucking both hands behind her as though he might reach for her again. "I . . . I should let Mammi know where I am." She paused, blinking at him, his little lost owl again, but with red flyaway curls and a stubborn chin and worry still darkening her eyes and . . .

Dear Gotte. I do love her.

Of course he did, or her rejection wouldn't have hit so hard, and knowing he'd made her cry wouldn't have hurt so much. The bands around his lungs tightened even as he sucked in a sharp breath, fisting his hands against the sudden ferocity of the emotion swelling inside him.

He shouldn't be surprised. The second the proposal popped out of his mouth, he should have known. This had been building for some time. When he'd fallen in love with Hope, he had no idea. He'd always liked her. Always noticed her. Appreciated things about her, like her kindness to everyone. But the relationship between their families had held him back. That hadn't changed.

More than that, though, he'd gone and messed everything up. She'd never believe him.

"Unless . . ." Hope's sweet voice dragged him from his thoughts back to the moment. Back to his mater, who needed his full attention. "Unless you don't need my help anymore now that you and your bruders are here?"

"Can you stay?" Selfish of him, but he wanted her here. Hope brought a sense of calm he sensed might desert them all if she left.

Her eyes softened. "Jah. I can stay."

"And your dat?"

"I'm helping a neighbor. He'll understand. Especially if Amity is here."

Aaron nodded slowly. "I'll walk you over."

She shook her head, backing away from him like a cornered deer. "Nae. You worry about getting Amity here."

Before he could argue, she turned and whisked herself away. It seemed Hope was always running away from him.

And take that lesson to heart, he urged himself. *No matter what Daniel says.*

It hurt more every time she did it. Eventually his heart would get the message.

"Hope?"

In the vague, misty space between awake and asleep, she was aware someone was shaking her shoulder and murmuring her name. But it took another shake and call before Hope managed to blink herself awake.

With a sharp inhale, she jackknifed up in her seat and smacked her head into something hard above her.

"Ow!" Aaron grunted softly.

"Ow," she whispered-grumbled at the same time, lifting a hand to the top of her head. Then she tipped her head up to find him standing behind her chair rubbing at his jaw.

"Sorry," she hissed.

Aaron grinned, so familiar it made her heart stutter. "I wanted to check on you. No need to give me a black eye."

Her lips quirked despite herself. "I'm pretty sure your jaw isn't your eye."

"Huh." He grunted, but she still caught a lingering hint of that goofy grin.

Taking the seat beside Hope, he turned his gaze to his mother's face. Ruth was finally sleeping still and peacefully in her bed. Based on the pitch-black sliver of night showing through the small gap in the drawn curtains, Hope guessed it had to be around two or three in the morning. Aaron had said he'd relieve her around then so she could get better sleep on the couch downstairs while he watched.

Mammi and Hannah had said that of course she should go help Ruth, and Mammi had promised to tell Dat about it. With the wedding fast approaching and having been at the store so much, Hope had reluctantly left them to it. It felt like she'd hardly seen her sister during the last weeks, and soon Hannah would be gone to her own home. Things were changing so fast.

But Ruth's health was more important than her silly worryings.

"She looks a little better," he said.

Hope patted Ruth's hand, lying on top of the covers. "I think her fever finally broke."

For over twenty-four hours, they'd taken turns sitting with her. Trying to get soup or milk or water into her and cooling her with cold compresses. Hope had changed the sheets twice, as Ruth soaked through them. Daniel had tried to get ahold of Joseph, but the boys' father was two towns over, set to stay with the blacksmith he'd been trying to earn as a vendor before returning home. At least he was due back in the coming afternoon. Finally.

"Thank you, Gotte." Aaron whispered a prayer she knew wasn't meant for her ears, his relief pouring from him out loud without thought.

Hope had sent the same prayer heavenward earlier tonight when Ruth had calmed, her skin cooler to the touch. As though they'd won a great battle.

Aaron turned his head, pinning her with a gaze filled with such tender gratitude, she had to swallow past a lump in her throat.

"There are shadows under your eyes." Absently, he lifted a hand and traced her skin with a single finger.

Hope held her breath as the touch electrified her, bringing all of her exhaustion-wearied soul back to brilliant, bubbling life. With a mere touch.

"Plenty of time to sleep when she's well," she murmured. Because she had to say something . . . anything . . . to break this connection that always hovered between them. Unspoken.

Any connection you think you feel is just convenience for him. A way to do what he wants. She reminded herself of this fact ruthlessly.

Except a quiet sense of belonging settled over her like the warmth of a fire on a winter day, or her mater's arms hugging her close. Maybe because of the way Aaron stared, which didn't remind her of anything like convenience. She returned his stare, unable to stop herself. Not with expectation, more . . . contentment.

A soft smile tugged at the corners of his mouth, jolting her out of her reverie.

What am I thinking? "I should—"

Before she could move, Aaron sat on the chair beside her and scooted closer. "Hope, there's something I need to tell you."

She stilled, captured again by warm dark eyes. Only now, a smidge of nervousness vibrated from him. "What?" she asked.

"Promise to hear me out?"

An answering nervous fluttering took up residence in her own belly. Was he going to propose again? The part of her that mourned her original reaction and how she'd ruined her chances with him quivered. The other part, the part that didn't want to marry a man who only wanted her for convenience's sake, quaked in the other direction. Both sides pulling on her like a game of tug-of-war until she didn't know if she was coming or going.

"I'm not going to propose again, if that's what you're thinking. I wouldn't . . ." He paused and grimaced, distaste pulling at his mouth. "I know you don't want that."

Everything inside her deflated like the balloon she'd begged Mamm to buy her at the flea market in Shipshewana as a little girl. One morning, she'd woken to find it wilted and pathetic on the floor.

Now she said nothing. What was there to say? Aaron seemed to take her silence as a sign of encouragement and blew out a breath as though he'd been worried she'd refuse.

"That night at singeon, when you overheard me . . ." He waved a hand.

Heat rushed up her chest and neck and into her face. No way did she want to talk about that again. The humiliation was too much. "I don't really think—"

Aaron reached for her hand, his warmth and strength seeping into her skin, his grip tight and urgent. "You promised to hear me out. Please?"

She settled under his touch and the urgent undertone to his voice, though the heat continued to flush through her body, pounding in her ears.

She gave a small nod, though she couldn't relax into her seat.

"Denki." The next words came out in a rush. "I *was* interested in you, Hope. Wonderful interested. I had been for—" He stopped and cleared his throat.

A new kind of tension stole into her, humming through her veins and buzzing inside her even as doubts plagued her like a swarm of gnats. This couldn't be right. He couldn't have meant that the way she wanted him to.

"Anyway, the only reason I hadn't approached you was your dat and how he obviously felt about my family."

Oh, help. He sounded so sincere, his dark eyes intent on

her face, as though he was willing her to truly listen to his words.

"Then why did you say it?" she whispered.

His eyes closed, squeezed tight shut for a moment before he opened them, shifting closer to her, gripping the hand that he was still holding tighter. "Because Luke Raber was doing the asking."

Lips parted with confusion, Hope leaned away, thinking back to that night. Was that true? She hadn't paid that much attention to the voices of the other boys, especially after Aaron said what he had. Had Luke asked the question? Why would he do that? She was his friend. "Why does that matter?"

Another grimace. "I know he's your . . . friend." He searched her gaze, for what she had no idea.

"Yes. He's my friend."

"And I wouldn't ever want to . . . hurt that friendship or speak badly of anyone." He turned her hand over in his, tracing the veins on her wrist, the touch searing into her even as he seemed hardly aware of what he was doing.

"Please just tell me, Aaron."

He stopped the distracting touch and looked her in the eyes. "Luke has a tendency to want someone else's toys." He shrugged. "And these days, that means girls. If another boy shows interest in a girl, Luke seems to . . . I don't know . . . swoop in and . . ." He paused, running his free hand through his hair. "I'm saying this wrong."

"No," she said slowly. "I've seen it, too. Only Luke has never been interested in me that way."

"Since we were fourteen, he's been asking to drive you home every Sunday." He glanced away. "Although this was the first time you've said yes."

Aaron had paid enough attention to notice that?

Hope scrunched up her nose, not really wanting to admit the truth, especially to Aaron, but . . . "It's an agreement we've had since I started Rumspringa. I was worried about hurting boys' feelings if I had to turn them down and Luke happened to find out. So he asks every time in case I need an . . . excuse."

Aaron went still, staring at her for a long time.

"Luke," he said, doubt rife in the name. "*Luke Raber* does that for you."

Hope allowed herself a small smile. "I know he acts . . . well . . . You know how he acts. But there's a gute person under all that."

And for good reason Luke hid it away, but she wouldn't betray his confidence about his home life. That was his story to share if he ever wished to. She'd offered the help she'd felt he'd allow her to offer.

"He's always been kind to me," she said. "But we're just friends."

Aaron frowned over that, then shook his head. "I don't think he sees it that way."

She sat up in her chair, her spine straightening with a snap. "Ach vell, he's never acted as anything but a friend, and I would know better than you, Aaron."

A tug on her hand and he released her. "I'm sorry," he said quickly. "Of course you would know better."

She gave a sharp nod of her head, irritation keeping her stiff. Even her face felt stiff.

"Anyway . . . I said what I did so that Luke wouldn't turn his interest more to you. Not because I actually thought it. I wanted to . . ." He blew out another breath. "I wanted you for myself."

Ach du lieva. What a tangled-up mess. Again, that internal tug-of-war had her where she didn't know if she was coming or going, sad or happy. Part of her thrilled to the thought, the other part growing wearier by the second. Aaron had said he wasn't going to propose again.

Aaron must've seen something in her expression, a reflection of the doubt, because he got to his feet, moving to the door.

"Why did you tell me this now, Aaron?" she asked quietly.

He stopped, his hand on the knob, and turned back to her. Twisting slightly, he looked directly at her, sincerity in his dark gaze. "Because I upset you with my words. I don't dare ask your forgiveness. But maybe by knowing why I said it, you won't . . . hurt as much."

Hope opened her mouth to say something. Anything. But the words just wouldn't come out. Lodged in her mind and unable to shake loose. Because she honestly didn't know what to think or how she felt about it.

"I hope it . . . helped," he said quietly.

The door closed behind him with a quiet snick that made her flinch.

Hope leaned her elbows on the bed, thinking through his words and what they all meant. Did she feel better? Mostly, she felt . . . confused.

"Oh, Aaron," she whispered.

Chapter Fifteen

✴

AARON KNOCKED SOFTLY at his parents' bedroom door. The scents of fried chicken and all the trimmings filled the house. Good thing he was a decent cook. Because they all worked in the shop, Mamm and Dat had come together to adapt to the specific needs of their family. Though Mamm did most of the cooking, the men shared the chore regularly.

"Supper," he called through the door.

A second later, the handle turned, the door swinging open, and Hope's sweet face appeared, tilted up to him with the rest of her in shadow. "I'll be right down."

Once Mamm had gotten through the worst, Hope had stopped staying overnight, returning to her own home in the evenings. However, Mamm was still weak as a newborn kitten, though she loudly and frequently declared her displeasure with that situation. They were all glad she was sitting up and able to fret about it.

If Aaron was honest, she'd scared him a lot more than

he'd allowed himself to acknowledge through the worst of it.

Instead of helping in the shop, Hope started coming over in the daytime to sit with Mamm while the rest of them worked, the men of the family trading off the daily chores like they always had. Mamm's chores fell to Hope, who'd taken them on without even being asked.

Behind her, framed by the open doorway, Mamm was sitting up in bed, her hair a single braid over her shoulder. The color had come back to her face, and she'd lost the gaunt appearance. Better each day.

"Hope was reading to me," she said. "But we can finish up tomorrow."

He tried not to let his gaze drift back to Hope and linger there. He'd promised not to bother her with his feelings again. And not to propose, but to his way of thinking, that was the same thing. Even so, he couldn't stop her from dominating his thoughts. Three days without her in the store and he'd missed her. Missed her off-key singing and perpetual good mood and the way she fit in with his family. For once, he was more than happy for his chore day, finally his turn to be at home. To help Mamm, of course. But even more to be near Hope.

Or was this a slow form of self-inflicted pain?

"The others should be back any second," he said. "Dat will want to eat with you, Mamm, but the tray is all ready. He can bring it up with his."

That earned him a grumpy snort. "I *could* come downstairs just fine."

But Hope turned to her. "Nae, Ruth," Hope said softly. "You know what Amity said. If you push too hard, you could get sick again."

"Oh, sis yuscht. I hate this bed."

Aaron grinned. "We Amish do not hate," he preached. "Besides, what did that bed ever do to you, Mamm?"

She glared at him, a tiny woman with a stare that usually got her boys moving in the direction she wanted, but he caught the small twitch to her mouth. "No lip from you, young man," was all she said.

"No getting out of bed from you," he shot back.

She harrumphed at that, arms crossed, but waved them away. "You two go ahead."

"Are you sure? I could wait for Joseph to arrive first." Hope visibly waffled, not looking at Aaron, but he could figure out her reasons just the same. She'd been avoiding being alone with him for three days. Not that he'd pushed. He didn't want to make her uncomfortable with his selfish actions.

"Go, go, go." Mamm waved again.

Hope ducked her head as she scooted past him out the door. Following more slowly, Aaron racked his brain for what he could say to her. Talk about. A nonthreatening subject, preferably. Nothing about marriage, or love, or Luke Raber, or still feeling bad about hurting her the way he had.

Quietly, they both filled their plates, then sat down at the table, offered their silent prayer, then dug in.

Hope groaned and Aaron took a quick bite of his, worried he'd messed it up. But it tasted fine. "What?"

"Ach du lieva, you really can cook." Hope glared at her chicken leg as if this were all its fault.

Aaron's chuckle brought her scowl up to him. "What if fried chicken is the only thing I can make?" he asked.

"Is it?"

"No. Because of the shop and the way we split the work there and here, Mamm made sure we could all cook, though she usually does it, even though she doesn't like it."

Hope sighed, the sound so forlorn, he couldn't help another chuckle.

"I'm sure your cooking is not hopeless. That would go against your name," he teased.

She flashed him a look that she clearly meant to be irritated, but he caught the sparkle of reluctant mirth dancing in her eyes. "Mamm got sick before she had a chance to give up, but Hannah's washed her hands of me. Mammi doesn't even try." She scrunched her nose adorably suddenly. "It's . . . unnatural. Isn't it? Like I'm not living the life Gotte set for me."

She plopped her chin on her hand, obviously trying not to let it bother her, but the downturn to her kissable mouth said otherwise. "Unnatural has nothing to do with it," Aaron insisted, glancing away.

"Easy for you to say. You can cook. I don't want much in life, but I would like to be a wife and mother and keep a proper house. Like my Mamm. Like Hannah will. But I'll just end up an old maid aendi at this rate."

"Nonsense." Aaron slapped an emphatic hand on the table and made her jump.

"Sorry." Hadn't he already proposed once? Didn't she realize at least one boy out there wanted her? "Do you help keep the house and make sure your family is taken care of?"

"Jah," she agreed slowly.

"Do you work hard every day?"

"Jah."

"When you do marry and boppli come, will you love them and care for them and raise them?"

"With all my heart."

He resisted the urge to rub at the sudden sharp ache in

the center of his chest. "Are you faithful and do your best to obey Gotte's word?"

"Of course."

Will you work in a shop making beautiful things and happily chatting with customers and singing off-key and lighting up my life? Aaron pushed the thought down deep. Selfish to still hold on to any hope. "Then don't worry that Gotte made you anything other than what He meant you to be, Hope Beiler. Bad cooking and all."

In answer, Hope took a bite of her chicken and thoughtfully chewed. "You make gute sense. Sometimes," she murmured.

"I know." He winked.

A small snort that might've been a laugh escaped her. "I would still like to learn to cook better yet."

Aaron pondered that while he demolished a chicken breast. "Okay, then. On my next day at home for chores, we'll do one of my favorites together."

Suddenly her eyes widened. "But—"

"It's a casserole that can be frozen easily. We'll make extra so that my family has two meals ready. We'll eat the other one on Joshua's night to cook. I promise, he's way worse than you."

"Hey! I heard that," Joshua's voice suddenly boomed from the mudroom.

Aaron startled, a surprised laugh bursting from him. How had he not heard his family coming in?

"Gute," he called back. "Maybe you'll manage to cook the chicken all the way through the next time it's your turn."

"That chicken really was uncooked." Daniel's mutter floated in from the mudroom.

Aaron shared a grin with Hope, her shoulders shaking with silent laughter.

His dat came into the room, heading to the sink to wash his hands. "How is my fraa this day?" he asked.

"She's been sitting up most of the day." Hope put down her chicken to report. "And ate all her breakfast and lunch."

"Gotte segen eich." The quiet relief in his fater's voice as he asked Gotte to bless her in Pennsylvania Dutch told Aaron that he'd been right to worry about Mamm. Dat didn't fret over sickness unless it was serious.

"Tomorrow I think she'll be well enough to come downstairs and sit on the couch. She would probably like that. Don't you think, Hope?" Aaron turned to find her watching him with an emotion in her eyes that sent his heart stuttering.

But she blinked and the look was gone, if it had ever been. "Jah. She is getting irritated with being kept in bed."

Dat grunted. "No surprise there."

Aaron shared a shrug with his bruders. "Mamm never was one to sit on her haunches."

"Nae," Dat muttered with a shake of his head. "If we didn't take our Sundays for Gmay, that woman wouldn't know a day of rest."

"My mamm was the same," Hope said with a fond smile, one that didn't dim with sadness for once.

Slowly his dat turned to face her, thoughtfully taking in the fondness in her expression. "Jah. I could see that about your mother," he finally said, offering her a smile in return. "She was always the first to offer help to neighbors, I know."

Even his dat was falling under Hope's unique brand of kindness. Despite the reservations he'd had when they'd taken her on for the shop.

Getting to her feet, Hope took her plate to the sink and scrubbed it clean. "Unless you need anything, I should be getting home," she said as she set the dried dish in the cabinet it had come from.

I'll walk you. The words sprang to his lips, only to be swallowed back. The last thing he wanted to do was force his presence on her.

"I'll walk you," Joshua offered after a beat of silence, as though his family waited for him to offer first. Daniel had offered yesterday.

"Denki." She shook her head, same as yesterday. "But there's no need."

"Tell Ruth I said goodbye," she said. "And I'll be over in the morning before you leave again."

"Denki, Hope," Dat said. "You've been such a help."

She ducked her head modestly. "It's easy to care for someone you like," she said. Then gave them all a cheerful wave and disappeared out the door.

Joshua leaned casually against the counter, feet crossed in front of him, staring hard at Aaron. "I've never thought of you as stupid, big bruder, but . . ."

Only to receive a smack on the back of the head from Dat. "Do not call your bruder stupid."

"I didn't," Joshua protested, rubbing at his head. "I said that I never thought of him that way. Until now." He hopped to the side, avoiding a second smack. "He's messing everything up with Hope."

"For sure and certain," Dat agreed. "But that doesn't give you call to use that word."

Joshua pursed his lips but nodded after a second. "Sorry."

Aaron dropped into a seat at the kitchen table. The trouble was his family clearly knew that he'd fallen in love with Hope. They wouldn't give up unless they knew the rest of the truth. "She said no."

The words dropped into an awkward silence as his

brothers and father stared at him. "She said no?" Daniel asked slowly, as if he'd misheard.

"I asked her to marry me. She said no. I lost her before I ever could have had her." And the story came pouring out about what she'd overheard and how much he'd hurt her and how his proposal made it all worse.

"Oh, sis yuscht, Aaron," Daniel murmured. "Sis yuscht."

"Can't you fix it?" Joshua demanded.

"I explained it to her, which I hope helped with the hurt I caused." He shrugged, suddenly weary in a way he never remembered being in his life. Somehow, telling his family made it more real. "But the most I can hope for is forgiveness and friendship."

He kept Hope's dat out of it. No use borrowing trouble when he had no chance.

Dat, silent until now, crossed the room to lay a heavy hand on Aaron's shoulder, giving it a squeeze. "Don't give up on Hope. If Gotte means you to be, then it will be. Give Him time."

LUCKILY, THE RAIN paused long enough for Hope not to have to use her umbrella as she took her path through the woods to the Kanagys'.

Everything was dripping and soft, puddles gathering in dips from the natural formation of the land. Her galoshes sank into the earth with each step, gathering more and more mud. Twice she had to pause to scrape the boots on exposed tree roots. At this rate, she'd gain a foot of height by the time she reached her destination. These last days of constant, soaking rain had turned everything brilliant green, dulled by the mask of gray clouds overhead. Before she even reached her bridge, the sound of the water reached her. Not the usual soft trickle. Louder.

Sure enough, the creek had risen overnight from the higher point it had already been at just last night when she'd walked home.

They must be getting a torrential downpour north of here, feeding the rivers. She'd rarely seen the creek this high, and the drizzling rain they'd had wouldn't do this. Still not dangerous, but the edges lapped the underside of her bridge right at the banks. Hopefully it didn't get much higher. It would break its banks soon and spread out over the flats, making it impossible for her to walk this way. At least it ran into a large culvert farther down, which kept the surrounding properties from flooding.

Hope gathered a small handful of pebbles and paused on her lovely bridge, leaning on the rail to stare into the swirling water rushing by beneath, carrying leaves and debris with it. Had it not been so wet, she might've come sooner and spent real time here thinking.

Dat, surprisingly, had said nothing about her nursing Ruth the last few days, though Hope had no idea what Mammi had told him. She really needed to stop leaving all this to her grossmammi to deal with.

After the bed frame was finished . . .

The gray day seemed to dim more, the drip of wetness off the leaves onto the floor of the woods below only adding to the colorless existence she'd been living since Aaron had told her the truth about those words that had hurt her so badly.

A year of believing that was how he saw her. Just okay. And she'd been wrong all this time.

Then again, he hadn't said he loved her, and his proposal

was still about the convenience of how they worked together. Not the life she wanted. She wanted to be loved, like Dat had loved Mamm. Like Aaron's parents loved each other. Like Hannah and Noah.

Am I wrong to want more? She lifted her face to the sky, eyes closed. "Is this Your plan for me, Gotte?" she whispered.

The idea that Aaron was meant to be hers sent a giddy trembling through her. Images of the life they could make together piled up like wishes tossed into a well in a fairy tale.

But he'd said he wouldn't approach her again. That he'd leave her alone.

The thought of asking Aaron to propose again was . . . No Amish girl would dare. Then again, even Mamm had always said that Hope would dare anything. What had happened to that girl who would forge streams and run wild through the woods?

With a flick, she chucked one of the pebbles into the water, the ripples swallowed by the faster running water.

Even if she could get past not being loved, she wouldn't do anything without her fater's blessing first. She'd learned her lesson about keeping things from him. Her heart couldn't handle it, nor could her conscience, and this was too important.

With a sigh, she let the rest of the pebbles drop together and brushed off her hands. She'd say and do nothing until after her debt was paid for the bed. Then . . . maybe.

As she made her way through the woods, her steps unconsciously hurried faster the closer she got to Aaron. Not that he would be home today. This was Daniel's day to do chores. A soft knock at the mudroom door and she let herself inside, not wanting Ruth to feel the need to get up. "I'm here," she called out as she removed her galoshes and coat, setting everything to the side.

Then she turned and almost buried her nose in Aaron's chest.

The clean scents of line-dried laundry and something just Aaron hit her a beat before she gasped and backed up a step. Only to stumble over her boots.

Aaron's hands shot out, grasping her by the elbows to steady her, at the same time bringing them close together again. Warm dark eyes crinkled around the corners, silently asking her to join in his mirth.

"Steady there, tanglefoot," he murmured.

Hope buttoned her lips around a giggle. Mostly because it would have come out slightly hysterical. But that also meant that she continued to stand there, staring at him. And he seemed content to do the same.

"Everything okay?" he asked after a long pause.

Panic sent her mind into a frenzy of answers. "Of course." She briskly shook him off. "Why wouldn't it be?"

Then she brushed past him into the kitchen. Only to jolt to a halt at the sight of bowls and food all over the countertops. "What's going on here?"

Ruth would hate her lovely clean kitchen all messed up, and Hope had sworn that Aaron had already cleaned up from the fried chicken last night by the time she left.

"You and I are going to cook today."

"But your mamm—"

"I'm in here, Hope," Ruth's voice sounded from the family room. Scooting forward a few steps, Hope discovered Ruth sitting on the couch, her feet up, covered in blankets and with the book they'd been reading in her lap.

"Ach du lieva, I'm so glad to see you downstairs." Hope smiled as she moved around furniture farther into the room.

"It is wonderful gute to be out of that bed, for sure and certain." Ruth's blatant relief had Hope chuckling. All the while she remained painfully aware of how Aaron had moved to stand beside her. Close enough to feel his warmth, but not quite touching.

"Isn't this Daniel's day at home?" She directed the question to Ruth.

"He traded me for next week so that we could do this."

"But it's such a waste. I'm sure you have many other chores that need doing. I should be helping with those, or helping Ruth, or—"

"We're making meals so that Mamm doesn't have to worry about cooking for a while after she gets back on her feet."

"Oh." Hope bit her lip, torn. Time with Aaron was so tempting. "I'm sure you don't want me messing that up."

"I'll be right there with you," Aaron murmured. "I won't let you mess anything up."

Finally she moved her gaze from mater to son to find him watching her, amusement tempered by a steadiness that always seemed to be his core.

Still she shook her head at him. "Don't say I didn't warn you. Mamm and Mammi and Hannah have all tried a hundred times."

"Do they write their recipes down?" Aaron asked.

Hope frowned. "Nae. I've learned them from scratch since I was little. I wouldn't need to write them down."

"Maybe that's the trouble," Aaron said.

Hope gasped, startled suddenly that she and all her family hadn't seen such a simple solution. Maybe she *could* do better if she didn't have to worry about missing a step or getting the amount wrong. Write everything down. How could she not have thought of that before?

Deerich. Because it's the way her family had always done it. But there was nothing wrong with written recipes.

"I work from memory as well," Ruth said. "The way I was taught. But my boys were hopeless, so I started writing down the easy ones for them. Aaron at least bothers to read the recipes."

Having tasted both Joshua's and Daniel's cooking these last days, clearly they did not. Although maybe Aaron's bruders read the recipe, too, and still got it wrong.

Oh, help.

She swallowed back the thought of how embarrassed she'd be for Aaron of all people to witness her inept skills. But the girl from the bridge, the daring girl she wanted to find again, the girl she'd worried might have died with her mother, had her straightening her spine. "I'm willing to try."

"Gute girl," Aaron murmured, his pleased grin widening. Sharing the smile with his mother, he led Hope back to the kitchen. "Let's get started. I thought we'd go with one of my favorite simpler recipes to see if the experiment works first."

Made sense.

"Here's the recipe." He handed her a sheet, pristine white and unused with neatly printed lettering in a masculine hand. Had he written this down for her last night?

"So we start with . . ." He paused, the last word ending like a question.

She glanced at the page. "'Boiling the water.'"

Aaron grabbed a large pot, filling it up at the sink before hauling it to the stove.

"Shouldn't I do it?" she asked.

"It's heavy," he said, as if that explained it.

Hope narrowed her eyes. "I *can* lift a pot, Aaron."

"Not when there's a big, strapping man around to do the heavy lifting." His wink took away all her irritation.

Before he could light the propane stove, she nudged him out of the way with her hip, then got it going. She wasn't completely incompetent in the kitchen.

"Next?" he asked.

She turned back to the recipe.

"'Dicing the ham,'" she read.

She glanced down at the next few steps, all of which involved cutting things up—green peppers, onion, and shredded cheese. Easy enough. The cutting-up she could do without instruction. Moving to a board already set up with ingredients around it, she started on the ham. "This size?" she asked.

"Any size works for this one except maybe strips."

She nodded, cutting the ham into bite-size cubes.

Next came the green pepper, which Aaron washed and handed to her. While she cut that up, he moved around behind her. The crisp crunching sound that came from peeling the first layers of an onion reached her, but didn't register until the *snap, snap, snap* of chopping sounded.

Turning, she found him dicing the onion. "Hey. *I'm* supposed to be learning this."

Aaron turned, blinking tears out of his eyes. "I thought I'd save you the sting."

Oh.

Hope hid a snicker behind her hand at the ridiculousness of Aaron's goofy grin, like a proud child, while tears trickled down his cheeks in a slow leak. "My mamm always said if you hold bread in your mouth, it will keep the tears away."

That earned her a narrow-eyed look full of skepticism. "Why on earth would that make a difference?"

"Try it."

"You're not just trying to play a prank on me?"

"Nae. I promise, it works."

Still blatantly disbelieving, his face reminding her of Hannah's as a kid, when Hope would tell her those stories on the way to school, Aaron pulled a loaf from the bread box on the counter, cut a small piece, and stuck it in his mouth before returning to the cutting board to continue his chopping.

After a minute or so, a low chuckle reached her ears. "What do you know? It does work."

Hope sniggered at the way the words came out all muffled and wrong and how, at least with her view from the side, he looked to be holding his mouth open with a piece of bread on his tongue.

Aaron continued his chopping. "Laugh all you want. I'm using this trick every time I chop onions now."

"What? I can't understand you around all the food in your mouth," she teased. Then she whipped around and started chopping her pepper before he could retaliate.

The next steps passed quickly and easily until what appeared to be a fully formed casserole with all its ingredients in proper proportion—she hoped—was placed into the fridge. This one the Kanagys would try tonight. The other one went into the freezer.

"You're sure it looked right?" Hope stared at the closed refrigerator door, doubts converging on her now that they were done. What if she'd missed a step?

"Hope." Aaron called her name softly.

When she turned, he took her by the hand and led her to the recipe on the countertop. "Did you do this?" He pointed to the first step.

"Jah?"

"And this?" Second step.

She nodded.

He continued down the list, and as he did, her shoulders loosened with each item checked off. She hadn't forgotten anything or done something wrong or measured anything wrong. She'd done it all exactly right.

Granted, Hope wouldn't be completely convinced until they cooked it for supper tonight, but still. The anxious knots in her stomach got a bunch looser.

She lifted her gaze to find Aaron watching her with a small smile hovering around his mouth, and suddenly all she wanted to do was wrap her arms around his neck, and kiss him, and have him hold her. This was a gute man and she'd let her pride tumble her into the sin of not truly forgiving him. "Denki," she murmured.

He squeezed her hand. "My pleasure."

When did I fall in love with you, Aaron Kanagy?

Maybe she always had been, or his unwitting words wouldn't have stung as badly or settled as deeply as they had or had the power to undermine her confidence in herself.

His eyes crinkled at the corners, like he was laughing with her. That's how life would be with him at her side. Laughter and promises and a helpmate working with her, side by side.

"Ready to try another one?" he asked. "We have time."

"Jah," she managed to force from a throat closed off with emotion.

He squeezed her hand again, then turned away as though nothing had happened, as though her world hadn't tumbled upside down.

Chapter Sixteen

✳

READY FOR LUNCH—so what if he was earlier than usual—
Aaron stepped into the store and immediately his gaze
sought out Hope. Now that they were all back to working
in the shop, Mamm included starting today, he could feel
fully that when Hope finally left, returning to her usual life
with her family, she would take his heart and his happiness
with her.

She stood with her back to him, wearing a deep purple
dress today that he knew changed her eyes from pale gray
to almost a light blue hue. A few red curls escaped her
kapp, lying against her neck softly. Her sweet voice floated
to him as she explained the different types of canned foods
to an Englischer woman, pointing out her favorites. Aaron
hid a smile as she mentioned the mint jelly, still trying to
sell some for poor Dorcas.

Practically in mid-sentence she stopped talking and
glanced over her shoulder, as though she'd sensed his

amused stare. As soon as she saw him, she sent him a smile that lit him up from within.

Gotte, please let that smile mean what I think. Please tell me my hope won't be in vain. Maybe Daniel had been right. She couldn't look at him that way and not feel something . . . more. Could she?

She'd looked at him that way the other day, too. When they'd cooked her casserole and it had turned out perfect. She'd even moved to give him a hug. At least he thought so. She'd stopped herself.

Now her grin turned mischievous and she held up the jar of the green concoction, sharing the joke with him.

Aaron shook his head in such a way that a small giggle escaped her.

"Hope," Dat's voice boomed through the shop from the back room.

"Excuse me," she said to the customer before hurrying to the back.

Aaron followed with a frown. Dat did not sound happy.

"Ruth is more tired than she expected to be on her first day back," Dat was saying as he walked through the curtain.

"Do you want me to take her home?" Hope asked.

"Nae. I will do that. But it causes a bit of a problem. Daniel is home already today and needs to tend his bees or we'd send him back here. Joshua, meanwhile, needs another man to go with him to pick up a delivery of metalwork from the blacksmith in Skokegan. I hate to ask it, but would you be willing to stay by yourself, help the customers, and close the shop at the usual time?"

Ach du lieva. Dat must have really come around when it came to Hope to trust her with the shop this way.

"Of course," Hope agreed eagerly. "Whatever help I can give that's best."

That earned her a satisfied nod from his father. "It means you'll be walking home alone, but it won't be dark for hours yet after closing."

"I don't mind," Hope assured him, her expression earnest.

Aaron opened his mouth to protest, not liking the thought of her walking by herself, but everyone, including Hope, appeared perfectly happy with the arrangement, so he closed it without speaking. She'd probably walked home from town a hundred times without him even being aware of it. This time should be no different.

"Are you sure?" Aaron asked her later as they waved his parents off. "Joshua and I could go tomorrow. Or come back here and unload instead of stopping at home."

"Nonsense. Your horses will be tired after the trip, and Skokegan is in the opposite direction. Don't make them come farther. I'll be fine."

When he didn't move out of the doorway that led to the back alley, she put a hand in the middle of his chest, her touch like a brand, and pushed him gently aside. "You're worse than Hannah."

He watched her walk away, returning to the front of the store in time for the bell to jangle, announcing another customer.

"I still don't like it," he muttered.

But thirty minutes later, Joshua returned with the wagon rather than the buggy, hitched to their wagon horses, Mule and Marlin. Good thinking. All the metalwork would be heavy. At least Skokegan wasn't too far from Charity Creek, especially from where their house sat. Hopefully the small break in the weather, sunshine peeking through gray and white clouds, would hold.

They headed out, leaving Hope on her own. They

wouldn't even pass back by this way to get home, or he'd check on her, if only to settle his own concerns.

"Something on your mind, bruder?" Joshua asked after they'd ridden in silence a good long while. Practically to their destination. He slid Aaron a sly smirk. "Or someone?"

"The day you fall in love is going to be a lot of fun for me," Aaron muttered.

"Love," Joshua scoffed. "I have years yet."

"Jah. And I'm looking forward to laughing a lot."

His bruder set to whistling a tune, clearly not too worried, then stopped suddenly. "Besides, love isn't everything. When I marry, I want a fraa who will work hard beside me. A quiet, easygoing girl."

"You?" Aaron snorted. "You'll be bored silly."

"I'll be content."

"I already pity the poor girl."

"Here we are . . ." Joshua turned the buggy down a narrow dirt lane. Ahead, a small white house sat nestled in a copse of tall trees with an aging barn nearby that needed a new coat of paint. The barn dwarfed the house.

After unhitching the buggy, they walked Mule and Marlin to the barn, only to slide the door back and discover not a space intended to shelter animals, but an old-fashioned smithy. A tall, broad-shouldered man stood with his back to them, facing a blazing fire, which he held a metal rod in. Sweat stuck his shirt and suspenders to his back and curled his dark hair against his neck.

This had to be Adam Miller, the man Dat was wonderful excited to do business with. Blacksmithing was a dying art.

"Excuse us?" Aaron called out.

"One minute," Adam called back, not surprised, it seemed, and also not bothering to lift his head, his focus on his craft total.

"I'll hitch the horses by the house," Joshua said, and wandered off.

Meanwhile, Aaron watched with interest as Adam pulled the glowing, red-hot iron from the forge and took it to an anvil, where, using a hefty flat-headed hammer, he pounded rhythmically at the now softened metal, forming something else entirely.

Reminded of his own craft, Aaron could appreciate the skill that went into what Adam was doing. A glance around showed him various pieces of finished work, and he walked farther into the barn, taking a closer look.

"Can I help you?" Adam demanded.

Aaron straightened and turned to find the blacksmith had finished and laid aside his tools. He now stood facing Aaron, feet planted, arms crossed, and with a grumpy glare.

"Yes. My name is Aaron Kanagy. My dat is Joseph Kanagy. He sent me to collect the items you agreed to sell through our shop in Charity Creek. A Thankful Heart."

"Jah. I'm still not sure about that."

Aaron tried not to stiffen at the dismissive way Adam tossed that at him. Instead, he calmly cocked his head, studying the other man, no older than he. "Can I ask why not?"

Adam cast his gaze over the shop, as though assessing his work. "I'm not sure it's worth giving up a percentage of my profits. I get enough business directly. Also, I don't know you or your family. You seem like decent Amish folk, but appearances can be deceiving."

Good thing Joshua was outside with the horses or he'd be struggling to control his temper about now.

"All the vendors we work with have been more than pleased with the partnership. I'd be happy to provide any references for you to speak with directly, though I'm guessing Dat has already done that."

Adam nodded. "Jah. And you're right. Everyone I spoke to was more than pleased. But my work is different. I'm the only blacksmith that I know of in the state who uses these techniques."

Aaron glanced around. "I don't know too much, but your work is impeccable."

"Denki." The word seemed to pain Adam, as if he didn't often use it.

Aaron had meant it sincerely. Smooth, well-formed pieces of varying kinds—horseshoes, parts for bridles and harnesses, buggy wheel rims, but also more items perfect for a gift shop like bottle openers, knives, towel bars, coat hooks, and even decorative items. And that was just at first glance.

An idea sparked in his mind. One involving combining his own woodworking business with Adam's blacksmithing skills. Furniture that blended the two. But he was getting ahead of himself.

"I understand wanting to keep as much of the profit as you can, and also needing to trust anyone you partner with." Aaron rubbed at his jaw, the rasp of day-old beard growth loud in his own ears. "Would you be interested in visiting the shop? It may help you decide."

"I can't be away from my work."

Aaron picked up a horseshoe, testing the weight and feel in his hand. "I guessed as much. But tomorrow is Sunday."

He kept his gaze on the shoe in his hand, giving Adam a chance to think. Then Aaron lifted his head when the other man didn't reply, clearly waiting for more.

"We're not open on Sundays," Aaron explained. "I assume you aren't either, so it won't impact business. You won't get to see the shop with customers, but you could come look around and join my family in our district for

Gmay, then stay to supper to get to know our family. We'd be glad to have you."

A muscle ticked near Adam's eye. The man had loner written all over him. Unusual for Amish, who lived in such tightly knit communities. "Jah. That sounds gute," he finally said.

Aaron tried not to appear visibly relieved. Dat wanted this partnership. Now that Aaron had seen the smithy's work in person, he could see why.

"Wunderbaar. Why don't we meet at the shop in the morning early?"

Adam nodded.

Sensing the other man wouldn't appreciate a handshake or any such token gesture, Aaron gave a sharp nod to seal the arrangement. As he turned to leave, a shadow filled the doorway.

Joshua took one look at both men and frowned. "Hello," he greeted. "My name is Joshua Kanagy."

"My bruder." Aaron introduced the two men.

Adam didn't even nod.

"We'll see you tomorrow," Aaron said, then dragged a visibly confused Joshua away and out into the sunshine. A few seconds later, the barn door closed behind them with a decided thump.

"What was that about?" Joshua demanded in a low voice as they hitched an irritated Mule, who'd been happily nibbling at a patch of clover peeking out from under the house porch, back up to the buggy, followed by Marlin.

"I'll explain on the way home."

It didn't take Aaron long, once they were on their way, to tell Joshua about the conversation with Adam Miller and the offer Aaron had made.

"Dat isn't going to be happy," Joshua muttered.

"Jah. But he'd rather have Adam for a vendor, and this was the only way I could see to earn his trust."

He'd hardly finished the last word when his gaze landed on a small sign pointing off the road. "Wait! Turn here." Only years of working with horses kept him from grabbing the reins from Joshua's hands to sharply turn the team down the lane.

"What?" Joshua asked, even as he started the turn.

"Roses."

"Roses? What are you talking about?" Joshua searched his face in a way that spoke of a worry for Aaron's state of mind.

"I dug up an old, dead rosebush at the Beilers'. I think Hope would like a new one. The sign said they're selling rosebushes."

After a long, silent pause, Joshua snorted. "If this is what love is, then it's not for me, for sure and certain. Love drives a man to do the strangest things."

Aaron wasn't going to argue with that.

But already his mind had turned to Hope. Would she be at her bridge tonight? Probably. The rain had finally given way to prettier weather, and he shouldn't intrude. What if she was embarrassed or felt pushed if he gave her the roses? Maybe it would be better to have Mamm give them to Hope at the store on Monday.

HOPE'S STEPS DRAGGED with her thoughts as she walked around the shop going through the process Ruth had showed her to close up for the night. Things she'd seen and helped with often, though a small glow of pride lit in the center of her chest at the idea that they trusted her to do this on her own.

Put away that sinful pride, she told herself. This was nothing special and wouldn't have happened if Ruth hadn't been unwell. To be happy at the expense of another, what was she thinking?

The front door was propped open to the outside, something she'd done earlier in the day as soon as the sun poked its head out, both to invite customers walking by to wander inside, but also to let in the unexpected beauty of the day after so much rain.

A lark sang a glorious song of life from her perch on the bench just outside the door, and Hope smiled. She should be enjoying the warmth of the late spring sun, the breeze drifting lazily through the door, the fresh, after-rain scent of the air, even the clouds building to towering white heights in the distance hinting at more rain to come. Gotte's creation was wondrous, but she couldn't focus on anything but the image of a pair of dark, laughing eyes and the wishes building inside her like the Tower of Babel, sure to be struck down. Dreamily moving through the motions, she imagined this was her life. Working beside Aaron and his family, a part of his life and the shop forever.

The front door slammed shut, the glass rattling horribly, followed by a bellowed "Hope Beiler! What do you think you are doing?"

Hope almost jumped out of her shoes at her dat's shout.

Outside, the lark took to the sky in a fright. Hope's heart wanted to do the same—leap from her chest and fly away. Instead, it sank to the pit of her stomach, laden with dread. She'd only ever heard her dat use that tone when he was truly upset.

"Dat?" she said. "What are you doing here?"

The wrong thing to say. His face turned thunderous, like the clouds beyond when they'd turn dark and roiling.

Oh, help. Gotte, please help calm us both. Help me explain my actions. Help . . .

She wasn't even sure what to ask for. She would fess up fully, take her punishment. She'd earned it. She prayed that he didn't turn his anger on the Kanagys. She'd promised Aaron she wouldn't let that happen.

"What am I doing here? The question is, what are *you* doing here?" He glanced past her. "Abram Raber just took great pleasure in informing me that my dochder has been working in this shop for weeks. Weeks, Hope."

She swallowed hard. "I can explain," she said.

"I don't want to hear excuses." He slashed a hand through the air. "You knew what my feelings would be on this matter. Did you ask Mammi for permission instead?"

Hope winced. "Yes."

He pinched his lips shut so hard, they turned white, then he jerked out a hand, beckoning her. "Kumme with me."

He grabbed her by the wrist, set to drag her out of the shop, but Hope dug her heels in. "I . . . I have to close up."

"The Kanagys can do that," Dat snapped.

"Nae, Dat. I'm the only one here. Ruth has been sick and—"

"They left you to do their work for them?" Dat went all quiet, a sure sign his temper was worsening.

She tried again. "Ruth has been sick and—"

"Finish closing up. Now," he ordered. "I'll wait."

She didn't need to be told twice. Hurrying through the last steps as quickly as she could, she finished by leading her dat out the front door, locking it behind her. "I need to drop the keys off," she said.

"You can do that tomorrow at Gmay."

He didn't even wait for her miserable nod as they climbed into the buggy. Rather than try to explain again,

Hope sat quietly beside her visibly fuming fater, trying to make herself smaller, hands in her lap, eyes on them. He'd cool down eventually and might listen then.

Out of the corner of her eye, she could see her dat shaking his head, as if arguing with himself. They were more than halfway home before he finally spoke.

"I don't know what to say to you, Hope," he started, his voice low, controlled. Blank of all emotion. Not her father's way.

Even as her own heart shrank inside her, Hope pulled her shoulders back. She'd had good reason for the choices she'd made. "I did it for Hannah, Dat."

"Hannah?" He scowled. "Don't bring your schwester into this."

"I wanted to give her a wedding gift."

His brows snapped down over his eyes. "So you're working for it? Oh, sis yuscht, Hope. What must the Kanagys think of us?"

"Nae. It's all right. I'm doing a trade with Aaron Kanagy," she rushed to explain. "He's making a bed frame for her and Noah. In exchange, I'm taking his place in the shop, so he can have the time to work on it. It's a fair swap, Dat."

"With the Kanagys yet. You know how I feel about . . . that family. Now you've brought them into our . . . troubles. Without my permission, no less."

"Mamm would have let me," she insisted. Not a grumble but stating a fact.

He did not take it that way, hands clamping into fists around the reins. "We don't know that. Do we? Your mater is dead, and I'm your only parent now, Hope."

She sucked in a sharp breath at the agony lacing each word and the answering pain slicing through her.

But she couldn't let this go. "The Kanagys are wonderful gute people, Dat. I've got to know them, and I don't understand—"

"Enough." He ran a hand over his eyes as though they ached with tiredness, suddenly small and weary. Not her big, strong, invincible dat. The man her mother's death had left him starkly evident. "I don't wish to talk about this more."

"But Aaron needs to finish the bed—"

"He can sell it to someone else. You are not allowed to work there or see the Kanagys anymore. Do you understand me?"

She had to bite back the sting of tears threatening to clog her throat. She shouldn't blame her dat. This was all her fault. Her lies. Her sneaking. And now her consequences to face. "Jah, Dat," she said. "I understand."

Chapter Seventeen

❋

PILED INTO THE buggy in their Sunday clothes, Dat drove
Aaron and Joshua to the shop. Mamm and Daniel would go
in the other buggy to the home where Gmay would be held
today and meet them there. Despite the rain dropping
steadily and strongly on the roof of the buggy, making it
difficult to see out the windshield even with the wipers going full speed, they were making decent time.

This was no weather to be out in, for sure and certain.
After all the light rain they'd had already, even with the
tiny bit of sun the other day, the ground had already been
soaked. Now, after going strong all night, rushing rivulets
ran down the side of the road, pooling in the dips and coming into the street in spots.

More a fair-weather horse, Frank didn't like getting his
hooves too wet and balked anytime he had to cross a pud-
dle. Aaron's mind, however, wasn't on the rain, or Frank, or
the shop, or Adam Miller, or anything but Hope. He'd gone
to her bridge after he and Joshua had gotten home last

night, but she hadn't been there. He'd waited over an hour.
When he'd first arrived, rain had been falling softly, more
a mist in the air than droplets. But soon it had turned heavy
and thick, coming down on top of him like Noah's flood,
and he'd been forced to turn home. She wouldn't come in
such a downpour anyway. Not even to her favorite spot.

"You are sure the blacksmith will be there?" Dat asked
for the third time since hitching up the buggy.

"Jah. He doesn't talk much but seems an honorable man.
Even if he's still unsure, he'll be there. Or if the rain is a
problem, he'll call the shop when he knows we should be
there and reschedule."

Dat ran a hand over his beard, which he only did when
he worried. He had not been happy that, after all his efforts,
Adam Miller was still balking. Aaron glanced over his
shoulder and exchanged a grin with Joshua. Poor Adam
Miller had no chance against Joseph Kanagy when he got
an idea in his head about what would sell well in the shop.

As they pulled into the alley at the back of the storefronts, Aaron sat forward about the same time Dat did.
"Why is the door open?"

"I don't know," Dat muttered, brows meeting in the
middle over his eyes.

He stopped the buggy, and in a rush, they scrambled out,
crowding into the shop only to pull up sharply at the sight that
greeted them. It looked as though a tornado had been through
the back room, throwing things everywhere other than where
they'd been left.

Horror stole the words from his mouth as he stared at the
mess.

"We've been robbed," Joshua snarled.

They moved through to the front of the shop to find the
same chaos reigned there as well. But Aaron shook his

head as he picked up one of the small faceless dolls that had been on the other side of the room with all the toys when he'd left yesterday. "We'll need to check against inventory, but I don't think so. Somebody just messed everything up."

"Who would *do* such a thing?" Joshua demanded, hands fisted at his sides and practically vibrating.

At least Mamm wasn't here to see this. Still recuperating from being sick, she shouldn't have a shock on top of that.

"The better question," Dat said through white, pinched lips, "is how did they get in?"

Aaron closed his eyes as realization sank in. Hope. She'd closed up on her own last night. On the heels of that thought, urgency spiked through him. "We should check on Hope. What if she was in here when—"

Dat cut him off with a glance. "We would have heard by now if she'd been harmed."

Of course they would. If not from the Beilers, a neighbor would have come to inform them. Aaron frowned even through the relief sweeping through him. They *would* have heard, which meant this must have happened after she left and no one else knew.

"What is going on in here?"

Aaron grimaced at the rough voice behind them. Of course this would happen when Adam Miller was set to visit. Along with his family, he slowly turned to find the blacksmith standing at the curtained doorway, hands on his hips and a glower setting his lips in a grim line. "Is this how you do business?" he demanded.

"We've been vandalized," Joshua snapped, stepping forward with the obvious intent of getting in the other man's face. Aaron stepped between them, ignoring his brother's growl of irritation.

"Can't you see that we're in as much shock as you?" He shot the question at Adam.

"Vandalized," Adam snarled. "Then why would I ever trust my hard work to you?"

They all exchanged a glance before Dat stepped forward. "I assure you that were this to happen again—and it has never happened before—we would cover all the costs of your goods, of course."

"You're asking me to trust that you have the money to do that." Adam gave a hard shake of his head. "Nae. I don't need to see any more. Please don't approach me again."

Dropping those final words into an echoing silence, Adam walked away. A few seconds later, the splashing of his horse's hooves as he rode away drove a nail in the coffin with each *clop.*

Oh, sis yuscht. Aaron didn't dare glance at his father.

He needed to check on Hope, the need overriding the horror at what had happened, or perhaps adding to it. If she was safe, then he'd breathe easier. They could deal with the shop.

"Let's lock up and go to Gmay," he said.

"You want to act like this didn't happen?" Joshua demanded.

Aaron shook his head. "We can announce this there. Others with shops should know, in case the person, or people, is targeting Amish-owned stores. We'll have to close on Monday to clean everything."

There was no doubt in his mind that the community would step up to help put things right. While Amish life came with a plain and, as seen from the outside, strict way of living, the strong community they were blessed with— one that supported each other unconditionally and with love and care—came directly from Gotte.

"Not the Beilers," Dat snapped.

What? He couldn't be blaming Hope for this. "But—"

"I forbid you to speak to that girl," Dat said as he stalked past Aaron.

Using the extra set of keys they'd brought with them, he locked the door and climbed into the buggy. "Dat, I'm sure she didn't—"

At a single glance from Dat, Aaron snapped his mouth shut with a clack of his teeth.

"I will address her part in it with Hope's fater privately," he said. "None of you say a word about that."

He bent a particularly harsh look on Aaron, who had no choice but to nod and trust that Gotte would soothe his father's anger before that conversation happened. Amish lived peaceful lives, taking a vow against violence and trying to live a life of forgiveness, turning their backs on anger, but they were human yet, and anyone could stumble in their lives and faith.

Leaving the shop behind in all its appalling state, they piled back into the buggy and turned Frank's nose back toward their own home, where their closest neighbors, the Yoders, would be hosting Gmay today.

One of the first to arrive, Aaron and his bruders stood off to the side just inside the barn, out of the rain, with the other boys their age. Daniel and Mamm arrived not long after. Dat took her aside to explain quickly, her face visibly paling. Even across the yard her distress was obvious to Aaron. But Mamm, after a few words, laying her hand on her husband's arm as though urging him, nodded calmly before she went into the house to help and Dat went to stand with the older married men.

After an interminable wait, the Beilers' buggy and horse, with those distinctive white-socked feet, muddy today, finally appeared down the drive. Hope got out with her schwester, took one step toward the house, and then froze as her gaze landed on Aaron, and his heart stuttered. He'd swear she'd been crying.

He took a step in her direction, only to stop when she shook her head.

Heart pounding, he knew something was horribly wrong, because it was all there for him to see in her eyes. He cocked his head in question, mostly asking with the silent gesture if she was unharmed. If anyone had laid a hand on her, he didn't know what he'd do.

But she glanced over her shoulder at her fater then mouthed two words at Aaron. "I'm sorry."

Nae.

The breath punched from his lungs.

Nae, she couldn't have been the one responsible for what happened to the shop. But what else could she be sorry for?

"She's sorry?" Joshua's whisper was a harsh scrape over Aaron's nerves. "What does that mean?"

"Ach vell, we might find out in a second," Daniel muttered, canting his head in the other direction.

Dread careened into Aaron's stomach as Levi Beiler marched up to his dat and held something out. What could Levi possibly have to give him?

Not the keys to the shop, surely?

Levi handed off whatever he held, then spoke a few words, not seeming to care that Aaron's dat's face turned redder with each utterance. Until Dat took him by the arm, pulling him off to the side for a certain amount of privacy. After another round of exchanged words, both men appeared solemn faced and relatively calm, but Aaron knew his parent. Dat was furious.

"Hope." Levi's voice cracked like a whip.

Having moved up onto the porch, out of the rain, Hope

stilled. After an expressive grimace, not even glancing in Aaron's direction as she went, she hurried over to where the two men stood. Far enough away that Aaron couldn't even catch the tone of the conversation, let alone any words.

Whatever was said, it didn't go well.

Hope shook her head. Several times. Harder each time, the ties of her kapp knotting together with the motion. Her hand flew to her mouth, then she said a few more words, after which her own father's expression turned to stone. He said several low words, seemingly in control except for the way his hands kept forming into fists, as though holding back physical violence with sheer will—a reaction that sent a splinter of shock through Aaron.

"This doesn't look good," Daniel said.

Joshua's grunt said enough. His bruder was too angry even to speak.

Dat spoke again, short and clipped, only a few words. Hope shook her head again and said a few words before her face crumpled and she turned and rushed away. Not inside to join the women for the service but down the lane away from her family and friends.

Away from him.

Her dat watched after her but didn't call her back. Instead, he said a few brief, clipped words to Aaron's father, whose face flushed from red to purple, then walked away to join the men, all of whom had watched this progress with wide-eyed interest.

"Anyone want to guess how long it will be before we get a visit from the bishop?" Daniel asked.

Aaron hardly heard him, his gaze on Hope's back as she got farther and farther away from him. Like she was leaving him and not the situation. Like he'd lost her completely. He took a step in her direction.

"Aaron—" The crack of his father's voice left him in no doubt. He wasn't to go after her.

Another figure rushed past him and down the lane, seemingly intent on catching up to Hope.

Luke Raber.

RAIN SOAKED THROUGH her dress, plastering the material to her skin, the ties of her kapp lashing the sides of her neck with each step. Arms wrapped around her middle, Hope plodded, not paying much attention to where her feet were taking her, just so long as it was away from the terrible results of her lies and the nasty accusations that had been thrown at her by Aaron's family.

And he'd stood back, not coming close to defend her. The man who'd said he wanted to marry her. How could he believe it?

"Hope."

Vaguely she was aware of someone calling her name, but the pain of what Joseph Kanagy had accused her of lodged in her mind, forcing everything else to the corners. He'd called her a snake in the grass. Said she'd left the back door unlocked on purpose. Maybe even arranged to let in the vandal.

As soon as she'd heard the words "break-in," she'd considered her fault in this. She was fairly certain she had missed the step of locking the back door. Her father's presence making her both rushed and worried, her mind was not on her actions as it should have been.

But on purpose to hurt them? How could he think that of her after everything she'd done recently? Hadn't she proved herself a hard and trustworthy worker and a true friend to their family?

Not that she could blame him. Dat had started it, angrily

accusing Levi of taking advantage of Hope, getting work from her without his permission. Hope had tried to step in, explain things to Dat, but he hadn't wanted to listen.

The rest had happened in a sluggish, horrendous way, Aaron's gaze like knives in her back. Neither man—her dat or Aaron's—had wanted to listen to anything she said. Both men apparently forgot their Christian roots, faces flushed in anger with each new word uttered, and Hope caught in the middle. So she'd run. It seemed she was always running when Aaron was involved. Even when she wanted to run to him instead of away.

Who would hurt the Kanagys like that anyway?

Hope racked her brain. Had she left the back door unlocked? She thought she remembered setting the bolt, but maybe, in her rush to leave with her fater so angry and waiting, she'd forgotten that important step. Which she'd tried to tell Joseph.

"Hope." The voice was closer now. Whoever had followed her clearly wasn't going away.

She jerked to a halt and spun to face . . . Luke.

Disappointment wrapped an icy fist around her. Not Aaron.

Luke ran to catch up, stopping in front of her, breathing hard. His gaze took in her face, wet and no doubt pinched and pale. "You run fast for a girl."

A comment that didn't need a response, her muddled mind not coming up with one anyway.

"Are you okay?" he asked.

Hope couldn't speak. Didn't want to. She managed to shake her head, her mouth buttoned tight trying to hold back the emotions threatening to drown her.

"Kumme," Luke said, taking her elbow. "Let's get you home."

In silence they trudged through the mud and the rain, the brisk breeze sending shivers cascading through her, clenching her muscles.

Before she knew where she was, he'd walked her up the front porch of her house and turned her to face him. "Do you have a key?"

Oh, help. Dat had the keys.

The widening of her eyes must've been enough, because Luke patted her shoulder awkwardly. "Don't worry. I know the secret way in."

She blinked as he disappeared down the porch and around the side of the house. A minute later, the front door opened from inside. He must've gotten in the way she'd showed him when they were kids. How that realization made it through the numbness, she wasn't sure.

Luke helped her take off her shoes to leave them, muddy and wet, on the front porch, then brought her inside.

"Denki," she whispered. "Please go on back. I wouldn't want you to miss Gmay."

In a haze of numbness, she turned for the stairs and plodded her way up, her feet sticking to the wood flooring as she went. Inside her room, she stood for a long moment, staring and seeing nothing.

Then, the sob she'd been holding on to with sheer will burst from her, echoing in her small room. Somehow that sound shut down everything, as though shocking the building tears away. Even more numb, she managed to strip off her soaked clothing and put on a warm and dry dress and stockings, not bothering to repin her hair or put on another kapp, then lay down on her made bed and watched the swirling clouds out her window. Rain battered the glass, distorting the view and coming from different angles as the wind changed.

Hope lay there in a lump. Staring. For who knew how long.

"Liebling?" A soft knock sounded along with her gross-mammi's voice.

She lifted her head as the door opened and Mammi came to sit on the side of her bed. "Ruth Kanagy told me what happened at the shop."

At the sight of worried, faded blue eyes, Hope moved into the circle of her comforting embrace, laying her head on her shoulder.

Mammi gathered her into her frail, bony arms and patted her back and murmured words that didn't register. They sat there like that while Hope willed herself to feel anything. Maybe Gotte, in His wisdom, had cut her off from her emotions so that she wouldn't break with the pain of it. After a while, Hope took a deep breath and sat up fully, letting Mammi's arms drop away.

"What do I do?" she asked.

Thin lips went even thinner. "First, you thank the poor boy waiting downstairs looking like a young, skittish horse that wants to bolt."

"Luke's still here?" she asked on a gasp. Ach du lieva. People in their community truly did underestimate him.

"He said he didn't want to leave you alone."

"Oh, help."

Mammi nodded. "I have a much better opinion of Luke Raber after this."

Hope managed a small smile. "Jah."

"I'd say you should marry a boy who would look after you like that, but your heart is already taken by another."

If her eyes hadn't been attached, they might've popped out of her head. "How—"

Mammi waved her off. "Because I know my Hope." She

tipped her head, taking in Hope's expression. "Aaron loves you, too, you know."

"Nae."

"He started to go after you, but his dat forbade him from taking another step. In front of all the men."

Hope shook her head, waiting for any emotion to find her. But none did. "Even if that was true, everything is ruined now, Mammi. Dat won't let me. And Joseph won't let him. I've messed this up horribly."

"So fix it."

Fix it? "Where do I even start?" she muttered, having to pin down a chin wobble before she started wailing.

Mammi took her by the shoulders and gave her a little shake. "Start by finding the fearless, kind girl I know you are. This isn't like you to give up. Especially when others are hurting, too."

Hope straightened. Mammi was right about that. She wasn't the only one hurting.

"Then," Mammi continued, "make things right with the Kanagys. Blowing at the smoke doesn't help if the chimney is plugged."

Hope bit her lip. "Dat says I'm not to speak to them or see them anymore. I can't—"

"We'll come up with something." Mammi patted her knee.

Something to make amends at least. Taking a deep breath, Hope nodded, then got up and made herself go downstairs to where Luke waited. He got to his feet as she came in, expression anxious and very un-Luke-like.

"I'm sorry," she said contritely. "I thought you'd left."

He shifted from foot to foot. "It didn't seem right for you to be alone."

"Denki for your help. You are a true friend."

He twitched like he didn't want to be thanked. "Are you okay?"

Not ready to answer that question, Hope forced a small smile. "Of course."

Luke seemed to accept the answer and the smile, his shoulders relaxing. "I'm glad. I . . . guess I'll go."

"Not in this rain, young man," Mammi said as she tromped loudly down the stairs. "You can escort an old woman in her buggy to your house, where you'll change into dry clothes, and then back to the Yoders' to attend service."

Hope almost laughed at his expression, which said he wanted to do anything but that. But Luke went along with Mammi like a lamb, leaving Hope alone in the house with her thoughts.

She made her way quietly back to her room to sit on her bed, knees pulled up to her chest, and watch the rain.

"How do I make amends?" she whispered to Gotte.

Then sat in silence and waited for His answer.

The answer came not while she sat staring, and not when her family returned home from Gmay. Not when Hannah came upstairs and hugged her tight. Nor when Dat came upstairs, grim and angry yet.

"You will have nothing to do with the Kanagys," he ordered.

Hope nodded.

"Imagine blaming you for their misfortunes."

"I must've left the back door unlocked when you . . ." She stopped herself from blaming her own dat. "When we left. I must not have been careful enough."

"Still . . ."

"I understand. I won't see them." She turned her head away.

The bluster seemed to go out of him, like the stillness after a storm, despite the rain still pounding away at the house outside. "Ach vell . . ." The next words came out almost carefully, as though he'd had to search for the right ones. "I see so much of your mater in you."

She lifted her head at that, searching his solemn face. "You do?"

He nodded slowly. "So much sometimes I think she's here with me again, and it hurts to realize she's not."

"Oh, Dat," Hope whispered, hurting for him.

He straightened and cleared his throat. "Anyway . . . we won't speak of this again."

Hope gave another nod.

As he closed the door behind him, Gotte answered her prayer. Still numb, but at least with a plan, she got out a piece of paper and a pen from the small desk in her room where she used to do homework when she'd been a scholar.

She stared for a long while at the blank page, trying to form the words in her head, words that might heal a bit of the damage she'd caused.

Then, slowly, she began to write.

Chapter Eighteen

✳

AARON'S DAY TO stay home for chores came like every other day since that awful Sunday, with a gaping sensation of emptiness the second he opened his eyes. Emptiness he pushed aside as he tried to pick up his life where he'd left it the day Hope suggested her trade. He'd worked all day, trying to drown out his thoughts by physically making it impossible to dwell on them. With quick, rough motions, Aaron mucked out the stalls.

The sun was doing its best to peek out of the clouds that still obscured its rays, the first they'd seen of it in a week. If it did finally break through, it wouldn't be for long, already sitting low on the horizon.

Only Aaron wasn't all that interested in sunshine, the gray dullness reflecting his mood exactly.

If he could talk to Hope . . .

His family hadn't discussed what happened with Hope or with Levi. Dat, at least, had appeared to cool down, but no one had brought it up. Moving back into their usual routine as though nothing had happened, in spite of the tension that had bled into every moment between them since. No longer his happy, comfortable family, but strangers.

He gave his head a shake and wheeled the barrow out of the stall, then set about adding fresh straw before he moved on to the next stall over. The telltale clopping of a horse's hooves signaled the return of his family from the shop just as he finished the last stall. Putting away the pitchfork, Aaron took the wheelbarrow outside to dump it, only to slow to a halt at the sight of two buggies nearing the house instead of one.

He stared. Who could be visiting before the supper hour?

The other driver pulled up beside where Dat parked their own buggy, so Aaron didn't get a decent look at him until he came around the side.

"Adam Miller." The name burst from his lips as the blacksmith appeared.

Adam gave him a single nod in greeting, curt and silent as usual. "Aaron."

"What are you doing here?" Given how tangled up in his mind Aaron had been with everything that had happened to cause him to lose Hope, the words came out sharper than he'd intended.

"Aaron," Mamm admonished. "He is our guest."

Aaron opened his mouth to argue.

"And he's decided to sell his work through our store." Dat cut him off with a significant look.

He had? After declaring in no uncertain terms that he'd never do business with the Kanagys. "What changed your mind?" he asked slowly.

"This." Dat pulled a folded envelope from his inside pocket and handed it to Aaron.

There, with the sun shining down on his head, and his bruders moving around to care for the horses, and everyone else watching, Aaron pulled out what appeared to be a letter, unfolded it, and started to read.

Dear Mr. Miller,

You don't know me. My name is Hope Beiler, and until recently I worked at A Thankful Heart, the gift shop owned by the Kanagy family in Charity Creek.

Aaron's hands jerked at the sight of her name. Hope had written to Adam Miller? Why? He glanced up to find Mamm and Dat both watching him closely. Mamm waved him to keep going.

I write to ask you to reconsider selling your metalwork through their store. I've known the Kanagys my entire life. They are the best of people. Faithful, honest, and hardworking. I know you won't regret partnering with them.

The incident involving the break-in at the store was entirely my fault. I had been given the responsibility of closing the shop on my own for the first time and I failed to lock the back door. In addition, two more shops experienced vandalism before two Englischer boys were found to be the culprits. Not that that is an excuse. Such a thing would never have happened with the Kanagys in charge, and I take full responsibility. If it sets your mind at ease, please know I no longer work in the shop, so this mistake won't happen again.

I feel I don't deserve any forgiveness, not in the least, but would like to apologize to you directly be-

cause my actions impacted your decision about your business. A decision which not only hurts my dear friends, who were so excited to partner with you in this way, but, I believe, hurts you as well. Having seen first-hand how they treat their vendors and how those folks sell so much through the shop, I know your business would only benefit from such a partnership.

Someday, I will also apologize to the Kanagys, though it won't cover the least of the many blunders I made. But my hope, from a pure and faithful heart, is that you might reconsider your decision.

Sincerely,
Hope Beiler

Hope had written Adam Miller and made a plea on his family's behalf? Aaron read it again, and again, then lifted his gaze to Adam. "You reconsidered?"

Adam nodded. "I dropped off my first load of goods this afternoon."

Dat stepped closer and put a hand on Aaron's shoulder. "We misjudged Hope. *I* misjudged her."

"I always knew that," Aaron said slowly, his mind abuzz. "But you're like me, Dat. You have to make up your own mind."

Dat huffed a laugh, though his creased face relaxed in what appeared to be relief. "I'll ask Hope and Levi for forgiveness."

Emotion, raw and eager, surged through Aaron, almost painful after a week of holding it so closely contained inside himself, trying not to feel anything. "I want to marry her, Dat."

He met his father's eyes straight on, steady in his decision.

Only Dat grimaced. "You have my blessing, of course. But Levi Beiler is the one who will need convincing."

And Hope herself. Aaron kept that particular, gnawing doubt to himself.

"I have an idea about Levi." One that couldn't wait. "I have to speak with someone. Don't wait supper on me."

Then Aaron sprinted in the direction of the woods. Not to Hope, or to Levi, but to her grossmammi.

If anyone would help him—could help him—Rebecca Beiler could. Though it might be tricky speaking to her privately. He had to try, though.

HER FACE SHADED by a wide-brimmed straw hat and her hands protected by the gloves Mamm used to wear, Hope knelt by the neatly turned rows she'd spent yesterday afternoon getting ready for today's plantings. The garden had become her place to escape from all the wedding preparations, which had turned almost frantic in the final days leading up to the event, helpers overrunning the farm with their kindness. Really, she should be helping Mammi cook more pies or finishing sewing her new dress for the occasion. She'd make up for it later. Sleep had been eluding her. Maybe sewing would pass the long hours of the night.

The early morning air remained crisp for late spring. The rain had finally cleared two days ago, but the ground had been too wet for planting then. Today, though still a bit soggy, things had dried enough. Combined with the warmth of the sun on her back, and the blue skies above, and the birds in the trees singing, it made for a lovely day to be outside working the garden.

At least, that's what Mammi had insisted before sending Hope out after they'd cleaned up from breakfast.

Only Hope didn't hear the birds, and the sky didn't seem all that blue, even after the constant gray of the rainy skies. The breeze had turned warmer as summer neared and the sun made her sweat. She wondered how long it would be before she stopped thinking about Aaron.

Questions chased around in her head like a dog after its own tail. Did he really believe she'd left the door unlocked on purpose? Was he glad now that she'd said no to his proposal? Did he think about her? Had he finished the bed frame and sold it? She hoped so. Starting his woodworking furniture business was important to him.

Hope went to dig a hole for the next seedling, only to realize she wasn't holding the trowel but the seedling in her hand. A puff of irritation passed her lips.

Keep your thoughts on your task, she reminded herself. She had to remind herself of that a lot lately. Much to Mammi's and Hannah's annoyance.

With a *tsk* at herself, she set down the seedling and picked up the trowel. The danger of a late frost was minimal, so she'd decided to set the warm weather plants to growing in the earth, starting with tomatoes and eggplants. Hannah would love that. Tomato was one of her favorites. She often ate them right off the vine the way one would eat an apple.

Hope's hands paused in her task as realization struck. Hannah wouldn't eat *these* tomatoes. She'd enjoy her own soon.

Her sister's soft voice reached her from the open window above her head. Hannah singing—perfectly on key, of course—getting ready to go over to Noah's house to meet more folks. With the wedding fast approaching on Thursday, family and friends from other Amish settlements across the states were arriving by train and bus daily. Her sister practically glowed with happiness. Hope was happy for her. Hannah deserved all the gute things in life, and Noah would be a faithful and loving mann.

Things would be different soon. Noah had bought his house. He and Hannah would move in after the wedding, leaving only Hope and Mammi and Dat here. Noah would start helping Dat work the farm.

Different. Maybe better. Certainly Noah's help would be better.

A shadow fell over her hands, blocking out the sun, and she glanced up to find her dat standing over her.

Since the incident, he'd remained the quiet man he'd been since Mamm's death, going out to work his fields, coming home late, and sitting with his Bible in the evenings.

Which made his appearance now all the more concerning. He never came home at this time of day. "Dat? Is something wrong?"

"Nae." He held out a hand to stop her getting to her feet. "I am taking Mammi into town for an errand for the wedding. A surprise for Hannah, it seems. She didn't tell me what exactly, just that she needed me to go."

Into town? Without Hope, of course. Dat was being careful to keep her at home since the situation with the Kanagys. Not wanting to risk her seeing them, no doubt.

"Ach jah. She's inside." Hope lowered her head and continued her methodical planting.

But the shadow didn't move.

She lifted her head again to find him watching her.

"Dat?" she prompted.

He gave himself a shake. "Your mater loved working in the garden yet."

Hope waited for tears, but the numbness was still all

she felt. "I'm wearing her hat and gloves. I should have thought—"

"So you are." Dat gave a brusque nod. He still didn't move inside to go with Mammi.

Hope raised her eyebrows in question.

"I'm surprised you're not singing," he said slowly.

Hope blinked. Singing?

The question must've reflected in her expression because he continued. "You always sing when you work."

He knew that? Hope often hardly realized when she was singing, it being as much a part of the work as what her hands were busy doing, making it more enjoyable as she went, even if the notes were wrong. She guessed she hadn't been singing lately, though. Then again, she didn't feel much like it. "I only got started," she said. "I'm sure the singing will come. Eventually."

Dat searched her face as though looking for an answer he wasn't getting. Then he visibly collected himself. "I'd better get going."

"Jah." Hope managed to muster a smile for him, then bent her head to her task.

After the garden, she cleaned herself up, muddy from the still damp ground, then decided the bathrooms all needed a good scrubbing, though Hannah had gone over them only days ago. The house needed to be spotless for the wedding. After that, she got on her hands and knees to clean the floors downstairs, even shouldering the furniture aside to get underneath it. That took her until the time came to get supper ready. Hannah was still at Noah's, and Mammi had gone with Dat into town to run their errand.

Should I make it?

Almost without thinking, she got out food, setting each item on the counter, then blinked at what she'd pulled out.

The ingredients for Aaron's ham casserole. He'd managed to invade every part of her day, it seemed. Still, maybe she could surprise her family with an edible supper this time. Feet slow on the stairs, she went up to retrieve the folded piece of paper with the recipe written out in Aaron's neat, masculine hand.

Hope paused and traced the letters with her fingertips, the ache inside her pulsing in time to her heartbeat. "Oh, sis yuscht, Aaron. Why'd I have to go and fall in love with you anyway?"

Needing to escape her own thoughts, escape this house, escape everything, Hope dropped the paper and ran. Down the stairs and out the front door.

The woods welcomed her, the cooler air sliding over her sun-warmed skin as she hurried. The path was faint, the rain having blurred the lines with mud and debris. Her shoes sank into the soft earth, and for a brief span of seconds, she debated going back to change into the muddy ones from gardening.

But the need to find peace, even if for a moment, drove her farther down the path to her bridge. The dense woods of maple, elm, and pine glowed green and lovely from the rain and now the sun. Hope hadn't let herself come here since the rains stopped, not wanting to risk bumping into Aaron. But in the middle of the day, she didn't have to worry. He'd be at work. The sound of the water reached her before the sight of the stream. She frowned. It didn't sound lazy and meandering. It sounded rushed.

Her feet sped up down the path until the water came into view. She slowed at the sight. Her beautiful, peaceful waterway had turned violent, a torrent of muddy water carving a path through the trees. It had broken its shallow banks, spreading out about ten feet to either side.

"Oh, help," she whispered.

Then she gasped. *My bridge*, the words a wail of anguish in her mind.

Breaking into a run, she had to navigate through the trees in several spots where the waters overtook her path. At one point, she worried that she'd passed where her bridge stood. Then she broke into a small clearing, recognizing the gnarled pair of trees that had guarded her spot for almost twenty years.

But her bridge wasn't there.

Hope's hands flew to cover her gasp, to try to hold in the pain. The one place she could always come to think was gone. Washed away. Was this Gotte's punishment for her sins?

Hope's shaking legs wouldn't hold her up as everything hit her all at once. All the emotions she'd been holding at bay behind the numbness, behind her chores and getting ready for Hannah's wedding and returning to her life as it had been, slammed into her with the force of a storm.

The tears that wouldn't come before, no matter how she tried to find them, came now. Her sobs were swallowed by the sounds of the waters that had taken away her bridge to Aaron.

Chapter Nineteen

✱

AARON'S SHIRT STUCK to his back as he put all his strength into sanding the curved wood in front of him. A glance at the clock had him moving faster, pushing harder into the wood. He needed to finish this before Thursday. Having to work in the shop again had put him back to how it had been before Hope, squeezing in his craft between hours.

Hope.

Every day stretched to forever, dull and uninteresting without her here. Without her smile and her laugh.

His gaze fell on the piece of paper that had given him the courage, and the hope, to take a bold step.

No way was he accepting things as they stood. With her so far from reach. He loved her too much to give up. Hopefully the plan he'd hatched with Rebecca would help.

Another glance at the clock. They were late. If they were coming at all. He kept moving, kept working, trying not to let his fears steal his thoughts. If they didn't come, he'd try a different approach.

A soft knock interrupted his spinning thoughts. Aaron threw a sheet over his project and moved to open the door, relief sweeping through him in the face of one determined Rebecca Beiler and an equally irritated Levi Beiler. Scratch the relief, nerves twisted knots inside him at the other man's glower.

"Please come in," Aaron said.

"I don't know what this is about," Levi said, brows meeting over his eyes. "But I have no wish to speak to you."

"And I'm still your mamm," Rebecca snapped at her son. "You will come in, and you will listen to what this boy has to say."

Levi blinked, whether from her tone or her words, Aaron wasn't sure. But Hope's dat suddenly appeared like a little lost owl, the same way Aaron had seen Hope look before, the expression so like her, he almost smiled. Only the tension gripping him kept that from happening.

"Make it fast," Levi ordered, then stomped into Aaron's shop, only to stumble to a halt. He reached out and smoothed a hand over the bed frame Aaron had made for Hannah.

"Is this—" He cut himself off and glanced at Aaron.

"Jah. The bed frame Hope had me make for Hannah."

Levi stepped closer, inspecting the work. "Did Hope come up with this design?" He pointed to the posts with their unusual details.

"Jah."

If he hadn't been watching closely, Aaron would've missed Levi's small smile, which came and went.

Then he turned to face Aaron, his expression closed. "Say what you need to say."

Aaron drew his shoulders back, knowing this was possibly his only chance. "I want to right whatever wrongs are keeping our families from healing the rift between us."

Levi stared at him, unmoved. "That's up to your dat."

"But maybe it can start with me . . . and Hope."

That only deepened the lines around Levi's mouth. "What does this have to do with Hope?"

"I love your dochder. With all my heart. I wish to marry her, with your blessing, of course."

Levi took a step back, then shot a glare at his mater. "*This* is what you dragged me here for?"

He went to stomp to the door, but Aaron jumped into his path, desperation making him move fast. "I don't know what happened between you and my dat, but Hope is my life."

"Your life?" Levi snapped, crossing his arms. "Is that so? What, exactly, do you love about my dochder?"

Aaron smiled, unable to help himself. Talking about Hope was as easy as talking of his faith. "I love her heart for other people and for Gotte. The way she sings off-key and doesn't seem to know or care because it makes her happy anyway. How she sees the world in colors. How she makes every customer in the shop comfortable and takes time to help them find exactly the right thing. The way she'd dare anything, even if it hurts her, for the people she loves." He waved a hand at the bed frame. "I love that you and her mamm couldn't keep her away from that stream when she was a little girl. I want to spend the rest of my life making her happy, providing for her, caring for her, and sacrificing for her."

Levi stared at him in silence when he'd finished, the absence of sound turning heavy, filling the room. Then Levi shook his head, dropping his gaze to the floor, and Aaron closed his eyes, hands fisting as despair filled the hole in his heart.

It hadn't worked. He hadn't changed a thing.

Nae. I'm not giving up. He snapped his eyes open. "May I show you something?"

Levi eyed him suspiciously but didn't say no, so Aaron moved to the worktable and snatched the paper up, handing it to Levi.

"What's this?" he was asked.

"This is not only about my happiness, but about Hope's," Aaron said. "I believe she loves me, too. At least I hope and pray she does."

That brought another scowl. "She wrote you?"

"Nae. And she's never said she loves me. If I'm wrong and she doesn't, then I'll leave her alone. But please read that before making up your mind."

Frown not lifting, Levi lowered his gaze. As he read, he seemed to delve deeper into the words. Words Aaron knew without seeing them after reading the letter so many times.

Finished finally, Levi lowered the letter. "You truly love my dochder?"

"She's a blessing from Gotte."

Levi glanced at his mater.

Rebecca snorted. "Don't look at me. I've been telling you for years to work this thing out with Joseph Kanagy. Anger on my account was never what I wanted, and now you could have ruined Hope's chance at happiness."

On Rebecca's account? Aaron frowned, glancing between the two. What did that mean?

Levi let go a long breath, the starch oozing from his shoulders. He shifted his gaze back to Aaron. But said nothing, falling silent. Aaron glanced at Rebecca, who held up a hand, and they stood there together, quietly waiting for Hope's fater to work through whatever was in his head.

Finally he drew his shoulders back. "I'll think about it."

Aaron had no idea what to take from that. At least it wasn't an outright refusal.

Levi nodded brusquely. "We'll see you and your family Thursday at the wedding."

He moved around Aaron and out the door, Rebecca following in his wake. "What does that mean?" Aaron whispered to her.

Rebecca pursed her lips, watching her son walk away down the alley. "If you want a place in the sun, you will have to expect some blisters."

Which left him even more baffled.

She shook her head like he should've understood. "There's still healing to do between our families. Even then, my Hope has to agree."

Hope had already said no to marrying him once. Aaron was well aware that his chances were slim. But maybe, just maybe, he'd made it past the first, and biggest, obstacle. Maybe.

Her letter to Adam, apologizing for her part in the store being broken into and proclaiming what gute and trustworthy people the Kanagys were—a heartfelt plea for him to reconsider and an endorsement despite essentially being fired—had been the first ray of hope in Aaron's world since it fell apart that Sunday morning.

Please, Gotte, Your will be done, but please let Your will be Hope.

AFTER CRYING UNTIL it felt as though she'd run out of tears, Hope hauled herself up to her feet and back to the house. There she changed out of her now muddy dress, splashed her face with cold water, and got started on supper, intending to have it on the table when her family returned from their errands.

The soft snick of what sounded like the front door closing caught her attention as she slipped the dish into the oven. She straightened and listened. Had somebody come home or was she hearing things now?

After closing the oven door and setting the battery-operated timer, Hope made her way to the front room, which was empty, then up the stairs, where she stood at the top and listened again. Nothing. Maybe her ears were playing tricks on her.

As she turned to go back to the kitchen, a tiny squeal of sound caught her attention. Hope spun back around. That was crying. She should know, after today. Steps hurried now, she didn't even bother knocking, barging right into her and Hannah's room to find her schwester sprawled across her bed, with her face buried in her arms.

"Hannah?" Hope ran to the bed and took a seat.

Only Hannah didn't look up.

"What's wrong?" Hope asked.

Her sister shook her head hard, her kapp slipping its pins and pushing over to set askew on her head. Only Hope didn't pay much heed. Not like Hannah, who always strove to appear neat as a pin.

Rubbing a hand on her back, Hope debated how to help. "Talk to me. Did something happen on the way home from Noah's?"

"Nae," Hannah snapped, then shoved herself to sitting, red-rimmed eyes brimming with tears. "It happened *at* Noah's."

What could possibly have upset her this much? Hope waited, giving Hannah time to collect herself.

With a great sniffle and running the back of her hand

inelegantly under her nose, Hannah's face crumpled. "I'm not enough for Noah," she wailed and flung herself into Hope's arms.

Stunned, Hope patted her sister's back, and opened her mouth several times, but no words came out, because she honestly had no idea what to say.

Finally, Hope landed on brutal honesty. "That is the most deerich thing you've ever said to me." She scoffed.

Hannah jerked upright with a glare, swiping angrily at her tears. "See! Even you think I'm stupid."

"I didn't say stupid, I said foolish." Hope shook her head. "Hannah, you are perfect. Annoyingly perfect sometimes. You do everything well. Say the right things, act the right way. You can cook, and sew, and clean, and you're wonderful gute with boppli and kinder. You have a kind heart and love Noah with all of it. He is lucky to have you."

Hannah sniffed, frowning, then shook her head. "I pretend to have a kind heart. Not like you. You're nice to everyone in ways I never think to be, and I have to think about it to act that way."

"I work at it, too," Hope assured her softly. "The point is you try."

Hannah's expression didn't ease. "And I have pride. I shouldn't take pleasure that my thumbprint cookies are better than Mary's. Or my stitches are neater than yours. Or that Noah is so handsome. Those things don't matter in Gotte's eyes."

"Everyone's thumbprint cookies are better than Mary's," Hope teased. "Even mine."

As she hoped, Hannah huffed a watery laugh at that.

"Now . . . what got all this started?" Hope prodded.

Hannah took a deep, shuddery breath. "I overheard his sisters talking about the state of our farm and how Noah would have to work so hard to fix it. How our family must've pushed us together because Dat needed a boy who could take over. But it *wasn't* that way." The tears welled back up in her deep blue eyes. "I love Noah."

Hope reached out and brushed the wetness from her sister's cheeks. "I know you do, and so does Noah. That is all that matters."

"But—"

"No buts. Would it break Noah's heart not to marry you?" She knew the answer already, but Hannah needed reminding.

Hannah paused at the question, then slowly nodded. "He loves me a lot."

"Yes. He does."

Hannah's tremulous smile was all Hope needed, for the moment her own troubles forgotten. "Now . . . wash your face and come downstairs to help me finish getting supper ready."

Hannah paused climbing off the bed. "You made supper?"

Hope laughed at the horror her sister was trying her best to hide. "It's a surprise and I think you'll like it."

"Of course I will."

Hope shook her head at the forced certainty lacing the words, the same way one might talk to a child who'd tried a chore for the first time. At least she'd be able to prove to her family that she wasn't hopeless in the kitchen, if not in love or obedience, or in so many other ways.

They were finishing setting the table and putting the food out to be served when Mammi and Dat walked in through the back door.

"Supper smells appenditlich," Mammi said. "Did you have time to cook, Hannah?"

"Nae. Hope did."

Both Mammi's and Dat's crestfallen faces almost made her laugh. Almost. Smiling still hurt.

Quickly, they sat and offered their silent prayers to Gotte, then served the food. With her first bite, Hope breathed a sigh of relief. She'd done it right, even without help.

"This is wunderbaar." Dat's exclamation had her glancing up.

She offered a nod. "Denki."

"We haven't had this before," he said. "Where did you get the recipe?"

Oh, help. She hadn't thought about being asked that. But she'd promised herself no more lies, even by omission. "Um . . . Aaron Kanagy taught me."

She waited for the explosion or, at the very least, an irritated frown. But instead, Dat's expression turned thoughtful. "*Aaron Kanagy* taught you to cook," he repeated slowly.

She bit her lip. "Jah. Just a few recipes." All they'd had time for that one lovely day at his home. "He wrote the recipes down and that made it easier for me not to mess it up."

"Ach du lieva, why didn't we think of that!" Hannah said, shaking her head.

"I had the same thought," Hope said. Then, assuming the conversation was over, she dropped her gaze to her plate, the meal suddenly not as appetizing.

Her bridge was gone. Aaron was a memory she needed to forget.

"When did Aaron teach you?" Dat asked next.

Hope's gaze shot to Mammi's, but she got no help from that quarter. Her grossmammi wasn't even looking, apparently too busy eating.

"When Ruth was sick, and I was helping take care of her. He stayed home one day, and we made a few recipes and froze them so that she wouldn't have to cook when she got better."

"Ruth was sick?" Dat asked, blinking.

"Remember. It's why I was closing up the shop on my own . . . that day?" She glanced at Mammi, who now didn't seem to so much be interested in the meal as avoiding her gaze. "I thought Mammi told you I was helping them?"

"I see."

Mammi lifted her head. "I told you she was helping a sick neighbor. You didn't ask who."

Dat leveled a hard stare on his mother. "You implied it was one of the Price girls."

"Did I?" Mammi blinked. "I don't remember exactly what was said."

Dat's lips flattened. "That's convenient."

"Well, I'm old. I don't find that convenient at all."

Beside Hope, Hannah choked down a snort of laughter. Mammi tended to bring out being old as a surefire way to get her son to stop asking questions. Dat lifted his gaze to the heavens as though asking Gotte for patience.

"I hope you didn't catch Ruth's cold and give it to Hannah," Dat finally said. "You both look like you're coming down with something."

Beside her, Hannah stilled. Hope managed to keep chewing, the bite turning to sawdust in her mouth. Even with her new everything-in-the-open policy, the last thing she wanted right now was to have to explain to her family why she'd been crying.

But Dat let it go, returning the table to silence as they all finished their meal. Though, when she glanced his way, her fater watched her with a speculative light in his eyes.

"After supper, I need to visit a friend," Dat suddenly said.

"At this time of night?" Mammi demanded.

He ignored the question.

"Do you want one of us to go with you?" Hannah asked after a beat of quiet.

"Nae. I won't be gone long. It's not far."

After almost a full year of his silence during and after supper, and his reluctance to go anywhere, finally a ray of hope that her strong, loving fater was returning to them broke through the clouds that had hovered over their family since Mamm's passing.

"It'll do you gute to get out," Mammi finally said.

Dat thumbed his suspenders. "Jah. It will."

Hope sent her thanks to Gotte. Even in the midst of sorrow, beauty and life and miracles abounded, thanks to His faithfulness and goodness.

She would try to remember that from now on.

Chapter Twenty

❋

HOPE STOOD ON the front porch in her new green dress she'd finished sewing last night with Hannah's help, and an equally new, pristine white kapp and apron. Hannah stood with her in a matching blue dress, radiant with happiness as they greeted friends and family gathering in their home for the wedding. Noah looked fine and appropriately proud in his Sunday black coat and white shirt and now wearing the wide-brimmed hat customary for adult men.

Because over three hundred people had accepted the invitation to the wedding, they'd decided to hold the ceremony in the barn, which had much more space. Luckily, the day had dawned gloriously sunny and warm, and it had been dry enough the last few days to allow them to set up the tables for the afternoon and evening meals outside.

For a long time, they'd been preparing with various members of the community—a veritable army of helpers. A trailer with propane-powered refrigerators had arrived the week before to store much of the food. All the cakes and pies had been baked ahead of time and brought over. Potatoes had been peeled on another day. The benches were already in place in the barn. And now, after all the planning and decision making and hard work, everything was ready.

Except Aaron and his family weren't here.

The last few guests were arriving, and no more buggies were coming down the lane. Were the Kanagys still so angry with her and Dat that they were staying away? A few folks had mentioned helping clean up the store and put it back to rights, asking where Hope and her family had been. Questions she'd skated over with mumbled words about the wedding or a change of subject.

Turning away, trying not to let the disappointment swamp her, she spoke to several women without even knowing what words were used. No one gave her an odd look, so hopefully she'd said sensible things.

Then a flash of color caught her eye and she paused.

"Hannah?"

"Jah?" Her sister stepped closer.

"When did we replace the rosebush?" She racked her memory but couldn't picture it there yesterday. It was beautiful with bright peach-colored petals in full bloom. She was tempted to step closer to see all the nuances of the color and inhale the heady scent.

"I don't know," Hannah said.

"Did Dat—"

"What on earth are the Kanagys bringing that requires a wagon?" Hannah suddenly leaned over to whisper in Hope's ear, gripping her arm.

Her heart hopped at the sound of the name, and then jumped even higher at the sight of Aaron driving a team to pull a larger wagon, following his parents and bruders in their buggy down the lane.

He didn't bring the bed . . . Did he? He couldn't have had time to finish it.

"I don't know," she whispered back.

Aaron drove the wagon off to the side, tucked in between other buggies already parked, those horses already cared for and turned out into a nearby fenced-in field thanks to the boys who'd been volunteering but were already gathering for the ceremony. Aaron jumped down to tend to his own horses, Joshua and Daniel joining him quickly. At the same time, Ruth, already out of the buggy, made her way to where Hope and Hannah stood watching.

Tension expanded and wrapped around Hope with every step Aaron's mater took toward her. But Ruth smiled wide, eyes clear and kind, when she reached them.

"Hope. I am so glad to see you," she offered.

Hope opened her mouth but only a squeak came out. Luckily Ruth had turned to Hannah, offering her many blessings on her wedding day. "Would you mind coming over to our wagon? We have a gift that is too big to take out."

Hannah's eyebrows shot sky-high as she glanced at Hope.

Only Hope had no idea what to say.

"Of . . . of course," Hannah said.

She moved to follow Ruth, but also grabbed Hope's hand as she stepped off the porch, dragging her along in her wake. Then Joseph appeared from the barn, not only with Noah but he'd brought Dat over as well, and shock reverberated through Hope like a clanging gong.

She tried to hide behind Hannah as they approached the wagon. But she couldn't help her gaze from wandering to Aaron, standing so tall and strong, in his black Sunday jacket like Noah's. He caught her eye and offered a wink.

An actual wink.

Though not with his normal grin that crinkled his eyes and made her want to laugh. A somber smile, tentative, as though he wasn't sure of himself. Which made her heart hurt. She'd done that to him. Aaron was always sure of himself.

Only she couldn't smile back. Shock had frozen her face.

"Hannah and Noah," he said. "Hope has been working in our shop for weeks so that I would have the time to make this for you."

He drew back a blanket that had been over the bed frame. Beside her, Hannah gasped, then took Noah's hand as the two stepped closer for a better look.

Hope took one glance at the bed—beautiful in both its simplicity and the obvious care that had gone into making it—then her gaze flew to Aaron, silently asking so many questions. Aaron stared back at her with an expression that made the empty ache inside her shrink a tiny bit.

How she loved this man.

She hadn't finished working off her debt, but he'd finished the bed anyway. He should have sold it to someone else. How many late and early hours had he worked to be able to do this these last weeks?

And why wasn't Dat angry?

She dragged her gaze from Aaron to her fater, whose stoic expression gave nothing away. But he wasn't angry. In fact, as she watched, he ran a hand over the wood and nodded. "You do wonderful gute work," he said to Aaron.

Confusion left Hope dizzy, her mind spinning. How was this happening? What was going on?

"You did this for us?" Hannah spun to face her sister, her voice choking on the words, and she threw her arms around Hope's neck.

Hope closed her eyes and hugged her back, basking in

the warmth of her schwester's love. Then a heavy hand fell on her shoulder and squeezed. Dat's hand. And suddenly what she'd done was all right somehow. Hannah was happy, and Dat was okay with it.

At least she had that.

She pulled back, wiping at the tears that snuck out, leaving her lashes damp, and gave a watery chuckle. "I love you," she whispered.

"Only you would do something like this, little schwester." Hannah put her forehead to hers. "I love you."

"What are you all doing over here staring at a wagon?" Mammi asked as she marched up to them. "The wedding is going to start without Hannah and Noah if we don't get a move on."

Laughter broke the tension that had been binding them all together there, and as a group, they each moved to join those they would sit with during the service, the same as on Sundays for Gmay. Together they all filed inside in order, many having to stand, and started the first hymn, slow and deliberate and all the more beautiful because today was a wedding.

Only Hope could hardly contain herself. Every time she lifted her gaze, Aaron was there, across the way, his steady gaze on her with an expression she wouldn't let herself believe. Her heart couldn't take more breaking.

Hannah and Noah, after having met with the ministers during the singing, exchanged their vows at the end of the three-hour service. Those five minutes, their voices solemn as they made their promises, sealing an eternal and holy bond, brought tears to Hope's eyes yet again. Happy ones . . . wishful ones.

After the vows were spoken, Hannah resumed her seat beside Hope, and the bishop offered a prayer for them, fol-

lowed by the ministers' words of blessing. The congregation then knelt for prayer, and the ceremony was over.

Hope grabbed Hannah's hand and squeezed it tight.
"You're married now," she whispered. "Hannah Fisher."

Hannah's smile could compete with the sun, she radi-
ated with such joy. "Jah. May Gotte guide us in our new life
together."

Then they were both whisked away as the festivities
began—the afternoon meal and desserts, singing and
games and a few harmless pranks, enjoying fellowship with
family and friends alike, leading into the evening and another meal. Hope hardly had time to breathe, let alone
think, busy with helping through it all. Never far from Hannah's side. Though she was horribly aware of where Aaron
was at any given time, he didn't approach her, and she
didn't approach him.

Gradually, folks started to take their leave, heading to
their own homes or where they were staying if they were
from out of town. Including Aaron, who climbed into the
wagon with his bruders and left.

That was it.

Everything was over. She'd see him at Gmay or singeon
and they'd do as they'd always done, a nod here and an ac-
knowledgment there, but otherwise, nothing more lay between them.

Hannah and Noah made their way dreamily inside the
house. They'd stay the night here and help clean in the
morning before moving the gifts they'd received and all
their other belongings, already packed, to their own home.

Mammi wrapped an arm around Hope's waist and
walked her inside. "What a day," she said. "I'm asleep on my
feet."

"It will be nice to get to bed," Hope agreed, trying not to sound as listless as she felt.

"Jah. But not quite yet."

Hope frowned as they walked in the door to find Dat standing in the family room, his face somber, almost as if he were waiting for something. Hannah and Noah, looking both curious and surprised, were already seated.

"Hope, please sit down," Dat said. "There's something we need to discuss."

Her heart dropped to the soles of her feet with a thud. "If this is about the bed—"

"It's not. Please . . ." He waved.

When she and Mammi had both taken their seats, Dat remained standing, watching the door, which was still open.

"Are we waiting for something?" Hannah asked.

"Jah." Dat had hardly gotten the word out when a knock sounded from outside, making Hope and Hannah both jump in their seats.

Dat, however, didn't appear remotely surprised. "Come in," he called.

Hope's eyes would've jumped out of her head if they weren't attached as Aaron and his entire family entered the house.

But if this wasn't about the bed, what was going on?

Another sizzle of shock flew through her as Dat clasped Joseph Kanagy by the hand, murmuring a few words she couldn't catch.

Once they were all settled, with Ruth seated and Aaron and the rest of his family standing, she looked back and forth between the fathers.

Joseph spoke first. "I want to start by offering an apology to you, Hope, for my accusations about the store. I spoke in anger and never should have even thought it. Of course you would never deliberately hurt my family in that way. Please forgive me. Forgive us?"

Hope swallowed. "Denki. I am so sorry for forgetting to lock the door."

Ruth reached across the space between them, patting her knee. "It's forgotten."

Then her dat cleared his throat. "I have already personally offered my apologies to Joseph for hurts long in the past and asked his forgiveness for my stubbornness."

Joseph nodded.

He had? When? The other night when he'd left so suddenly after dinner? That had to be it. Hope couldn't decide who to look at, so she kept her gaze fixed on her fater.

"What past hurts?" Hannah asked.

This was a night for surprises, because her soft-spoken sister would usually never dare openly question a parent.

Dat cleared his throat again. "I blamed his fater for my aunt Leah."

Hope frowned. Her great-aunt Leah had hardly been spoken of in their family, shunned for leaving the community. "Why?"

"I think I can explain," Mammi said.

Hope's gaze zoomed to her, her mind getting dizzy with each new speaker.

"Leah is my sister," Mammi said. "She fell in love with Joseph's fater, Moses, and he proposed. But then he fell in love with another woman who moved to the area shortly after and broke off the engagement and broke Leah's heart. In the end, she jumped the fence. Something that ripped my own family apart. My own fater never forgave Moses."

Dat stepped forward. "Growing up, I listened to all the blaming of the Kanagys, and, when we started at school, I told Joseph all this and said his family was to blame. We got in a fight over it, and I'm shamed to say that while I spoke words of forgiveness, I wanted nothing to do with the Kanagy family. To my way of thinking, they didn't take any responsibility for the hurt they'd caused."

This is what had caused the rift? Hope dropped her gaze to her lap.

Love was so hard, but to add the pain of an entire family to it . . .

"My sister ended up becoming a teacher in an Englischer school, marrying a fine man, and has been content with her life," Mammi said. "And I explained this to Levi, but the hurt left behind, especially for my fater, who Levi was close with, was difficult for him to move past."

"But I should have." Dat took a deep breath. Collecting himself, he continued. "My hard heart is the reason my own dochder felt she had to go behind my back to do a beautiful thing for her schwester."

Emotions snatched at his voice, breaking the words, drowning out Hannah's gasp. Hope raised her gaze to find him watching her with tears in his eyes. Without thinking, she got to her feet and wrapped her arms around him. "This was my sin, not yours," she whispered.

"Nae." He took her by the shoulders. "My sin begat yours."

She could only shake her head.

Leaning forward, he planted a kiss on her forehead, then took another deep breath. "As I said, I've asked the Kanagys for forgiveness, and they have been more than kind to give it, but I will also take this to the bishop, so that I may confess in front of the gmay as well."

Hope bit her lip, but her dat shook his head at her, cupping her cheek in his hand. "This is on my heart, not because of your actions. Do you understand?"

She nodded.

"And you have my blessing to marry Aaron should you wish."

Everything around her came to a grinding halt, even her breathing, the only noise the ticking of the clock in the silent room, before a rushing filled her ears as her heart slammed against her ribs, pumping the blood through her in violent bursts.

Marry Aaron?

She jerked back, her gaze going to the man she loved, who watched her with dark eyes, his expression giving away nothing.

Only . . . she still hadn't heard more than Aaron needing someone for his shop so he could pursue his dream of creating furniture. She couldn't say yes without love. If this was another proposal, what was she supposed to say?

Her fater was nodding. "Er is en faehicher schreiner," he said in Pennsylvania Dutch.

"I know he's an able carpenter." She said the first thing that came to mind.

"He'll be a gute mann, and take care of you all of your life," Dat continued.

But what about love?

Feeling yanked in a million directions, Hope took another step back, then another. Aaron lifted his hand as though to stop her. And everything crashed in on her at once, too much. With a cry, she turned and ran out the door.

She didn't stop running once she got outside, heading to the place where she found peace so often. Maybe there she could think. The cool, dark, silent woods greeted her like an old friend, branches seeming to reach out in offerings of comfort as she followed the path to her favorite spot.

Then she remembered, stumbling to a halt before the last turn. Her bridge was gone.

Only she couldn't go back. Not yet. Not until she got her head back on straight. Not until she was confident that she wouldn't run into his arms and beg him to marry her even if he didn't love her. She could say yes only if he loved her, no matter how much her heart wanted to be his forever. If he only wanted a convenient wife for the shop, she couldn't . . .

Slowly, Hope's feet moved again, taking her on to where her bridge had been. She'd sit on the bank of the stream and try to find a way back to herself. Gotte might whisper the answers to her if she waited patiently enough.

Turning the corner, she didn't lift her head from the path until she was almost there. Only to stumble again, her feet tangling up as she took in the sight of a bridge over the water. A new one. Wider, with a bench big enough for two to sit on built into one side.

Her lips opened on a gasp and she found herself running to it. The wood was smooth and almost soft against her palms, silky with a stain to keep out the effects of the weather.

Unable to help herself, she sat on the bench, smiling despite the chaos of questions in her mind. Then her gaze fell on the rail across from where she sat, and she was back on her feet in an instant, peering closer at the letters carved into the wood.

HOPE AND AARON

Their names were joined by carved vines and flowers similar to the design she'd painted on that little chair.

* * *

Aaron stumbled through the woods, chasing after Hope even as his shattered heart urged him to go back, get his family into the buggy, and go home, where he could lick his wounds in private and try to learn how to breathe again.

When she'd run out of the house, they'd all stood there in stunned silence.

Hannah had surged to her feet. "Should I go—"

"Nae. It's not your place." Levi had been the one to stop her. Then he turned to Aaron. "It's yours."

She'd run away from the very thought of marrying him. "She doesn't—"

Aaron's dat put a hand on his shoulder, squeezing to stop him. "You don't know what she does or doesn't want. Go talk to the girl."

Mamm slipped her hand through Dat's arm, smiling up at him then back at Aaron. "Go talk to her."

Even then, Aaron had hesitated. How many times could a girl turn him down before he got the message?

"Go, dummy," Joshua practically yelled.

Aaron had no idea why that galvanized him, but he'd shot from the room like the rock from David's sling when he defeated Goliath.

The center of his chest hurt as he rounded the path and paused at the edge of the clearing, watching Hope as she explored his bridge, his gift to her from the bottom of his heart. Finding her old bridge gone the night he'd tried to come this way to talk to her grossmammi, he'd worked tireless hours to finish this one before tonight. He felt stupid now, working so hard on it for a woman who didn't love him.

Aaron winced as she discovered their names, turning

away only to pause when she leaned closer to run her finger over the letters.

"Oh, Aaron." Her whisper reached out to him like a peace offering. Like a prayer.

Like the last line of hope he desperately clung to in a storm. "Why did you run?" The words tumbled from his lips, pushed out by his heart.

With a gasp, Hope jerked upright to see him there. She bit her lip—she'd been doing that a lot today and he'd so wanted to kiss her better.

She opened her mouth, then closed it, then opened it again. But he waited. He needed to know.

Finally, gray eyes trained on his, she tipped her chin up. "As much as I love working in the shop, I want a husband who loves me for me."

That's what she thought? That he only wanted her for what she could do? That he didn't love her with every part of himself?

Aaron stayed where he was, hardly daring to let himself try one last time. "I told my parents everything. About wanting to be a full-time carpenter and start a furniture business."

She opened her mouth, then hesitated. "What did they say?"

"They've given me their blessing, though they were disappointed about the shop." That had been a difficult conversation, but needed.

Hope nodded, understanding reflecting in her eyes.

"Dat even showed Gus Troyer the bed frame tonight, before we took it over to Hannah and Noah's new house. Gus says he wants me to work for them. Apparently, Benjamin has no interest in making furniture and Gus was already looking for an apprentice."

Hope's sigh whispered to him over the gurgle of the stream. "I'm so glad for you, Aaron."

Glad? That was all? Didn't she see? He'd messed up that first proposal by making it about the shop, and his dream, and the convenience. That was no longer a factor.

He walked closer until he stood on the bank of the stream at the end of her bridge, only a few feet away. "There's one problem, though . . ."

"What?" she whispered.

"None of it would be right without you at my side."

Her eyes widened, but Hope said nothing. What was she thinking?

Panic flooded his veins, setting his heart to a gallop. "I have a new dream, Hope Beiler, one that involves building a life with the woman I love more than anything. More than making furniture, for sure and certain. But more than my own happiness, and even, though it's wrong to say it, more than the happiness of our families or anyone else."

Still Hope said nothing.

"If I could spend the rest of my days seeing your beautiful face, and hearing your singing, and making you happy, I would count myself blessed. Marry me, Hope." He took a desperate step forward, onto the bridge. "Please marry me. I don't know what I'll do if you say no again."

Suddenly, Hope smiled, and the entire world lit with it, and somehow, Aaron knew everything was going to be all right.

The breath in his lungs punched from him, and he practically leapt to where she stood on the bridge. Gently, lovingly, he took her face in his hands, searching her beautiful gray eyes, which glowed with happiness.

With reverence and thanks, he placed his lips softly over hers, inhaling the springtime scent of her skin and absorbing her warmth and her sweetness. Unbridled joy slammed into him at the touch, at the knowledge that he'd be giving her many more kisses. He wrapped his arms around her waist, drawing her closer, and pressed his mouth to hers. Hope went up on her tiptoes, her arms finding their way around his neck, and she kissed him back. Molded her lips to his in the purest giving of herself, everything there in that kiss that he could ever hope for—trust and love and wanting.

Drawing back, he stared into her eyes, still amazed that he could touch her like this. "I love you."

"Jah." She grinned, a little breathless and teasing now. "I should hope so if you're kissing me like that."

Aaron snorted a laugh. "And?" he prompted.

"And I love you, too," she whispered, and he thought maybe his heart would soar from his body on wings of sheer joy.

"Marry me?"

This time her smile was slow and breathtakingly beautiful. "Jah. I'll marry you, Aaron Kanagy. With all my heart."

Epilogue

✳

AARON TOOK HIS bride's hand and slipped it into the crook of his arm. He gazed at Hope's upturned face, more beautiful today than ever. Her hair vibrant in the late summer sun, gray eyes closer to blue thanks to her new blue dress, and brimming with love, had his own heart spilling over. His cup was truly full.

Hope smiled, reflecting his own happiness right back to him. The months had flown by as they'd prepared for their wedding day. Hope's dat had grumbled that at least he got it all over with for both his dochders in less than three months. They'd decided to live in Hope's family home. With Hannah and Noah in their own house, there was plenty more room in the Beiler house. Plus, Aaron could help with chores here now on his day off while Noah and Levi took care of the farm.

His carpentry had moved to the Troyers' shop, which was larger with more tools available to him. Gus had been happy to have Aaron work on smaller furniture and toys for the gift shop, as well as larger items for the furniture store. Hope was thrilled, meanwhile, to be working at the shop permanently, happy to leave the farm in both her dat's and now Noah's hands.

I am a blessed man, with such a life and such a fraa.

Gazing out over their guests, who laughed and played and sang in the area in front of the barn where they'd set up the tables for the meals, just like at Hannah and Noah's wedding, Aaron could hardly believe this day had come when the path here had been rocky and uneven.

Gotte's will, for sure and certain.

Leaning over, he whispered into Hope's ear, "Want a quick break from all the well-wishers and the noise?"

He urged her with his eyes to say yes, because, just for a minute, he wanted to be alone with his new wife. To be allowed to hold her, away from the kind but prying eyes of their friends and family.

Hope cocked her head, eyeing him, amusement tugging at the corners of her mouth. "What are you thinking?" she asked.

"Kumme with me, Hope Kanagy."

She chuckled as he tugged her along. "I like the sound of my new name," she said.

"So do I." Aaron grinned. "I plan to use it often."

Together they walked to the path in the woods, the sounds of the festivities receding as they made their way through the cooling evening and the shadows of the trees to their bridge. They'd met here every evening these months leading up to their wedding. It had become their place. Their adventure. Hope would tell him funny stories about trolls marrying unsuspecting princes, only to turn into a princess in disguise. They played and laughed, skipped rocks, and shared whispered dreams.

He settled them on their bench with her in his lap and his arms around her. Hope's head dropped to his shoulders, and he took a deep, contented breath. "Gotte knew what He was doing when He put your name in your parents' hearts," he murmured, her vibrant curls tickling his mouth.

Hope threaded their fingers together. "Oh?"

He nodded. "You are the light of my life," he said, "and the hope of my future."

Hope turned in his arms and kissed him. Sweet and soft and stealing his breath, humbling his grateful heart.

"You are the blessing of mine," she whispered. And kissed him again.

Acknowledgments

No MATTER WHAT is going on in my life, I get to live out my dream surrounded and supported by the people I love— a blessing that I thank God for every single day. Writing and publishing a book doesn't happen without the support and help from a host of incredible people.

To my readers (especially my Awesome Nerds Facebook fan group!) . . . Thanks for going on this ride with me. Sharing my characters with you is a huge part of the fun. Hope and Aaron are my hope for what is good in the world with their sweet and deep caring for each other that grows from an unexpected start. I hope you love their story as much as I loved writing it. If you have a free sec, please think about leaving a review. Also, I love to connect with my readers, so I hope you will drop a line and say "Howdy" on any of my social media!

To God . . . Thank You for the journey and the gifts of imagination and words.

To my editor, Kristine Swartz . . . Thank you for taking a shot with me in this new Amish community that I absolutely love. As we learn and explore together, I appreciate all your guidance more than I can say.

To my Berkley family . . . Thank you for the amazing and appreciated support and all the hard work to make these books the best they can be.

To my agent, Evan Marshall . . . Thank you for helping direct my career and keeping up my wanting to do it all. You're the best!

To my author sisters, brothers, and friends . . . You are the people I feel most me with, and you inspire me every single day.

To my support team of beta readers, critique partners, writing buddies, reviewers, RWA chapters, friends, and family (you know who you are) . . . Thank you, thank you, thank you.

Finally, to my own partner in life and our awesome kids . . . I don't know how it's possible, but I love you more every day.

Amish Words & Phrases

THE AMISH SPEAK a variation of German called Pennsylvania Dutch (some speak a variation of Swiss) as well as English. As happens with any language spread out over various locations, the Amish use of language includes different dialects and common phrases by region.

As an author, I want to make the worlds I portray authentic. However, I have to balance that with how readers read. For example, if I'm writing a romance based in Texas or in England, I don't write the full dialect because it can be jarring and pull a reader out of the story. Consequently, for my Amish romances, which hold a special place in my heart, I wanted to get a good balance of readability and yet incorporate Pennsylvania Dutch words and phrases so that readers get a good sense of being within that world. I sprinkled them throughout and tried to use what seem to be the most common words and phrases across regions, as well as the easiest to understand within the context of the story.

If you read books within this genre, you'll note that different authors spell the same words in several different ways. Each author has her or his own favorite references, and not all references use the same spellings. I preferred to go with a more phonetic spelling approach.

The following are the words and phrases most consistently used in my books:

WORDS

ach jah—oh yes

ach vell—oh well

aendi—aunt

appenditlich—delicious

Ausbund—the Amish hymnal used in worship services

boppli—babies (alternate spelling: bobbli)

bruder—brother

dat—dad (alternate spellings: daed, daadi)

dawdi and/or grossdawdi—grandfather (alternate spelling: daddi)

deerich—silly, idiotic, foolish

denki—thank you (alternate spelling: danki)

dochder—daughter

fater—father

fraa—wife

Gelassenheit—yielding or submission to the will of God. For the Amish, this is a central tenet to living their beliefs. Translations in English include serenity, calm, composure, and equanimity—essentially the result of that yielding.

Gmay—capital *G* when referring to worship/church services held biweekly

gmay—lowercase *g* when referring to the Amish community who worship together

Gotte—God (alternate spellings: Gott, Got)

gute—good (alternate spelling: gut)

jah—yes (alternate spellings: ja, ya)

kinder—younger children

kumme—come (alternate spellings: kum, cum)

liebling/liebchen—darling (term of endearment)

mamm—mom (alternate spellings: maem, maam)

mammi and/or grossmammi—grandmother

mann—husband

mater—mother (alternate spelling: mudder)

nae—no (alternate spelling: nay)

narrish—crazy

Rumspringa—"running around," the term used to describe the period of adolescence starting at around age sixteen with increased social interaction and independence (alternate spelling: Rumschpringe)

scholar—student

schtinke—stink

schwester—sister

singeon—a Sunday evening social event for the older youth / teenagers / unmarried young adults. They bring tasty food, play games, sing hymns and other favorite songs of faith, and enjoy other social activities. Often part of courtship (especially offering to drive a girl home in a buggy).

vell—well

wunderbaar—wonderful (alternate spellings: wunderbar, wunderlich)

yet—used at the end of a sentence in place of words such as "too" or "still"

youngie/die youngie—young folks, usually referring to teenagers or unmarried young adults

PHRASES

for sure and certain
it wonders me
oh, help
wonderful gute ("wonderful," as a way of saying "very,"
    can be placed in front of many words)

PHRASES IN PENNSYLVANIA DUTCH

ach du lieva—oh my goodness
Er is en faehicher schreiner—He is an able carpenter
Gotte segen eich—God bless you
oh, sis yuscht—oh no, oh darn

SAYINGS & IDIOMS

"Blowing at the smoke doesn't help if the chimney is
    plugged."
"Difficulty is a miracle in its first stage."
"If you aim at nothing, you're bound to hit it."
"If you want a place in the sun, you will have to expect
    some blisters."

Keep reading for an excerpt from the next book in
Kristen McKanagh's Unexpected Gifts series

The Gift of Joy

Coming in May 2022

Joy Yoder tried not to limp or rub at her sore backside as she paused at the edge of the tree line to observe the area around her family's home.

The large barn where Dat kept the horses he trained—for Amish as well as Englischers—partially blocked her view. Beyond the barn lay their old family farmhouse, with its well-cared-for clapboard siding, flourishing garden, and sheets drying on the line. At this hour of the day, Dat would no doubt be either in the barn or the paddock, also hidden from view, and Mamm would be in the house, expecting Joy home soon to help with dinner.

If she could make it inside without anyone seeing her in this state, Joy could change her dress, and no one would be the wiser. Mamm wouldn't know that she'd tried to repair the fence in the back pasture. Anna Yoder didn't like her only dochder doing what she called "man's work." Not when she was trying so hard to get that same dochder married off.

Joy brushed at the large streak of dirt across the skirt of her blue dress to no avail. At least it wasn't her favorite yellow dress. Even if she could clean herself up, the additional insult of a large rip wasn't something she could hide from her parents' sharp eyes.

Guilt tweaked at her heart because she had been going against their wishes, even if she had just been trying to help. Unfortunately, the fence might be in worse shape now, for sure and certain.

The least of her worries at the moment.

Cautiously she made her way through the soft green summer grasses of the open field between the trees and the barn, accompanied by the hum of the bees working away at the flowers. Luck was with her, and she reached the red-sided barn unseen. Sticking close to the building, she scooted her way down the long side. A quick poke of her head around the corner showed no one in sight. With careful steps she moved toward the house. She was almost to the wide, open barn doorway when the sound of Dat's voice had her stumbling to a stop, her heart leaping like a hoptoad in the creek that ran through the woods.

"It saddens my heart to hear that, Joshua," he was saying.

Joshua Kanagy, no doubt. One of their closest neighbors; he was here often helping her fater with the horses.

Joy paused, and, to her shame, moved closer to the doorway.

Her girlhood fellow adventurer no longer paid her much mind, unless she made him. Not since he'd grown too old for such shenanigans, telling her she was a naïve child. It was a hurt that had worked its way under her skin like a splinter, but she'd been determined not to let it fester. Forgiveness had always come quickly for Joy. Even though all Amish practiced it, she never had to try.

"You know I have appreciated working with you." Joshua's voice sounded now.

Appreciated? But not anymore?

Dat's heavy sigh was easily distinguishable. "I must admit, I had hoped you might apprentice under me."

Joy had to put a hand over her mouth to hold in her gasp. Joshua *was* quitting. But he couldn't. He was *blessed* to do this work. Dat said his hands were blessed by Gotte, that Joshua was a born horse trainer. He was here every chance he had. Why would he give up such a gift?

"The buwes will eventually take over," Dat continued. "But training horses is wonderful gute business. There is enough to go around, and they won't be old enough for years yet. Are you certain?"

She wasn't sure what Joshua's reaction to that was, because only silence greeted her ears before Dat spoke again. "I appreciate that you must honor your parents' wishes and continue your family's work."

Understanding settled over her like her mamm's winter shawl.

The Kanagys owned a gift shop in the nearby town of Charity Creek. A family-owned and -run establishment for several generations, A Thankful Heart sold Amish-made goods of all kinds. They'd long expected their three sons to take over.

Joy clenched her hands in fists at her sides to keep from running into the barn and arguing. Crying out that anyone with half an eye could see that Joshua didn't want to work the shop the same way he did with horses. Gotte didn't give blessings of ability and passion to everyone, but He had to Joshua. How could he not honor that? How could his parents not see?

But, for once, a cooler head prevailed, and she stayed where she was.

"This is my choice," Joshua was saying. "Please do not say anything to Mamm or Dat."

Her own dat was silent, and no surprise there, because Joseph and Ruth Kanagy were part of their close-knit Amish community, but, as their nearest neighbors, they were also close and dear family friends.

"Very well," Dat said.

That was all? Very well and let Joshua walk away?

This is none of your concern, Joy Yoder. Her mother's voice sounded in her head. It was always Mamm's voice when common sense tried to override her natural spontaneity.

Silence inside again. What were they doing?

The sound of footfalls nearing where she stood had her jumping to scramble back around the side of the barn. She pulled up as she rounded the corner, plastering her back against the wood as Dat stomped away, off toward the house.

He couldn't be pleased about this.

She peeped around the corner again, waiting until he disappeared inside before hurrying into the darkness of the barn, with its familiar smells of sweet hay and leather and horseflesh. It took a moment for her eyes to adjust after the bright sunlight outside, but then she spotted him. Joshua stood at the other end, putting away equipment he and Dat must've been using.

The dark hair that all three Kanagy brothers had inherited from their dat was sticking up in all sorts of ways. Which meant he'd been running his hands through it, a sure sign he was bothered. He had the sleeves of his shirt rolled up, and her steps slowed as his arms flexed while hefting a freshly oiled saddle onto a rack on the wall. Joy wasn't sure when she noticed that Joshua had become a man, but she sometimes found it . . . distracting.

And improper, she reminded herself in that mental Mamm voice again. She should be interested in a person's heart, their character, not their physical appearance. Usually Joy didn't find that a problem.

"You can't mean to go," she called out as she got closer.

Joshua straightened abruptly and whirled around. "Joy?"

His gaze skated over her disheveled appearance and he gave her *that* look. The look he'd started giving her when he'd reached the age to start Rumspringa. Without her, because she was a little over two years younger. About the same time that he told her he was too old to play with her.

Joshua's face clearly said, *What did you do this time, Joy?*

What he said out loud was, "Ach du lieva. What did you do, Joy?"

At least he'd left off the "this time" bit. "You're a mess," he continued. "There's a rip in your dress, and where's your kapp?"

Her hand flew to her head and she grimaced at finding it uncovered, her dark hair no doubt a tousled mess. She'd tried to heft a fence post and ended up tumbling into the dirt and getting pinned under its weight. Now she'd have to go back to the field to fetch the dratted head covering.

"Ach vell, I fell, but I'm unharmed," she said with a dismissive wave of her hand. Then she stepped closer, tipping her head to gaze up at his face. "You can't quit horses, Joshua. You love them."

He cocked his head, arms crossed, though she caught a flash of sadness in his dark eyes. She wasn't wrong about this. "Eavesdropping again?" was all he asked, though.

She wrinkled her nose. "As if I do that often." She might get herself into unusual situations, but listening to others without permission was not usually her way. "You didn't answer me."

Joshua twitched a shoulder, tension settling across his broad back like a burden. He hated this as much as she knew he would.

Without thinking, she took one of his hands in both of hers, like he had once when she'd been a little girl and skinned her knee jumping out of his family's buggy. "Why are you doing this?" she asked softly.

She shouldn't be holding his hand. They were both in their twenties now, no longer kinder, so there was no way to excuse such an intimacy. They were certainly not sweethearts. But Joshua had always been one of her favorite people, and he was hurting. She could no more keep herself from offering comfort than her brothers could keep from mischief.

"It's time for me to grow up," he said. "Accept my responsibilities."

Always with the growing up.

"But Aaron doesn't work in the shop," Joy pointed out.

Joshua's older brother now worked for the Troyers making custom furniture. Obviously the Kanagys understood—

"Hope works in the shop now, taking his place."

Aaron's brand-new wife. Hope was a sweetheart and perfect for Aaron and for the gift shop. Joy *could* be perfect for it, too, except for her parents' own rules about working. Her mamm had watched several girls slightly older than Joy get jobs in nearby towns to help support their families. Englischer jobs—with the permission of their community, of course—thanks to the shrinking options in their region of Indiana. Several of those girls had jumped the fence or remained unmarried, and Mamm had made her rules.

Joy sighed, because no matter how she thought through it, she couldn't see a different answer for her old friend. "I'm sorry, Joshua."

He smiled his thanks, though it didn't quite reach his eyes, then glanced down. His hand tensed in hers a heartbeat before he pulled away.

Heat flamed into Joy's cheeks as he also stepped back, apparently not able to put distance between himself and her forward ways fast enough. Her impetuous heart would get her into serious trouble one day, and not just into embarrassing situations with boys.

Not that this was that kind of thing. This was just Joshua.

"A man is never old until his regrets outnumber his dreams," she said. Her grossdawdi used to say that before he died.

Her heart warmed at Joshua's chuckle, because he'd heard that phrase often enough. Then he sobered and nodded at her dress. "You'd better get changed before your mamm sees you like that."

Joy grimaced. He wasn't wrong. Mamm's wrath wasn't worth risking. "I'll see you tomorrow at Gmay."

Before he could say anything, she scurried toward the smaller door located at this end of the barn. She checked that no one was about.

"Joy," Joshua called, much louder.

"Shhhh—" She swatted a hand in his direction even as she turned to find out what he wanted. "What?" she whispered.

Joshua suddenly grinned, his handsome face turning into something else entirely. Into the boy who had once been her hero, dark eyes twinkling with the delight of a shared adventure. "Don't get caught," he whispered back.

"What are you doing, Joy?"

She practically jumped out of her shoes at the question and whirled to find her bruders—Amos and Samuel—standing by the door. No one had been anywhere near the barn two seconds ago. Sneaky buwes.

"Where did you come from?" she demanded, hands on her hips.

They might be her cousins in truth, but they'd lived here with her family almost all their lives, and Joy considered them her bruders. Everyone did.

Matching expressions that were a humorous combination of guilt and sly intent slid across their freckled faces. Angelic faces that got them out of more trouble than Joy had ever managed to get into.

"Nothing," they said in unison.

Knowing she'd get nowhere asking, she squatted and instead said, "Can you help sneak me inside? I don't want Mamm to see me like this."

"Corrupting your younger bruders, yet?" Joshua demanded from behind her, followed by a *tsk* of his tongue.

She shot him a quelling frown over her shoulder, and he held up both hands as though warding off her ill humor.

Turning back to the wide-eyed scamps, she raised her eyebrows in question. Amos looked at Samuel, who grinned, then ran off.

"Where's he going?" she asked, as he sprinted across the grass, past the garden, and into the house as fast as his six-year-old legs could go.

"He's our scout," Amos said, proudly, as though this was a longtime setup and they were letting her in on the secret.

Together—with Joy terribly aware of Joshua watching all this from behind her and doing her best to ignore his presence—they watched the house. Sure enough, after a few minutes, Samuel stuck his dark head out from the back door and waved frantically.

"Let's go," Amos said.

She swore a dark chuckle followed her out the barn door—Joshua, of course—as Amos took her hand and they ran. As soon as they were inside, Samuel glanced over his shoulder. "Go up the back stairs," he whispered conspiratorially.

Though his whisper was more like a harsh yell. Amos jumped at his bruder, clamping his hand over his mouth.

"Oh, sis yucht, Samuel," he muttered. Older by a year, Amos was the self-proclaimed wise leader of the two, though Samuel tended to be the instigator.

"Hurry," Amos said to Joy.

"Denki," she whispered. And received a gap-toothed grin in return.

Sometimes she loved those boys more than she thought possible. Mamm might tear her hair out over them, but she loved them with all her heart, too.

In her room, Joy blew out a breath of relief. She could admit that trying to fix that fence on her own had been a deerich idea. Except with Joshua around less lately, Dat had more work than he could handle. Not that he ever said anything, but she'd wanted to help.

Now that Joshua wasn't ever coming back . . .

Joy paused with her change of clothes in her hands, staring at the floor vacantly, trying to figure out why that left an odd little ache, akin to a pebble in her shoe, sitting in the center of her chest. She rubbed the spot. It had to be worry for Dat. Amos and Samuel were helpful around the barn, but too young to be able to do much with training horses—or mending fences, for that matter—and she wasn't allowed.

Mamm's edict.

No unmarried dochder of the Yoders was going to be seen doing a man's work. She was to help Mamm with the house and garden and find herself a wonderful gute man to marry and have boppli of her own. Joy had her doubts about that last part. Not that she didn't wish to marry. She did. Only it had always been in a distant future. When she was "old enough."

An age that had somehow crept up on her.

She straightened suddenly. Maybe her parents would make an exception if it meant keeping Joshua around to help Dat. After all, if she took his place in the gift shop, then he could stay. It had worked for Hope and Aaron.

In a flurry of activity, Joy threw a clean dress on, stopped in the bathroom to check her appearance and fix her hair under a fresh kapp—she'd go back to get the other one later—then ran downstairs to help her mater with dinner.

"Weren't you wearing your blue dress earlier?" Mamm asked.

She hadn't even turned from the sink, where she was peeling potatoes, to look at Joy. Eyes in the back of her head, that woman.

"Not recently," Joy hedged. Lying was a sin.

Mamm hummed, which could mean anything, but didn't say any more, and they got down to the business of preparing supper.

Finally, gathered around the table, after their time of silent prayer, Joy broached the topic. "Dat, I happened to be walking near the barn when you were talking to Joshua Kanagy today," she said.

"Ach jah," he murmured as he passed the bowl of boiled potatoes to Mamm. "Unfortunate, but I respect his decision."

"What's this?" Mamm asked.

Joy could hardly contain herself as Dat elaborated on how Joshua intended to devote himself fully to his family's business.

"That is too bad for us." Mamm frowned at her plate.

"You do need the help, Mervin. Do you have anyone else in mind?"

"Actually," Joy jumped in. "I had an idea."

"You are *not* training horses," Dat said, his beard twitching as his mouth turned down and he glanced at Mamm.

"No, no." Joy headed off yet another argument about that. She loved the horses, but she didn't have Joshua's passion for them. "But what if I worked in the shop in his place?"

Mamm dropped her cutlery with a clatter. "Joy Yoder, we have discussed this."

"But I wouldn't be working for money. It would be an even trade." Aaron's wife, Hope, had done something similar before they married.

"No," Mamm stated categorically.

Joy turned pleading eyes in Dat's direction. "I *could* use the help, Anna," he murmured.

"And who would help me around the house and with the boys? Nae." Mamm picked up her fork and knife, her mouth pinched.

Here it came.

Sure enough . . . "No dochder of mine needs to work like those girls going to Englischer jobs. She needs to focus on her own chores and responsibilities and finding a fine Amish man to marry and start a family of her own with."

Joy straightened in her chair. "Think of the nice Amish men I could meet working in the shop." People, Amish and Englischers alike, came from miles around to the quaint downtown of Charity Creek, and the gift shop was one of the most popular businesses.

Anna Yoder was not above using Joy's tender heart to get her own way. "Meet men from other districts so you would move away from me when you marry? Leave your family behind?"

"You know I wouldn't want that, Mamm."

Joy groaned in her head; she didn't dare groan out loud. Mamm only wanted the best for her. Though secretly, Joy was pretty sure her mater had set her heart on Leroy Miller, one of the ministers' sons.

She didn't have the heart to dash Mamm's hopes, but Leroy, a nice boy certainly, was too quiet. Not in the Amish way, but more . . . wimpy like. An unkind thought that she'd never share with anyone else. She felt guilty enough thinking it in her head. Besides, one of these days, when Leroy finally got up the nerve to ask to court a girl, it wouldn't be her, since Ruby Jones was who had caught his eye. If he wasn't careful, Ruby would give up waiting soon. That, or prim-and-proper Ruby was going to have to develop a new personality and break with convention to ask Leroy to drive her home in his buggy after singeon.

Joy didn't see that happening.

But Mamm would figure that all out on her own. Eventually. The same way Joy hoped Mamm would also realize that Joy would marry when she was ready. When she found a man who she could see herself standing beside for life. Her hesitation wasn't about finding her soul mate, as Bertha Miller, who was prone to reading Englischer books from the library, talked about all the time. Joy wasn't romantic in that way. Her dreams of a future were more about longevity. Her parents were partners in life, working side-by-side comfortably, and that's what she wanted, too.

Though handsome wouldn't hurt any. After all, she would have to look at him every day, too.

Her mater's expression softened, and she reached across

the table to pat Joy's hand. "Your heart is in the right place, but we must find a different way."

Joy just nodded, deflating inside like her favorite riding horse, who finally stopped holding her breath when she was cinched up.

She should have known Mamm wouldn't go for that idea.

The rest of the meal and evening went on as they usually did. Cleaning up, getting her bruders to bathe and settle, and finally getting into bed herself, her mind still turning over the problem of losing Joshua.

Part of her was tempted to simply ask the Kanagys if they realized that their expectations were holding their son back. Except that would be judgmental and disrespectful, not to mention hurtful to two people she genuinely liked. And Joshua had told Dat he didn't want his parents to be troubled by his decision. Even she wouldn't dare go against his wishes that way.

Why this was so important to her, she didn't dwell on. Joy put it down to not liking change. She never had. Mamm said that was what held her back from marrying. She stared at the wood beams of her ceiling and pursed her lips in contemplation.

Something had to be done.

THE NEXT MORNING she had to drag herself out of bed after a restless night. Sunday morning went the way it usually did—breakfast, chores, dressing for Gmay, and loading up in their buggy to travel to the gathering, which was being hosted at the Bontragers' house this week.

She lost herself in the flurry of activity when they arrived: bringing in the food they'd brought for the communal meal after service; greeting the other women; and finally, lining up to enter the barn, where service would be held. Joy sat with the other unmarried women her age, next to her gute friends Sarah and Rachel Price.

And through all of that her mind had been focused on running through and discarding ideas. Solutions. Any solution.

They started the first song. Knowing it by rote since she was a young child, Joy sang without thinking, though her heart was focused heavenward. Gotte must have a plan here. A reason for why this was happening.

She raised her gaze from her lap only to find Joshua directly across from her, with the men on the hard benches. He was sat tucked behind Eli Bontrager, but Joshua was so tall, she had no difficulty seeing his full face.

He did have a handsome face—strong-featured and square-jawed, with deeply dark eyes that often crinkled with laughter. Despite being a frustrating combination of too serious and not serious enough, depending on the setting, he was a fine and decent man. He'd been baptized in their shared faith when he was old enough to make that decision, as she had, and was a hard worker and kind, if a tad judgmental.

Joy's voice faltered, shock stealing the sound right out of her throat.

Because she knew. Right then and there, she knew exactly what she could do. As though he'd heard her thoughts, Joshua happened to raise his own gaze at that moment and caught her staring. Joy straightened and sent him a sunny grin. Because Gotte *did* have an answer, and He had just supplied it to her.

Joshua frowned at her, because smiling wasn't done in church. Nor was staring.

Dutifully, she lowered her gaze and took back up the song, which suddenly soared in her soul. She couldn't entirely squelch the smile, though. Now that she knew what she had to do, she needed to make plans. Tonight at singeon was probably the best place to take the action so clear in her mind.

Church was no place to be proposing marriage to Joshua Kanagy.